T0374578

THREE
MARID
DJINNS

Three Clicks

JUAN BERRY

ARCHWAY
PUBLISHING

This is a work of fiction. All of the characters, names, incidents,
organizations, and dialogue in this novel are either the products
of the author's imagination or are used fictitiously.

Archway Publishing books may be ordered
through booksellers or by contacting:

Archway Publishing
1663 Liberty Drive
Bloomington, IN 47403
www.archwaypublishing.com
1 (888) 242-5904

ISBN: 978-1-4808-6022-3 (sc)
ISBN: 978-1-4808-6023-0 (e)

Library of Congress Control Number: 2018903089

Print information available on the last page.

Archway Publishing rev. date: 04/05/2018

THREE MARID DJINNS IN:
THREE CLICKS

Contrary to certain myths and legends, Jinn's did not inhabit lamps to give three wishes. *This particular type* of Jinn inhabited humans and creatures. Since the first great war of the heavens an iconic Jinn named Iblis had sought to corrupt and oppress humanity. No Jinn's were more feared and respected for the task than three Marid Djinn's. Iblis had spawned the creatures within the magma, ash and water vapors of an erupting volcano.

Since the day of their creation his selfish nature has kept their faces hidden from all creatures, and they were forced to cover their faces with black silk scarfs. Their proud, arrogant and rebellious ways quickly moved them through the ranks of their father's army. They manipulated their human vessels by granting powers through seduction and increased strength for plots based on revenge. For this same reason Iblis lost his Marid Djinns to a king. A deal forged by a practitioner of black magic forced him to barter the services of the Marid Djinns to soldier's in peril. They displayed their vengeful nature by refusing to bow down to any creature and inspired characteristics that created legends for all cultures to follow. Many Greeks, Romans and Scandinavians referred to them as Moirae, Parcae and Norns. *The Fates.*

Every weapon they wielded or created was a design for death to any creature or god. They spawned legends within Spartan vessels and led 300 soldiers on a suicide mission against an unstoppable Persian army. They continued to weave fates in battle on the Tiber of Rome. Three Roman soldiers inseparable and unmatched in skill refused to surrender to an army on a bridge that led across the Tiber River. Now in present times their names are Gall, Sitoel and Banter. I'll tell you their story…

BANTER STYLES

Banter restlessly turns in his sleep before a hooded stranger gives him a warning, *"Don't move!"* When he opens his eyes from the recurring dream he finds his arm raised toward the ceiling. "Good morning Master Styles" greeted his maid. "Good morning Bella" Banter replied as he brushed off the tension. "Having problems sleeping again?" Bella asked as she placed a pair of slippers by the bedside. "It feels like I had it raised the entire time I slept" answered Banter. "I know a Greek woman that can help you sort out those crazy dreams" said Bella as she placed his breakfast tray by the bed. "I don't need a tarot reader or one of those crystal ball phonies" replied Banter. "This woman is no phony. She's helped several important people. She's highly recommended in her field" Bella explained while writing the address on a piece of paper. "If you have nothing planned for your Saturday morning I can arrange an appointment for you. I'm sure she'd be able to fit you into her schedule" added Bella. "Then make the necessary arrangements and bring back something casual from my wardrobe" requested Banter. "Right away Master Styles" replied Bella as she opened his closet doors.

Banter grabbed the remote control, and after three clicks activated a large plasma screen television in the center of the room. After two quick flashes the news channel appeared and Banter saw his father. "Fortune 500 ranking Morgan Styles also known on Wall Street as *The Mongol Corporate Raider* has just made another successful takeover, but the local authorities still have no suspects on the attempt made on Mr. Styles life after leaving a meeting the day before". The camera operator focuses on a reporter that quickly approaches Mr. Styles and asks, "How do you feel about the speculation that a terminated employee is responsible for the attempt made on your life?" "I feel the previous employees of this corporation should concentrate more on the question of their next employer. Which one were you, corrupt or stupid? After they choose they can find me on a remote island sipping rum from a pineapple debating the next take over" Morgan Styles boldly answered as two bulky framed bodyguards rushed him into an awaiting car. His father's response had quickly brought to mind a past experience in Banters life.

Before Morgan Styles had set his sights on businesses overseas he started in a small town called Scarsdale. Banter had just graduated from junior high school and his father had given him a realty internship in Styles Corporate building. While attending a town shareholder's meeting Banter became overwhelmed with boredom and strolled outside for a breath of fresh air. That's when an attractive damsel called out for his attention. "Can I help you?" Banter offered as he tried not to stare. Her pale complexion was highlighted by curly red hair and bright red lipstick. A tight red velvet dress complemented her figure and bared legs long enough to touch the ceiling. "I accidentally locked my keys in my car?" the woman pleaded. "I'll be glad to help" Banter eagerly replied.

The woman gave small conversation as she led Banter two blocks away from the building and stopped in a vacant lot. "Where's your car?" Banter curiously asked as he looked up and down the block. "I don't have one, and we won't have a home either when your father gets done!" she angrily shouted while five other boys crept out of a neighboring alley. Banter quickly learned of his surroundings as the teens gathered objects to pin him into a corner. The sound of broken glass followed Banter as he maneuvered through a hole in a fence to escape.

Unfortunately, the teens refused to give up their pursuit. They continued to chase Banter with bats and pipes until his anger built. For a brief moment it seemed as if he could see himself running, and the sight of him cowering enraged something deep within. It forced him to stop and face his enemy. As one of the teens closed in, Banter did just that. "Fight like a mannnnn!" the first teen yelled as Banter scooped him off his feet and tossed him in the air. Before the boy had landed, Banter quickly clenched his fist and punched the second hounding attacker in the throat. Both impacts had left the teens on the pavement crying in agony. He quickly made a defensive stance as the other three caught up, but before they could interact the screeching of car brakes suddenly gained everyone's attention. "Brimm!" Banter blurted as Morgan's personal bodyguard Brimm Straton jumped from the car and withdrew two electric batons. Within seconds a series of lightning fast strikes had immobilized the remaining group of teens.

Banter admirably watched before Brimm rushed him into the car. "You better learn now and fast. To be free spirited in my profession can get you killed!" Morgan shouted as the car pulled off. "She didn't seem like the type" Banter defensively replied. "In this business, they're all the type!" Morgan scolded. That experience had a serious impact on Banter. When he returned home he shaved his head bald and his only concern was protection. To his father's disappointment he left Styles Corporate and majored in several fields of science. He also studied several types of handheld weapons and practiced arts involving hand to hand combat. After mastering a skill or weapon, Banter would invent ways to combine them with others. Leaving no stone unturned Banter bought a picture of *The Last Supper* and hung it over his bed as an omen to ward off future temptresses and predators.

Banter's new interests left Morgan's hope for a successor to a nine year old son named Alexander. That morning he rushed into the room and jumped on the bed to gain Banter's attention. "Can I see you break Brimms record before I leave?" Alexander eagerly asked. "I don't have time right now" Banter replied as Bella brought him a jumpsuit. "Please!" Alexander begged as he continued to jump on the bed. "Okay! Get my batons and I'll meet you in the garage" answered Banter. Shortly after getting dress, Banter met Alexander in the garage with his driver and two groundskeepers. "They wanted to wager Master Styles" the driver explained as he folded two twenty dollar bills. Banter responded with a nod as he handed him the paper Bella had written Akantha's address on.

Alexander passed Banter his batons and escorted him to a water jug hanging in the corner. "How many hits did Brimm make before breakage?" asked Banter. "Ten hits!" Alexander excitedly replied. Banter quickly made a stance and took several deep breaths as he focused on the center of the jug. After seven strong blows he got a cheerful reaction from the crowd. "Breakage at Seven!" Alexander shouted after seeing water drip from a crack. The next two blows were crucial, and after nine hits the driver happily collected from the wager. "Awesome!" Alexander cheered as water from the broken bottle poured into a sewage drain. "Now put these back and get ready for Brimm. He doesn't tolerate tardiness. Especially after a broken record" advised Banter as he handed Alexander his batons and boarded the limo.

A long drive to the inner city of Manhattan made Banter wonder what life would be like if he lived on his own.

His father's reputation gave a list of enemies that placed a debonair lifestyle far from reach. His only friend was his servant Bella. He never knew his mother and female acquaintances rarely returned after spending the night under a picture depicting a betrayal of Christ. "We have arrived Master Styles" said the driver as he pulled in front of a luxury home in the upper west side of the city. "This fortune teller has done well for herself" mumbled Banter. He slowly made his way up the steps before an elderly woman with long silver gray hair unexpectedly stepped out to greet Banter. "No need for alarm Mr. Styles. I have been expecting you for some time" said Akantha as she waved for Banter to enter the house. Banter cautiously continued into her home and asked, "You said for some time? Have we met before?" "That was rude of me. Allow me to introduce myself. My name is Akantha, I've been a caretaker to several prestigious people before I offered my services as a spiritual adviser. Bella has told me so much about you. I feel like I practically known you my whole life" Akantha explained as she escorted Banter into the living room. "She mentioned you had a problem with sleeping?" she asked before removing a necklace from a small safe in a bookshelf centered by the door. "I have strange dreams about a hooded figure. He warns me not to move, and when I wake up I find my arm raised toward the ceiling" explained Banter. "The problem is that you only see bits and pieces of your dreams. Allow me to help you see the rest" Akantha replied as she held up the necklace and slowly approached Banter. He optimistically watched as it spun on the end of a thin silver chain.

Before Akantha reached the couch Banter had succumb

to its glare. "Watch this coin closely and tell me what you see in the center of it" instructed Akantha. "I see a hat with two daggers beside it" answered Banter. At that moment another mysterious light beaconed from the coin. "This coin was handed out by Brutus in honor of Caesars assassination. Do you want to become a solider?" Akantha continued to question. "No. After I get my degree I plan to open my own corporate security company" answered Banter.

"Do you know *your Fate?*"

"You mean my destiny?"

"No, I mean the Marid Djinn that possesses you"

The question unnerved Banter and he reached for his side arm. "Relax, no harm will come to you in my domain" said Akantha. Banter felt two large hands press down on his shoulders. "Someone else is here?" Banter nervously replied as the person behind him pushed him deeper into the sofa. He tried to see who it was but couldn't turn away from the luster of the coin. "Close your eyes and take a deep breath" instructed Akantha.

Banter did as she wished and listened to her story. "As one of many caretakers I often told children stories that warned them about the *Fates*. Before they became known to us, they were three Marid Djinns. They served their father Iblis from the day of their creation and his selfish nature kept their faces hidden from all but him. In honor of his defiance, Iblis offered the services of the Marid Djinns to mankind. Soldiers often called on them to display fates against enemies with great numbers.

One servant to Iblis eventually became a king. His name was Abraxas. He was a ruthless king with a want and need for everything within his grasp. During a time of war, Abraxas called on Iblis for the services of the Fates. This request would bare a slightly different twist. Abraxas didn't want them to soldier in the war. He wanted them to serve as personal bodyguards to Prince Aktaion. While in his service the prince was ambushed by a horde of assassins during a training session close to the palace. The prince and the Marid Djinn's fiercely fought their way back but when the prince had reached the gates, he lost his life. Do you know how Mr. Styles?" asked Akantha. "I feel a sharp pain. I turn to face my attacker and find he's wearing a hooded robe. I reach out to unmask him before a guard suddenly appears and warns me, *"Don't move!"* I turn cold after he removes the object that stabbed me in the back. Everything becomes dark. We were betrayed!" answered Banter.

Akantha quickly reached for his hand and consoled him while she finished explaining, "When King Abraxas returned from war he was informed about the death of his son. He cursed the Marid Djinn's for their failure. He immediately summoned Iblis for their punishment. To compensate for the king's loss Iblis granted King Abraxas three requests. For the loss of his son Abraxas requested rule over his enemies and all neighboring kingdoms. Within seconds a gold spiked crown was placed on his head and he was given an angelic carpet. This carpet was inhabited by earth angels. When asked it spoke all the weaknesses and strengths of his enemies. The second request was for the Marid Djinn's to spend an eternity in wars where death was a certainty. Iblis immediately cast out the Marid Djinns from their vessels. Then he individually placed markings on their hand, arm and rib cage. One Marid Djinn pleaded that a greater betrayal caused their failure, but it was to no avail. Their vessels were put to death. No one knew the last wish Abraxas made but one servant's warning stayed on Abraxas mind forever, "Never cross a Marid Djinn!" In time you will seek another. Her name is Sitoel Carrea and she harbors one of the beings we speak of. The third Marid Djinn and his vessel are already here. His name is Tibbigall Maxwell, but you can call him Gall. They will help you complete your tasks" Akantha explained as Banter fell back into a deep sleep.

An hour had passed before Banter woke to the sound of numerical counting, "98… 99…100!" A large muscular man with a frame that overlapped the bench counted as he pushed three hundred pounds back on the rack. Banter suspiciously watched as he lifted himself off the bench and used a towel wrapped around his neck to remove a hearty sweat. "Akantha had to leave but she asked me to stay and introduce myself. My friend's call me Gall" Gall greeted as he rose to his feet and approached Banter.

He extended his hand but Banter rudely shrugged away to check for his wallet. "Why would your mother name you after insect bile?" Banter asked while he rubbed his head. "My full name is Tibbigall Maxwell. I never knew my mother. A piece of paper said I was one out of five dumpster babies. The group home I grew up in had a Haitian caretaker with a strong accent. She always expected me to get into trouble. Every time the cops brought me back home she would answer the door and say *Typical*. It grew on me, so I went to the hall of records and made it official. *Tibbigall*

Maxwell, but you can call me Gall for short. By the way, *Gall* can also mean rude or imprudent. For example, there's the door. Now see yourself out!" Gall explained before he returned to the bench and continued his workout. "So the ogre has a brain" Banter amusingly mumbled as he made his way out the door and down the stairs to an awaiting driver. "Do you wish to go home Master Styles?" the driver asked. "Immediately" Banter answered as he jumped inside and picked up the receiver to the mobile phone. The session had left him with a bad headache and a strong sense of betrayal, so Banter dialed his father's top private investigator. "Virgil Price's office" answered his secretary. "Tell Price Banter Styles requests his services" replied Banter. Price's secretary immediately connected the call to Price's cellular phone. "What's up Mr. Styles?" asked Mr. Price. "I need you to run down these names and give me a full report as soon as you're done. No delay!" Banter instructed as he jot down the names Tibbigall Maxwell, Sitoel Carrea, and Akantha's address. "Just fax what information you have to the office and I'll start immediately" answered Mr. Price. "She'll need more than a cheap parlor trick to fool me" said Banter as he hung up the receiver and faxed the information.

Later that evening, in his Orlando villa, Morgan Styles boldly stood on the patio admiring the moon before the arrival of his youngest son. Alexander anxiously ran through the living room. "Are you going to liquid stuff before we go to Disney World?" Alexander asked as he jumped into his father's arms. "The term is liquidated and I already handled that part of the business" Morgan answered as he tossed Alexander in the air. "I had to give the pilot notice.

It was his third tardiness" said Brimm as he entered the room with Alexander's luggage. "Brimm is grumpy. Why is that?" Morgan amusingly asked as he playfully tossed Alexander onto the couch. "Banter broke it by seven" answered Alexander.

Morgan slyly walked over to his desk to get a game pack from the draw. "Take this up to your room. I'll play with you after I talk with Brimm" said Morgan. "Alright, but don't take too long" Alexander replied as he snatched the game pack and hurried up the stairs. "Make no mistake about my methods for measuring Banter's skills" said Brimm. "Your game with my son is of no interest to me. One of my sources told me Banter is inquiring about Akantha. After he gets the information he requested I want you to send a team to her home and make her aware that I don't like outsider's meddling in family affairs" instructed Morgan. "I'll handle the matter immediately Mr. Styles" replied Brimm. "After you do, give Alexander's tutor notice as well" requested Morgan. "And when she asks why?" asked Brimm. "Tell her I needed to liquid stuff" answered Morgan.

The following afternoon Banter arrived home from the university and found Mr. Price waiting for him in the living room. He had seen two thick folders planted in his lap as he walked over to greet him. "Is that what I asked for?" Banter curiously asked. "You've come across some unsavory characters Mr. Styles" Price answered as he stood up and handed Banter the folders. Banter quickly sorted through the files and suddenly stop to ask, "There's barely anything here on Akantha?" "There was nothing I could dig up on the woman. She has no known last name and runs a legitimate business as a spiritual advisor. Tibbigall Maxwell and Sitoel Carrea on the other hand have enough paperwork there to keep a fire going all night" Price replied as he wiped a trickle of sweat from his forehead. Banter sorted through their files while he explained.

SITOEL CARREA

"Sitoel, pronounced *See-too-hel* is of Romany heritage. Her gypsy tribe mainly traveled in Spain. In her mid-twenties she performed escapology acts in her tribe's circus. She was very popular too. They called her *The Great Secret*. The name is based on the gypsy superstition that everything comes to hand. People believed she had pins and keys surgically implanted in them. Her tribe benefited from the wealth she collected, but now she resides under stricter quarters" explained Price. "How could a woman this beautiful be in a secure unit for the criminally insane?" Banter asked as he looked over a picture of Sitoel on a flier. "Sitoel Carrea had a younger sister named Nina that she was close too. Her sister was a known adulterer. She had repeated affairs in every town the circus visited. Then one night her sister failed to return to the caravan. Everyone had their suspicions but there was no proof, and for gypsies there was no justice unless they handled it themselves" answered Price. "Let me guess, that's when she went crazy and started a body count" replied Banter. "To neighboring residents she did something worse. She moved into the community. She would steal items from people's homes and leave it in front of their doorstep with a note that read, "*I want answers*". The act created a big scare for residents that kept items under pillows and in safes. She tormented them for months and local authorities were never able to make an arrest. So at a town meeting residents decided the only way to get rid of her was to capture her and have her committed. One night after a mysterious bump on the head, Sitoel Carrea woke up in the custody of the local authorities. They say the mayor made a citizen's arrest after catching her with some stolen jewelry and it's been downhill ever since. Several prison fights, riots and attempted escapes are all on file. "She did all this?" Banter skeptically replied. "Everything up to the present day. They keep her in solitary confinement at the Rampton" answered Price.

TIBBIGALL "GALL" MAXWELL

A smirk appeared on Banter's face as he tossed the file aside and asked, "What about Gall?"

"Another piece of work" Price replied after he swiped a drop of sweat from his forehead. "Mental illness or junkie. Those were the assumptions circling a mother who left three babies by a dumpster. Then drove to the next borough and left the other two in the same predicament. He's been in and out of group homes since he was seven years old. Just before turning eighteen he ran away to join his eldest brother's crew. They called themselves the Abominables because of their size and strength. By his mid-twenties Tibbigall Maxwell had reached the status of a high level enforcer. Rumored to have an embrace similar to a boa constrictor. After the death of his younger brother he became the prime suspect in the death of a rival gang leader named Lenox Blaine. Mr. Blaine never left his apartment, but when forensics analyzed the body they found fractures similar to a man that jumped off a five story building.

A detective ordered patrol units to bring Tibbigall Maxwell in for questioning and they cornered him in a store in Crown Heights. When he spotted the units waiting outside he quickly thought of a scheme that would've been worthy of reality television's *Daring Escapes*. In a neighborhood filled with racial tension, Tibbigall Maxwell bought a box of Matzos. After paying for the item he places his firearm on the counter and politely asks the cashier to remove her bra. After she complied, he withdrew a knife and cut two long curly locks from her hair. Then he removed two hairpins. After removing one of the bra cups Mr. Maxwell pinned the long curls on each side and exited the store impersonating a Hasidic Jew. To start a riot Mr. Maxwell repeatedly shouted *gavalt* and *shanda* while resisting arrest" explained Mr. Price.

"Gavalt? Shanda?" Banter asked with a puzzled expression. "It's Yiddish for shame and scandal. Words that instantaneously provoked a response from the Jewish community. They started to protest in his defense and during the riot the community recognized the real *shanda*. The crowd turned violent and threatened his life over the outrage. After that Tibbigall Maxwell was more than willing to go with the authorities. They couldn't pin the murder they wanted on Tibbigall Maxwell but the store clerk filed charges and a lawsuit. During his court battle he fell into the company of Akantha. She strongly supported him through the ordeal and paid for his legal fees. Since then he hasn't left her side" explained Price. "Why would she think I'd want to run with these people?" Banter mumbled as he pushed their files aside. "I'd like you to put a tail on Akantha" Banter ordered as he sat behind his desk and began to search the internet for everything he could find out about Marid Djinns. "I'm afraid I can't help you with that" Mr. Price nervously replied as he wiped another trickle of sweat from his forehead. "What do you mean you can't help me, and why are you acting so strange?" Banter questioned as he looked up from the screen. "Your father had sent word that he didn't want any more dealings concerning the Greek woman or the company she keeps. I'm supposed to drop the case when I hand you those files. You can just wire the money for my services to my account" Mr. Price replied as he made his way out the door. "Why would he be concerned about Akantha?" thought Banter. There were too many questions and Banter needed answers. Even if he had to go through Gall to get them. Banter quickly changed into a sweat suit and packed an electric baton with his glock before instructing his driver to return to Akantha's residence.

That same evening, Gall and Akantha caught wind of Morgan's surprise. "How many of them are out there?" asked Akantha. Gall peaked around a curtain in the living room and counted the passengers in a car parked outside. "I count four. *If he sent them,* they're probably Special Forces or mercenaries. Hand me my mask from out the safe before you go to your hiding place" Gall requested as he walked to the bookshelf and removed a large silver case. "Do not spill blood in this domain" Akantha warned as she withdrew a black Venetian bauta mask from her safe. Gall acknowledged with a nod as he armed himself with two tekken's and a kusari fundo chain before closing the case. When Akantha climbed the staircase she uttered a few words that spiraled down a mist around the house. It grasped every word spoken on the street, and carried it into the house while Gall sat in a position for meditation. When he was done, the sight of a symbol appeared on Gall's chest. It confirmed the bond with the Marid Djinn within. Two connected arms in the shape of a U.

The symbol defined a deadly embrace and gave Gall the design for a fate before he turned off the lights. Gall discretely made his way to the window and eavesdropped on the words carried by Akantha's mist. "They're retiring for the evening" said the driver. "Let's wait another hour and then will deliver Mr. Styles message" replied a soldier on the passenger side. He adjusted his infrared goggles to close proximity. Gall playfully twirled his kusari fundo chain while he patiently waited for the assailant's to make their move. After an hour had passed, the sound of metal clicking echoed in unison while the men loaded and checked four MP5's with suppressors. A broad smile appeared on Gall's face as they jumped out the car and raced up the stairs to the door. Two soldiers stood guard while the other two picked the lock and electronically jammed the alarm.

They cautiously entered the darkness of the house when the sound of loose change dropping on the floor echoed down a long stretched corridor connecting to the kitchen. "Be brief with the problem" the group leader instructed as he headed toward an open safe in the living room. Two glowing green eyes nodded in agreement as a soldier slowly made his way down the corridor. When he crossed the kitchen threshold, they quickly disappeared. Gall's forearm tightened around his neck and the loss of air muffled an agonizing cry. "You were fortunate enough to pass out before the breaking of your cervical vertebrae" Gall mumbled in a tone that echoed a hiss. He slowly released the body onto the floor and removed the goggles from the corpse. He positioned them in his right hand and sturdily held his arm at the estimated height of the intruder as he entered the corridor. The glare had put the other soldier at ease before he turned and focused on the safe.

He removed a miniature flashlight from his belt holster while Gall approached. "Did you identify the problem?" the soldier loudly whispered as Gall adjusted the tekken on his free hand. *"You!"* Gall blurted as he delivered a blow to the back of his head. The impact had caused the soldier to hit the safe in front of him and while dazed, Gall quickly tied his hands with the kusari fundo chain. When he was done, he spun the man around to face him. The sight of the mask provoked a cry for help, and it was just the opportunity Gall needed to insert the pocket flashlight into his mouth. He forcibly positioned it within the brink of the man's oral cavity before embracing him. When all limbs had cease to move, Gall released the corpse onto the floor and the light fixed on his symbol. "Only two left and lucky for me their outside" said Gall. He retrieved the firearm and headed toward the door. Just as he turned the doorknob a black limo pulled in front of the soldiers. When Banter exited the car he immediately recognized them as members of his father's corporate security team. "What are you two doing here?" asked Banter. "You shouldn't involve yourself" the soldier warned as he placed his hand on Banter's shoulder.

Before he could make another bad decision Banter quickly withdrew a baton and immobilized him with a blow to the throat. "If you still value your job, pick up your friend and take him home!" Banter commanded as he made his way up the stairs. Before reaching the door Gall charged out the house and shouted, "When you're done with that loser you can carry out the other two!" Startled by the response Banter quickly withdrew his firearm. "I already told you there will be no need for that here" Akantha warned as she unexpectedly stepped from behind Gall. "You expect me to be subtle after I see an ogre charging out of a house with a mask and automatic weapon?" replied Banter. *"Ogre!"* Gall angrily blurted. "I want answers" demanded Banter. "Come inside and you shall have them" said Akantha. When Banter entered the house Akantha began to explain, "It is wise to be cautious, but keep in mind that it's insulting to those who mean you no harm". "Caution is an understatement when there's a body lying in the middle of the room with a light stemming from his mouth" Banter responded as he stepped over the corpse. "Iblis placed three symbols on the three Marid Djinns before sentencing them. The one on Sitoel's hands symbolizes an opening, and the symbol on Gall's chest stands for embrace. You will have a symbol of a forearm making a clinched fist on your right arm. It symbolizes the word cease. It was the best advice Iblis could give them before sentencing them to an eternity of danger. When you see an *opening, cease* the advantage and *embrace* the moment.

Gall wears that mask to bond with the Marid Djinn within, and the Marid Djinn returns the favor by revealing his symbol. You would be wise to do the same. It will emerge to give you a design and bond with you to weave the fate" instructed Akantha. Banter replied with sarcasm as he tried to contain his laughter, "I've just about seen and heard it all. Can I have three wishes after all this takes place?" "You won't be so amused when you find a gold spiked crown and a carpet that explains the route of your father's fortunes in his possession. I granted your father the audience to obtain it and I believe it's kept in the sublevel of his corporate building" replied Akantha. "Only my father has access down there" said Banter.

"Then you'll need Sitoel to help you get it out" replied Akantha. "Now you're really pushing it. You expect me to steal from my own father?" asked Banter. "You said you wanted answers. The carpet will help you find them. You must not hesitate. *There is an opening!* The Rampton has just completed a new wing with high level security. They'll be transferring Sitoel and it may be the only chance you have to free her" explained Akantha. "They're dead?" the soldier interrupted as he entered the living room and looked over the corpse. "You haven't heard the last of this!" he angrily shouted. "Thanks to Banter. If he hadn't had interrupted, you and your buddy would've been on the same ghostly journey" Gall replied as he adjusted the laser sighting on the gun to the soldier's forehead. "Call Brimm and have him deal with the matter. If my father is involved he wouldn't want anybody else finding out about it" instructed Banter. "Where will you be when I explain it?" asked the soldier. "I'll be talking to my father!" Banter answered as he stormed out the door. After leaving Akantha's residence, Banter jumped into his limo and called his father from the car phone. "Hello" Morgan politely answered.

Banter calmly spoke to lure his father into a conversation, "Is Alexander enjoying Florida?" "It's a little late if you called to speak to Alexander" said Morgan. "That's okay because I need to ask you something. Is Brimm there?" Banter continued to question. "You know Brimm is always by my side unless I send him for Alexander. Now stop stalling and ask me already" insisted Morgan. There was a slight pause before Banter gave an answer, then he heard a cell phone ring in the background. "I think I know what this is about" said Morgan.

"You do?" replied Banter. "You'll be receiving your degree in a couple of months and you probably thought you had everything planned out, but now you're starting to have doubts. You need some reassurance. Well I bought you a building to start your corporate security business. I even had a lab and firing range built in the sublevels. I was planning on surprising you after graduation. We were supposed to drive to the entrance and cut the ribbon on the door, but I guess I could put that idea to rest" explained Morgan. "I don't know what to say?" replied Banter. "I would like to finish this conversation but something urgent has just come up" said Morgan. "Fine with me, just make sure you tell Alexander that I called" replied Banter.

The change in Morgan's tone had confirmed Banter's suspicions and after hanging up the phone he called Bella. "Bella, do you remember the mask I wore at father's masquerade party?" asked Banter. "Yes Master Styles. You wore a black Venetian volto mask with a gold sabre tooth trimming and cloak. Would you like me to retrieve them for you?" asked Bella. "Leave the mask on my bed" requested Banter. "I wasn't informed of a party. Would you like me to leave an overnight guest package as well?" asked Bella. "No, just leave the mask on my bed and prepare a steam bath" answered Banter. "They shall be ready on arrival Master Styles" assured Bella.

Whenever he was troubled about a test or problem nothing proved more favorable to Banter than a steam bath. There he could figure out how to deal with Akantha. He leaned into the backseat and allowed his thoughts to circle while looking out the window. "I'm sure father had his reasons for sending those men over to Akantha's. One reason would be the discovery of her plan to infiltrate his corporate building for something in the sublevels. If that was the case, why didn't Morgan warn him? Moreover, why would Akantha involve me in her plans? She could've easily used Gall to spring Sitoel. Why bother feeding me a silly superstition or fairy tale?" questioned Banter. He continued to ponder on the subject as he removed a laptop from a pouch tucked in the seat. After he opened it he continued his research on Jinns.

At that same moment, a call from Brimm sent two professional bodybuilders disguised as carpenter's to Akantha's home. Polex and Winston Deluca were identical twins and contract killers. They kept their hair gelled in spikes to hide the small pikes they used for private torture sessions. They dragged three giant rolls of carpet up the stairs and rang the bell until Gall answered. He opened the door with his weapon drawn and cautiously watched as they dragged the carpets inside. "They're over here!" the soldier shouted. The twins quickly unraveled one of the carpets and placed a corpse in it. "You'll have to help me with the next one. My brother will prepare the other" instructed Polex.

Winston quickly unraveled the carpet and after placing the second corpse in the center the soldier suddenly realized the purpose of the third carpet. "Wait! It wasn't my fault!" he pleaded before two muffled shots fired from behind. "You fool!" Akantha angrily shouted as Gall aimed his gun over her shoulder. "How dare you fire a weapon in my domain. You have no idea of the consequences!" she scolded. Gall maintained a position that wouldn't involve her in his line of fire. "Mr. Styles wanted a message delivered" Polex answered as he unraveled the last carpet and tossed the body in it. "When you see this marking again it will mean the end of you!" said Akantha. She extended her arm and displayed Sitoel's symbol in her open palm. "Move swiftly lackeys" she warned as she made her way to the stairs. Unconcerned with the warning, Polex shrugged his shoulders and helped his brother carry out the carpets. "Sloppy" Gall taunted as they exited the house. He wondered if the fourth man was worth mentioning, but as the twins descended the stairs an empty car erased his concerns.

At the Styles estate Banter looked over pages he printed off the internet. In a mythical sense Jinns were magical creatures that lived in oil lamps. There were some elemental types, but the Marid Djinn's were the worst and most feared. In some religions Jinns could possess humans for several reasons. Granting a vessel an increase in physical abilities to serve as tools for plots with mischief, revenge or lust. Banter recognized the name and character of Iblis, but there was no story or information similar to what Akantha had spoken of.

As foolish as it may have seemed, Akantha's story more than peaked his curiosity. He entered his room and found the mask on his bed. He quickly scooped it off the mattress with his robe and two towels. Before entering the steam room Banter pulled the mask over his face and acted out a scene from a movie. "I can grant you three wishes!" boasted Banter. Then he stood on a bench and slowly lifted his arm to check for a symbol in a mirror on the wall. "Nothing!" he disappointedly blurted. He sat and stared at the ceiling. As foolish as the act was, Banter felt relieved. If there was any truth to Akantha's story he wouldn't know how to deal with it. Gall and Sitoel's profile were a perfect fit for a Marid Djinn. To entertain the thought of him being one made him shutter. It would also mean that a gold spiked crown and angelic carpet was in his father's possession. Silly notions he slowly brushed off. "I'll tell Father about Akantha's plot to free Sitoel and infiltrate the corporate building in the morning" Banter mumbled as he fell into a deep sleep.

The slumber carried Banter into the battle Akantha had previously spoken of. "Something's not right. The assassins are holding back!" Banter shouted as he opened his eyes and wielded two scimitars. He looked over his shoulder to check on his companions and seen them sturdily holding their ground while the prince made his way toward the palace gates. "What's delaying the palace guards?" he thought as he closely followed the boy from behind. Three assassins jumped out of a neighboring brush and loaded their crossbows. Banter removed a sharp dagger from the belt on his waistline and aimed it at the closest assassin before he threw it into his chest. He timed the impact of the arrows the other two fired from their bows, and barely dodged an arrow after hacking one in half. The near miss placed a graze on his shoulder.

Shortly afterwards a sickness followed and placed smiles on the faces of the assassins. At first he thought they were gloating about the wound the arrow had made, then he heard a cry for help. "The prince!" Banter shouted as he caught sight of the boy falling to the ground. It quickly motivated an emotional charge from Banter's Marid Djinn, but he woke up in the mist of the steam room before he could retaliate. He immediately recognized the tension in his arm as he wiped the sweat from his body. He paused to look into the mirror and seen the symbol Akantha had spoken of. "How could this be?" said Banter. He closely observed the imprint of a forearm with a clenched fist, and almost lost his balance as he raced from the steam room to look in the bedroom mirror. For a brief moment he saw the luster of a black opal jewel in his pupils. When he realized another set of eyes were staring back at him, the mirror mysteriously shattered into pieces. The occurrence was so overwhelming Banter passed out from the experience.

The following morning Banter woke up to the sound of broken glass funneling through a vacuum cleaner. "Good morning Master Styles. What a night you must've had" Bella greeted as she paused to set up a breakfast tray. "Good morning Bella" Banter answered as he checked his arm for the symbol. He disappointedly removed his mask as he sat up and asked, "Bella how well do you know Akantha?" "I've known her for years. She's gifted and has a natural talent for helping people out. Then again, what else would you expect from a woman named Akantha" joked Bella. "What do you mean?" Banter asked as he retrieved a schedule planner from his desk draw. "She was named after the female caretaker of Zeus. We joke about it because it's fitting for her profession" Bella answered as she unplugged the vacuum. "Would you like me to arrange another appointment for you?" she asked before leaving the room. "No" Banter replied as he pushed aside his breakfast tray. He skipped classes for the day, and before he would consider seeing Akantha again there was one stop he had to make.

Shortly after getting dress Banter arrived at Styles Corporate building. It was an unusual building with three floors above ground and three sublevels. It contained 53 cameras and access to the lower levels could only be granted to Morgan Styles and a selective group of corporate security guards. That was all Banter knew about the facility. He boldly walked through the double glass doors and quickly thought of an excuse as he approached the security desk. "Mr. Styles, this is a surprise? Were you supposed to meet your father today?" the lobby guard asked. "No, I'm here on business. I received some disturbing news about a group trying to infiltrate the lower levels. I'm here to make sure everything down there is up to standards" explained Banter. The guard quickly looked over a manual on procedures and questioned, "This is highly irregular. Why didn't your father send Brimm?" "It's highly irregular that I would have to explain myself twice. If you keep your ears open at the water cooler during company gossip you'd know I'm about to start my own security business. This inspection can be beneficial to me as well as my father. Now get on the phone and arrange a tour!" demanded Banter. The guard quickly nodded his head in agreement. Shortly after making a phone call two men in suits approached Banter. "You must be new. I haven't seen you before?" Banter asked as he looked over the twin's appearance. "I guess you can say we're replacements. I'm Polex and this is my brother Winston. We can begin your tour" greeted Polex. "Lead the way" replied Banter as they headed for a large metal door with a key coded door handle. "No elevators or stairs?" asked Banter. He looked down two levels that lead to the basement. "Nope, if there was a fire we couldn't use them anyway. That metal door is air tight and after we pass through it, nothing upstairs is of our concern. In the event of an emergency we would have to go through a passageway leading to the sewer" explained Polex. He continued to escort Banter to the basement. "On this level there's a long stretched corridor that leads to the second building. It houses the guards and has a kennel" added Polex as they passed a group of rooms on their left side. They approached two double glass doors on their right. "It houses the black dogs. Brimm calls them Hellhounds" said Winston. Banter paused to peek through the glass and within seconds a pack of Great Danes viciously pressed their jaws against it. "What is the purpose of the medium sized door at the other end?" asked Banter. He looked over a pile of bones that rested at the base of the door. "It's a shortcut to the sewer and your father's trophy vault. It has a magnetic lock that automatically releases when someone triggers the alarms planted there" answered Polex. He proceeded to guide Banter to the lower levels. "The next two levels contain two armed guards that stand watch over five large vaults. We have electrified gates bordering the passageways to the vaults and they only shut them off during a change of shift. Our final floor is a guard station. It harbors three guards and our audio video technology. They monitor the 53 cameras, perimeter gates and emergency sewer exit. A thief would quickly realize they stood a better chance swallowing a container of Drano than infiltrating these vaults" explained Polex. At that point he ended the tour and led Banter back to the main level. "Thanks for the tour and you should know that I'll give a good report to my father" Banter replied before leaving the building.

After the driver opened the door Banter requested the next stop to be Akantha's residence. The drive gave him time to think to himself as he held his mask. "Infiltrating father's vaults would be a tough task for any thief. Sitoel must be a Marid Djinn if Akantha believes she can do it. Unfortunately, the other Marid Djinn's would need three wishes to break her out of a heavily secured facility, and then break into another" thought Banter. Realistically wishes wasn't a luxury he could factor into the equation.

When he arrived at Akantha's home, Banter eagerly jumped out the car and rushed up the staircase with his mask. Then he rang the doorbell until Gall opened the door. "What do you want?" snapped Gall. "For starters you can show me how to call it back" Banter answered as he held up his mask. An outburst of laughter followed and spilled onto the street. "Welcome to the family!" Gall happily replied. He stepped aside to allow Banter in. "I had my doubts at first. You seemed snobbish and spoiled. I started to change my mind after I saw the way you handled that guard, but that ogre remark took off a few points. While you're sorting things out with Akantha I'll start packing my things and prepare my special briefcase" said Gall. Banter suspiciously watched while Akantha approached with a tea cup. "Still troubled Banter? You once thought of telling your father about me infiltrating his vault" said Akantha. She stirred a mist of steam around the rim of her tea cup.

"You read minds too?" Banter nervously asked. "No, it's one of my defenses. From the time you left all your thoughts have carried back to me" explained Akantha. "Of what importance is the crown and carpet to you?" asked Banter. "Not to me Mr. Styles. *To you!* History has always found a way to repeat itself and a chain of events have begun. I can help you read the carpet and allow your Marid Djinn to redeem himself" answered Akantha. "Why would I need the carpet if I already know my father is Abraxas?" asked Banter. "Abraxas? Don't be silly. No one knew Abraxas third wish but Iblis, and Morgan Styles is not an Immortal. He's no different from any other tyrant that forged a deal with Iblis. What do you know about Alexander's mother?" asked Akantha. "Morgan never discusses his relationships with women. Bella brought Alexander home the same way she brought me. A newborn wrapped in a blanket" answered Banter. "You never investigated the whereabouts of your mother?" Akantha continued to question. "I made a few attempts before I seen a darker side of Morgan. He doesn't trust himself to pass gas for fear a stain might lead back to him. Past experiences convinced me the breakup was too heartbreaking or tragic. I still love Alexander like a brother. What does this have to do with us?" asked Banter. "There are rules Morgan would have to follow to keep the power and fortune of the carpet. Morgan will have to choose between you or your brother to keep it" hinted Akantha.

"Choose?"

"If you allow Morgan to complete his path, one of you will perish"

Akantha briefly displayed the same coin she used to

place Banter under hypnosis. "I'm ready when you are" Gall interrupted. He placed two large duffle bags and a large silver briefcase by the door. "If you show me how to communicate with my Marid Djinn I wouldn't need his help" suggested Banter. "Don't be foolish Mr. Styles. You will need all three Marid Djinn's to complete your task. You have wisely bonded with one. It will surface in times of battle and danger. Now seek out the brotherhood that has bonded the Marid Djinns since the day of their birth and made them a force that no army could reckon with" advised Akantha. "We have to make a stop in the Bronx" requested Gall. "Why?" Banter curiously asked. "I made arrangements for the tools will need to free Sitoel" Gall answered as he picked up his bags and walked out the door.

Shortly afterwards, Banter and Gall arrived at a home on Earley Street in the Bronx. Banter stepped out the car and admired the view of the neighboring bridges. "Does this house belong to your family?" Banter curiously asked. "I guess you can say that. This house belongs to the Abominables. Before we go inside I'm going to give you some helpful tips. If you're not making any business arrangements, do not stare at them directly. Do not make any sudden moves around them. Last thing and try not to forget it. Don't interfere in any argument or fight. Just wait until it's over!" explained Gall. "You're asking a lot of me. If there's something I need to know you have to give me a heads up" replied Banter. Gall took a deep breath and explained, "I left the Bronx after the death of my younger brother Paul. We were out joy riding one night and ran into some trouble. There was a fallout with one of my older brother's rivals. To make a long story short, Paul didn't make it back home and my eldest brother blames me for his death. Things didn't get any better when I turned down the contract for that crew's kingpin".

"You didn't get revenge?"

"I wouldn't admit that I did"

Banter took a minute to ponder on the response and left an extra firearm before stepping out the car. As he made his way up the stairs, Gall's older brother Victor opened the door to greet them. "The prodigal son has returned. So what do you want?" he asked with sarcasm. "You already know" replied Gall as he made his way into the house. Banter quickly hurried behind him. When he crossed the threshold, a large hand grabbed his shirt and raised him toward the ceiling. "You know how Kaleb feels about outsiders. Why do you have to find ways to anger him?" Gall's second oldest brother Matthew asked while he searched Banter with his free hand. "Unhand me behemoth!" demanded Banter. "Allow me to introduce you to my brother's, Victor and Matthew. Leave your gun with them and wait for me in the living room" Gall instructed as he climbed the stairs. When he had reached the second landing he slowly approached a room with a large wooden door. It had a camera directly over it, and as Gall approached a voice echoed through an intercom, "The door's open!"

Gall took a deep breath before entering and found his eldest brother standing at ease behind a large oak tree desk. In the corner of the room hung a broken punching bag and sand was still pouring out of a recently made hole. Gall approached the desk and found two sets of tekkens resting on top. "Tekkens. Not my preference but still effective. Is that what you used on Lennox?" Kaleb curiously asked. "Let it go already!" warned Gall. "Or what? You'll put on a mask!" Kaleb continued to taunt. "I speak to the Greek woman from time to time. Unlike you, I know the responsibilities of being my brother's keeper" added Kaleb. He looked over Gall and picked up the tekkens. "Don't try your luck. I just came to get what I paid for" Gall replied as he slowly stepped away from the desk. Kaleb adjusted the tekkens over his knuckles as he stepped from behind it. "Where was that spirit when they riddled Paul's body with bullets?" Kaleb asked as he scooped the second pair of tekkens off the table. "I'm warning you. Let it go!" said Gall. Kaleb threw the tekkens at him to make his actions clear. "Let it go? Like you let Paul go!" threatened Kaleb. "Don't!" warned Gall. "That explains why you're the youngest. *Typical!*" replied Kaleb.

Kaleb added a punch with the remark and it pushed Gall back into the doors. An action that instantly unleashed Gall's Marid Djinn. The sound of furniture breaking and the pounding of flesh followed and echoed through the house. Banter looked up to the ceiling as glass shards vibrated on the chandelier. After fifteen minutes had passed, the house suddenly became still. "Go check on them" said Victor as he leaned against the doorway. Matthew acknowledged with a nod. When he had reached the second landing, the doors flew open and Gall charged out. "I knew I couldn't count on you. I expect a refund!" Gall demanded as he angrily marched down the stairs. "Let's go Banter!" he continued to shout as he charged out the front door. Banter complied and after boarding the car, Kaleb stumbled out of the house. He approached the car after wiping a trickle of blood with his sleeve. It was at that point Banter realized how accurate Virigl Price's intel was about the Abominables. Kaleb was on his knees and still casted a shadow that appeared eleven feet tall. Victor quickly raised him to his feet and aided him to the car. Matthew followed with a large duffle bag and cylinder canister that contained a layout of the Rampton.

Within a few feet from the car, Kaleb pushed Victor away to stand on his own. "I have something to say!" shouted Kaleb. He applied his weight to shake the car for Gall's immediate attention. "You better answer him before I have to give him a bill!" shouted Banter. "Open the trunk" Gall told the driver as he jumped out the car. "Everything you ordered is in there and if you need me, you know where to find me" Kaleb offered as he extended his hand. "You know where to find us!" added Matthew. He placed the bag and canister in the trunk. A smirk appeared on Gall's face as he responded with a mild embrace. "Watch my ribs!" warned Kaleb. Gall quickly released him and before entering the car he bided his brother's farewell. "Abominables!" he boasted as the limo pulled away. "So where to now?" Gall asked as he made use of the bar. "My father had a building built for me. I figure we can use it as a base until we free Sitoel. I can use the lab to modify my guns and mask. "Your mask?" Gall asked after a swallow of bourbon. "Did you think Banter Styles would expose himself to the public? I can already see the headlines. Mogul's delusional son commits crime under Marid Djinn identity. I estimate at least a day of freedom before we all get admitted into the Rampton" explained Banter. "Understood. I prefer to work with my mask anyway, but what modifications are you speaking of?"

asked Gall. "The type that won't get us killed or harm the guards" said Banter as he picked up the phone to dial his father. "Banter? I'm busy right now" answered Morgan. "I apologize for the interruption father but I have a potential employee interested in my field of business. I was hoping to give him the same reassurance you gave me. It would be appreciated if you could relay the address" requested Banter. "It's in Suffolk New York. Go to the Rockville Centre. The entry code is Banter One. Now if you don't mind I have a matter that needs my immediate attention" explained Morgan. After hanging up the receiver Morgan stood up from his desk to address Brimm. "So Banter visited the vaults at Styles Corporate. He didn't discover their contents. Why bother?" asked Morgan. "The excuse he gave Polex was sensible but irregular. I'm also bothered by the failed attempt at Akantha's residence" explained Brimm. "Do you honestly believe my son would infiltrate my vaults?" Morgan asked as he walked to the flames of a stone framed fireplace. "Infiltrate? I still have the bones of the city worker that accidentally triggered the door to the hell hounds. I'm not worried about a break in. I'm concerned if we capture a team and Banter is among them" answered Brimm. "Banter is not involved in my plans. If he should cross that line, detain him and I'll handle the rest" answered Morgan. "That's when you'll make your decision?" asked Brimm. A long pause of silence fell over the room and Morgan angrily replied, "You may leave now".

Within a few hours Banter and Gall entered a newly renovated building and prepared for Sitoel's extraction from the Rampton. "My brother came through with the security passes. The fake ID's were last minute, but they'll pass without question" Gall explained as he handed Banter a packet that included an old Dutch style beard and eyebrows. "Dr. Vernon Tiberius" said Banter as he looked through his packet. "A psychological analyst should get you a close look around the facility" added Gall. "So who will you be pretending to be?" Banter asked while he closely observed the authenticity of his new identity. "Montgomery Lang. A new orderly at your service" answered Gall. He removed a curly wig, thick pair of glasses and a skin tanning lotion from his bag. "Now make sure you handle your end" replied Gall. He looked over crates labeled weaponry.

It only took a few days for Banter to prepare the tools he needed for the job. A proud smile appeared on his face as he handed Gall a new Venetian bauta mask. "I kept the color and installed a pair of padded earplugs for comfort" said Banter as he retrieved a small cage containing a lab rat from the table behind them. Gall anxiously fitted the mask to test the upgrades. "Good fit. Now why do I need the earplugs?" asked Gall. "There's a small knob under your chin plate. Slowly turn it until you've seen enough" Banter instructed as he put on a pair of ear plugs. Gall watched the cage in amazement as he slowly turned the knob. After one complete turn, the lab rat frantically rolled over and pawed at his face. The response provoked Gall to turn the knob without regard. The result gave the rat a case of nausea and after vomiting Banter quickly interrupted, "Do you have to see his head pop?" "Does it have the same effect on humans?" Gall asked after removing his mask. "Yes, there's a neural disruptor in the mouthpiece and I installed a sonic disruptor in mine" answered Banter. "Is that the M-107 sniper rifle?" Gall eagerly asked as Banter packed his firearm. "Yes. Making additional modifications wasn't easy. So don't touch it!" warned Banter. "You'll be using this for reconnaissance and extraction" he added as he handed Gall a pair of shock gloves and battery pack. "Thanks, but I prefer my kusari fundo chain" replied Gall. He tossed the gloves back on the table with a smirk. "Suit yourself. Just remember no harm is to come to the guards" said Banter as he packed several rounds of stun ammo. "No fatalities" Gall disappointedly mumbled as they exited the lab.

The following day Banter and Gall arrived at the Rampton. Gall reported for work and Banter kept an appointment with the staff's senior psychologist. "It's a pleasure to meet you Dr. Tiberius" greeted Dr. Pompeli. "Likewise Dr. Pompeli. Your name presides you" replied Banter. "I understand you're writing a thesis on patients with compulsive disorders?" asked Dr. Pompeli. "That is correct, I have done some research on one of your patients and I'm interested in having a session with Sitoel Carrea" answered Banter. "*The Great Secret*. She's now our *Great Headache*. I doubt if you'd be able to get any information from her. She's uncooperative with all the staff members and refuses to speak to our psychologists. The only progress she's displayed is her art work. She's painted some beautiful pictures. She was the artist that painted this" said Dr. Pompeli as he pointed to a picture of two barbarians and a warrior woman. "Who are they?" asked Banter. "It's a portrait of Conan, Subotai and Valeria" answered Dr. Pompeli. "Conan of Greystokes?" asked Banter. "Conan the Cimmerian. Didn't you see the movie?" Dr. Pompeli replied with an outburst of laughter. "If my son was here he'd call you a prude or accuse you of smoking the devil's lettuce" joked Dr. Pompeli. He laughed until he entered his office with Banter. "Unfortunately Sitoel Carrea regained her desire for escape. We had to increase the dosage of her medication and replace her art tools with crepes. Now she draws pictures like these" said Dr. Pompeli. He paused to hand Banter a paper from his file cabinet. "Did she succumb to other disorders?" Banter questioned as he observed three large blotched figures. "No, those figures are distorted because of her sedation. They represent three imaginary figures that she calls Marid Djinn's" explained Dr. Pompeli. Banter disappointedly leaned back in his seat as he thought, "Gall will have to carry her!"

Later that evening Banter phoned Gall's cell phone to inform him of the inconvenience. "They keep her sedated for a good reason! She's featured in the training video on how to handle hostile patients. Her part highlights the mistakes. Before today I enjoyed a flexible woman. After I seen what she did with a paintbrush, I developed a difference of opinion. One positive you can add to the list is the new wing. After they gave me the tour of my new station I discovered we'd have a better shot taking her during transport" Gall explained as he unpacked his belongings. "Lucky we have the route and guard detail" said Banter as he looked over the sketches of the Rampton. "I hope your marksmanship is on point during the time of extraction. The guards are well trained and a couple of them are in my weight class" replied Gall. "This should be a piece of cake for a man who achieved the status of a high level enforcer" encouraged

Banter. "I didn't say that out of worry. The stakes have changed and considering the circumstances, so does our agreement" warned Gall. "No fatalities!" demanded Banter. "Then don't miss! I don't plan on being an inmate or patient. I'll probably maim a few while carrying the woman, but if they don't stay down". "I get the picture" Banter interrupted before hanging up the phone.

Before he retired for the evening, Banter retrieved Sitoel's drawing from his briefcase. He slowly moved his index finger around the frame of the distorted characters while he asked himself, "Is she worth it?" He repeatedly mumbled the words until he fell asleep. In the midst of a deep slumber Banter found himself floating through a cloud of smoke. It carried him to the ledge of a palace window. Inside was a small boy and a beautiful woman in armor that bared a resemblance to Sitoel. He leaned closer to eavesdrop on their argument. "Aello! Hand me my robe and slippers" commanded the prince. "I'm not your handmaiden runt!" shouted Aello. "I am prince Aktaion and *you are* whoever I command you to be!" replied the prince. "*I am Aello.* I do not hold the title of warrior and personal guard for my female attributes. I have earned this title for the slayings of men beyond your size and muster. So be weary of your tongue or I'll..."

Before she could finish her sentence another palace guard unexpectedly entered the room and made Banter feel like he was staring into a mirror. "Aello keep your composure" commanded Adrastos. Aello attempted to hide her smile, but Banter could still see an attraction. "You must forgive my outburst. I hunger for a more glorious task" replied Aello. "You'll have no need for a robe and slippers this time of day my prince. Your father has requested me to start your battle training. Seek your armor. Your personal guards are awaiting to escort you to a camp beyond the Gala woods" Adrastos instructed. The prince eagerly grabbed a sword resting by the bed and exited the chamber. "Battle training outside the palace walls? Is the king aware of the dangers?" asked Aello. "I don't question the king. We have our orders. I suggest you take this time to muster all your weaponry. I feel your cry for battle is about to be answered" advised Adrastos.

Banter continued to ride the mist and it carried him three miles from the palace walls to a forest. Two miles beyond the forest was a tundra. A favored battleground against invaders. "Not an unusual choice for training" said Adrastos as he looked over the territory. Their numbers gave him some ease. The royal guard comprised of twenty men, and beside the prince stood three personal bodyguards with black silk scarves covering their faces. Adrastos, Aello and Aethon cautiously watched as the prince practiced until noon that day. By that time the blistering sun took its toll on the prince and forced him to make a request before returning to the palace. "Adrastos, we will set up camp near the river in the forest. I wish to take a swim before returning to the palace" commanded the prince. "I don't think that's a wise decision my prince. There are many dangers to be wary about" Adrastos advised as they approached the border of the woods. There a scent gained Aello's immediate attention. She looked over to Adrastos and coyly made a signal with her hand so she wouldn't alarm other's lying in wait. Then she slowly made her way to the lead of the caravan. "Snakes" Aello whispered as she steered her horse to the side of Adrastos and the prince. "Snakes are not uncommon in these woods" replied Adrastos. "A poisonous Naja is! I smell the carcass and poison of many. It's as if they were just feasted upon" answered Aello. "After standing guard in this sun it's your own scent you've grown weary of!" joked the prince. An outburst of laughter carried from the surrounding guards as a cold feeling crept over Aello. Adrastos had great respect for her keen sense of smell. After fighting in wars and sailing to different lands she could identify many exotic fragrances and poisons. So without question he gripped the hilt of his scimitar.

Aello clenched her shield and withdrew a spiked triple ball mace. In one leap she tackled the prince to the ground. "Have you gone mad woman? I was toying with you!" snapped the prince. "I now occupy this shell!" Aello warned with a voice that carried a hiss. *"Marid Djinn!"* blurted the prince. A dark feeling overwhelmed Adrastos as his Marid Djinn emerged. "Seek cover!" he warned with a voice that also carried a hiss. A storm of poisonous arrows soared through the air and quickly slayed ten of the royal guards. "Ambush!" Aethon yelled. Banter also noticed the echo in his tone as he clenched his shield and withdrew one of his battle axes. "Raise your shields!" Adrastos instructed as another barrage of arrows soared through the air. "Their trying to keep us in the tundra!" Aello shouted as arrows cluttered her shield. Already aware of the intentions of their attackers, Adrastos threw down his shield and withdrew another scimitar. "Aello stay with the prince and try to keep up!" he commanded. Adrastos turned to lead a charge. He jumped into the brush with Atheon and put to use the powers their Marid Djinn's granted them. "The assassins are cowardly and foreign!" said Aethon as he kicked a corpse off the blade of his axe. "They descend from the same place as Aello's Naja" said Adrastos. He turned to check on the status of the prince and caught sight of him on the back of Aello. Her speed had kept them ahead of the guards and unknowingly placed them in another assault. "Hurry! The prince is within our grasp!" an assassin shouted as he charged with three others. Aello tightly gripped her shield and mace. Then she elevated her arms to use them both as weapons as she gracefully spun through an approaching group of assassins. "I can feel your heartbeat pounding against my back" Aello amusingly responded as a severed head rolled across the bridge of her shield. She kept the edges on it sharpened for such a purpose. "After today you will never confuse my title or scent again!" she added before yanking the implanted spikes of her mace from an assassin's neck. "I agree" uttered the prince.

A sudden knock on the door pulled Banter through the thick mist as a nurse called for him. "Dr. Tiberius are you awake? It's your morning wakeup call!" a nurse shouted from outside Banter's door. "I'm awake. Thank you!" Banter groggily replied as he forced himself up from the bed. A smirk appeared on his face as he pushed aside Sitoel's picture and prepared for the day. At noon, Banter was able to meet with Gall in the employee's cafeteria. "The living arrangements here are very accommodating for a mental hospital" Banter commented as he took a seat across from Gall. "It's still a prison" Gall grumpily replied. Banter nodded in agreement and asked before he sipped from a spoonful of soup, "Were you able to find out anything?" "They'll be transporting her with three others. Two serial killers and a cannibal. Four guards and two orderlies" whispered Gall. "Day and time?" asked Banter. "They won't disclose that till the day before. Now if you don't mind, I have other duties to attend to" Gall disappointedly replied. Alerted by Galls tone, Banter grabbed him by the arm and asked, "You should let me know if something's going to get in the way of you doing your job". "You can see for yourself in solitary confinement" answered Gall. "I'm scheduled to go there after lunch" said Banter.

When Banter was done with lunch, Dr. Pompeli escorted him into solitary confinement. Bone chilling wails carried from a corner cell at the end of the row and it worried Banter. "Don't worry. She's not in that cell. *She's in this one!*" Dr. Pompeli pointed out as he looked up at a camera positioned over the door and signaled to unlock it. Two orderlies followed them in and they quickly scooped Sitoel off the bed when they entered. "Wake up!" shouted the orderly as they both checked her restraints. She kept her head low, and her face hidden behind the long curly black tendrils of her hair. Banter curiously reached out and parted it to get a better look at her face. "Stop! We're not finished checking the restraints" warned the orderly. "I don't think all that is necessary" Banter replied as he stared into a pair of bright green eyes. "Don't let those pretty green eyes fool you. They get darker as the weather gets colder. You must let us do our job and check all the restraints" advised the orderly. Banter patiently waited and tried to communicate with Sitoel during the process. "Sitoel, I'm Dr. Tiberius. I would like to ask you some questions" greeted Banter. "If I get my hands free you'll never want to speak again!" Sitoel groggily replied as the orderlies tightened her restraints. "I guess you're still enduring the effects of your sedation. I'll come back when you're in a better mood" Banter amusingly replied. "This is as good as it gets. I told you she's uncooperative with staff. Don't expect this mood to lighten now or in the new wing" said Dr. Pompeli as they exited the room. "Then lessen her dosage before our next meeting" insisted Banter. "I'll relay your request to the staff" replied Dr. Pompeli. "Imposter! Another imposter! I knew you'd come for me. I can sense your deceit and worry. When I get free I'll have your fingers in Shaobing sandwiches!" an inmate shouted from the last cell. "That's enough Mr. Blaine!" warned Dr. Pompeli. "Blaine?" Banter mumbled as he attempted to familiarize the name. "Quinton *The Delicacy* Blaine. You might have heard about the tragic death of his older brother. A crime boss named Lennox Blaine. His younger brother Quinton was the only one left alive the night of those murders. He suffered from a severe contusion in the back of his head. It caused mental disorders that made him cannibalistic and strangely heightened some of his other senses. The newspaper's nicknamed him *The Delicacy* after a neighbor turned him in for serving Kinilaw with his caretaker's toes. No need to worry though. He's not one of your patients" explained Dr. Pompeli as they both entered the corridor.

After the tour Banter returned to his room and angrily

mumbled to himself, "All that tough talk, *Don't miss or I'm going to have to put people down.* That was just Gall thinking of excuses to finish what he started" said Banter as he reached under his bed to retrieve the case carrying his sniper rifle. After doing so, he calmly carried it over to Gall's room. When Gall entered that evening Banter greeted him with a shock from an electric baton. "Liar!" Banter shouted as Gall fell to the bed. "You weren't interested in freeing Sitoel. Quinton is your hidden agenda" Banter loudly whispered as he leaned over him. Gall laid stunned for only a few minutes before he angrily lifted himself from the bed. "This better be the last time you do something crazy like that" Gall warned. "I came here to free Sitoel. That hasn't changed, but I'm also responsible for Quinton. Him being alive wasn't intentional. Milk done more for his bones than the others. He's the only one that knows what I did and he chose to keep it a secret. There's only one reason someone would do that. He plans to settle the score! I'm not the type to spend my life looking over my shoulder. So you can either turn your head or fire a headshot. Your stun projectiles are the same size as the regular bullet. If you like, I can lift him up". "No! We planned for one job with no fatalities. Quinton is of no concern to me and shouldn't be any of yours. He resides here now. Unable to harm himself or others. Now I need to know if you're still willing to do the job?" asked Banter. Gall thought to himself for a moment and responded with a nod. "Good. Now I need you to find a hiding place close to the roof for the rifle. It'll be easier for you since you have more access" requested Banter. "It's a good idea placing the rifle up there now. It'll be ready when it's time. I still feel like we're passing up an opportunity with Quinton" Gall replied as he stashed the rifle case under his bed. "Let it go" said Banter.

That same evening, Morgan and Alexander returned home from their trip. "Banter!" Alexander repeatedly shouted as he ran through the house. "Your brother hasn't been home since you left Master Styles" said Bella. She stepped out of the kitchen to assist with his bags. "What has been occupying so much of my son's time?" Morgan suspiciously asked as he entered the house with Brimm. "He called once last week to say everything was okay. He said he had to leave town to do some research. He also requested that I prepare the guest house upon his return" explained Bella. Morgan curiously looked at Brimm and then hurried to the privacy of his den. He quickly put on the speakerphone and placed a call to Virgil Price. "Where's Banter?" asked Morgan. "Playing doctor with his new friends at the Rampton" replied Virgil.

"Akantha's friends?"

"Yes sir" answered Virgil.

Morgan disappointedly hung up the phone and walked over to the fireplace. "I didn't want to be right about this one. Now what do you need me to do?" Brimm eagerly asked as he rubbed his hands together. "Call our contacts in Columbia and tell them to get things ready for Alexander's arrival" requested Morgan. "What about Banter?" Brimm asked with a smirk. "Send a team out to the Rampton to stir things up. I hear *The Delicacy* has a home there. Tell them to reach out and enlist his services. Also have Bella fumigate the guest house when Banter gives notice of his return" instructed Morgan.

The following day Banter arranged a private conference with Sitoel. They silently stared at each other for fifteen minutes while two orderlies waited outside the door. "I believe you're innocent" said Banter as he scribbled on a pad. "Now I know I'm over medicated. I told my story to every authority figure and psychiatrist from here to Spain. All they gave me was straitjackets and happy pills twice a day at 7:30. Now a Dr. Tiberius waltz's in here with the belief that I'm innocent? I'm in no predicament to make demands, so take this as a suggestion. Whatever it is you're on, don't prescribe it for me!" Sitoel angrily replied as she laid down on her mattress. "Aethon, Aello and Adrastos. Leonidas, Polynikes and Dienekes. Horatius, Lartimus and Herminius are true warriors that you should consider painting" Banter advised in a final attempt to make a connection. Sitoel's left eyebrow raised with a sense of familiarity and she curiously asked, "Was there ever a time you dreamed about being one of the three?" "More often then I'd like to remember" answered Banter. "Let's start over. We can begin with what you were looking for in other people's houses?" asked Banter. "There were no other people. Just one woman who was the mayor of a small town" answered Sitoel. "Are you telling me people filed complaints because you existed?" Banter doubtfully replied.

Sitoel explained while she struggled to get back in an upright position, "Evelyn Ortega has a lot of power in that town. She wanted to get rid of me before I found out where she buried my sister". "I found my ring and a gas receipt in their house dated on the same night my sister went missing. It came from a gas station not far from a coffee plantation she owned. I questioned the gas attendant and he said he seen a woman matching my sister's description with the Ortega's that night. I returned to town to tell the sheriff about it but he was out investigating another burglary. So I stopped by the cantina to have a few drinks until he came back. I blacked out on the way home. When I came to I was being booked for every burglary that occurred since my arrival. Moreover, the ring and gas receipt was no longer in my possession" explained Sitoel.

"What about the gas attendant?" asked Banter. "Bought. He gave the sheriff an entirely different story" answered Sitoel.

Banter studied Sitoel's expressions and curiously asked, "What is so special about the ring?" "There is a ruby bloodstone that every male teenager in my tribe has the right to earn if they beat the trials. On the day of the final trial every teenage boy in my tribe was assembled and given the challenge of retrieving a small purse from the coat of a thousand bells. If they could remove it from the inner pocket without a ring the bloodstone would be his. I spied on the event with my grandmother and laughed at the failure of others. I felt compelled to win it, so I did. My grandmother woven a lock of her hair around it to make a ring, but I never wore it. I gave it to my sister on her eighteenth birthday as a gift. She never took it off. It's unique and no one could've mistaken it if they saw it!" explained Sitoel. "This will be the end of our session. I'll let you know what I can do for you" Banter replied before leaving the room. As he walked down the corridor he continued to hear Quinton's wailing. "I better tend to that" an orderly mumbled as he passed by.

After he left the hospital, Banter stopped by a beauty supply store while touring the town. As a precautionary measure for Sitoel and himself, he bought a barber set and red hair dye to upgrade their disguises for the underground trip back to New York. When he returned to his room he found a sealed envelope on the floor. He quickly scooped it up and opened it. Inside was Gall's directions to the hidden sniper rifle and time of transfer.

We'll bump heads tomorrow at midnight!
Left a loaf of bread in the bread box of my new apartment,
middle room, third floor. Adjacent the watchtower magazine.
Your friend,
Ali Baba

Banter quickly placed the store bought items in a duffle bag and prepared his gear for the following day. The next morning the facility had heightened security before and after visiting hours. Two hours before midnight security did a final sweep of the building and courtyard in preparation of the route to the new wing. An hour before transport Gall peeked out of a custodial closet on the first floor wearing a black coverall suit and his Venetian mask. He patiently waited for a guard to pass and discretely made his way across the hall into a room facing the courtyard. Shortly afterwards, Banter arrived in a pair of black hooded coveralls and a Venetian mask. He patiently waited for a patrol to pass before scaling a fire escape. "Third floor" whispered Banter. After disabling the alarm on the window he quickly slipped inside and followed the instructions in Gall's note. He made his way into the middle room with a window facing the courtyard. It was a medical examiner's office and it had a side room containing a tomagraph machine in the shape of a bread box.

A broad smile appeared on Banter's face when he recovered the silver case from under the bed trimmings. After assembling the rifle Banter propped a chair against the door and lifted his sleeve to check for his symbol. "I guess it's just me" said Banter as he tested the rifles electro optics. He calmly focused on a two tier Valencia fountain resting in the center of the yard. Admiring the ripples from sprinkling droplets helped him regulate his breathing until a glare of light gained his attention.

Two guards exited the building on the right side of the courtyard. "Stay in a single profile!" one shouted as he stood aside to allow the prisoners to pass. Banter immediately focused his optics on Sitoel. She was third in line, and followed two average looking men that Banter assumed to be the serial killers. "Move it Blaine!" the rear guard shouted. A bald tan skinned man about seven feet and weighing approximately three hundred pounds strolled out of the building. There were dark heavy bags under his eyes and a connoisseur mustache rested above his lip. "Call me *The Delicacy!*" corrected Quinton. Two orderlies pushed him from behind in response. Banter knew that somewhere Gall was watching, and probably drooling from the mouth as *The Delicacy* curiously looked around the courtyard with a smile. When Banter had everyone in his sight, he picked

his first target. He calmly placed his finger on the trigger
before a cold chill suddenly swept over him.

Four rounds from a sniper rifle unexpectedly picked
off the guards and Banter hadn't fired a shot. He quickly
pinpointed two shooters on his right and left side. He also
became aware of another assailant overhead as he shouted
for Quinton to take cover. Everyone in the courtyard took
his advice after three grenades landed in the center of the
fountain. The debris from the detonation killed one of the
orderlies and it provoked Quinton's cannibalistic urges. He
wailed as he crawled to the sight of a cracked cranium and
feasted as if it were a split lobster tail. "Hurry up Blaine!
Jump into the sewer drain underneath. Someone will be
waiting for you at the end of the tunnel!" shouted one of the
sniper's. Banter scoped through the dust screen and found
Sitoel motionless on the ground. He couldn't tell if she was
alive or dead. When he thought the situation couldn't get
any worse, the dust screen settled and Gall entered the field.
His kusari fundo chain slowly unraveled down the arm
of his left sleeve as he turned his neural disruptor to full
blast. The effect instantly crippled Quinton's heightened
senses and gave Gall the advantage he needed to creep
from behind. While Quinton vomited over the body, Gall
wrapped his kusari fundo chain around his neck and raised
Quinton to his feet.

When he had leverage, Gall lifted Quinton seven feet
in the air and angled him into a head first position over the
ground. The act forced the flow of blood to his head and
Quinton began to gag on his own vomit. Gall then looked
to Banter's position and gestured for him to complete the act

with a head shot. It would've been an act of mercy, but Banter was more concerned with the snipers on opposite sides of him. They were no longer stunned from Gall's bold display and aimed their rifles in Quinton's defense. "Fool!" Banter scowled with a hiss. He quickly exchanged the cartridge in his rifle from stun to live ammo. He turned his sonic disruptor full blast to break the large glass window in front of him and as the shattered pieces rained over the courtyard, it created a distraction that quickly gained the attention of both snipers.

Banter fired two rounds and they carried the shadow of an eagle. They screeched over the courtyard with the same skill and precision of the predator as it penetrated the optic lens of both snipers. When the *fate* was complete, the blood splatter casted a shadow of an eagle ripping an eyeball out the parietal of a cranium on the back wall. An act that provoked the third assailant to launch another three grenades into the courtyard. The detonation forced Gall to release his hold on Quinton, and as he crawled through the debris he heard a man shouting, "Run for it!"

Cover fire followed as Quinton regained his bearings and franticly ran to the broken border of the fountain. "The next time we meet I'll cater the party with over a dozen herbs and spices. No one will leave until the plate is clean!" Quinton threatened before he jumped into the sewer. Banter jumped out the third floor window while Gall occupied the attention of the third assailant. He aimed his rifle to the rooftop and with increased speed he ran through the courtyard until he locked on the target. A loud thump followed the squeeze of a trigger before the corpse fell into the courtyard. "What took you so long?" Gall shouted with a voice that carried a hiss. "We had an agreement!" Banter angrily replied as he knelt down to check Sitoel's pulse. "She didn't move, so I took advantage of another opportunity" replied Gall. "She's still alive! Hurry up and grab her before this courtyard becomes an open forum" instructed Banter. "Where are we going to go? There must be over a dozen guards and witnesses at every exit. Furthermore, the authorities will be on their way" said Gall as he lifted Sitoel and threw her over his shoulder. "We'll follow Blaine" replied Banter. He ran to the opening in the fountain and jumped into a sewage drain. Gall followed close behind, and it wasn't long before they heard Blaine heckling.

The sound of his laughter kept Gall's hatred and Marid Djinn fueled. "Besides him being alive, he threatened to eat me!" Gall angrily whispered. "Forget Quinton or risk your freedom" advised Banter. He tried to keep Blaine in sight with the rifle's electro-optics. "I'll spit in every clip until I get him!" snapped Gall. "Freedom!" Quinton repeatedly shouted. The word echoed through the sewer as he reached the cage door at the end of the tunnel. A getaway driver had just finished blow torching an oval shape hole before Quinton had reached the exit. "Hurry up and get this jacket off of me. I'm being followed!" Quinton demanded as he crawled through the hole. "Don't worry, I brought something extra for surprises" said the driver as he withdrew a knife and cut through Quinton's restraints. A smirk appeared on Quinton's face as his jacket fell to the ground and the driver opened the backdoor to hand him an RPK-47. "Get down!" warned Banter. Quinton returned to the entrance with the weapon in hand and opened fire. "You want to cancel *The Delicacy!*" Quinton shouted as a steady stream of bullets riddled the surrounding pipes. "Perhaps you like something a little spicy?" added Quinton. Steam and water flooded the area. "Now I really don't like him!" replied Gall. "I can't get a clear shot" said Banter as he peeked around the corner. "Then fire at random!" demanded Gall. Banter waited for a pause and returned fire. He was able to get off three shots. Two knocked off the metal bumper of the getaway car, and the third barely missed Quinton before he boarded. "Until next time!" Quinton threatened as the sound of tires peeling from the tunnel followed another round of fire.

Banter and Gall quickly made their way through the outpouring of water as they carried Sitoel toward the end of the tunnel. An element that was a factor in reviving her Marid Djinn. "Now what are we going to do?" Gall asked as Banter crawled through the fencing. "Hopefully the authorities will believe we all escaped by car. It should by us some time" answered Banter. Gall placed Sitoel on the ground and after crawling through the fencing he pulled her by the ankles until she angrily responded in a tone that carried a hiss. "Put your hands to better use and release me from my restraints!" demanded Sitoel. Gall surprisingly looked to Banter before he willingly complied. When he was done, Sitoel stood upright and stretched out her stiffened muscles. Then she tore off a piece of her gown and wrapped it around her face. A pair of dark green eyes emerged as she turned to face Gall and Banter. "Follow me and I will guide you through this. The trek is just a mere walk for a Marid Djinn!" instructed Sitoel. "Do you think she knows what she's doing?" asked Banter. "I have no doubt. She carries the voice!" answered Gall.

The Marid Djinn's raced with increased speed. Surrounding sites became nothing more than a blur. As they approached a river a page of their history unfolded. "Swim?" Banter disappointedly replied with a hiss. Sitoel acknowledged with a nod as she dove into the water. Gall removed his mask and revealed eyes that carried the luster of a black sapphire gem as he removed his T-shirt and wrapped it around the bridge of his face. After he dove into the river, Banter did the same. They swam to the bottom while their thoughts circled in unison, and a familiar mist brought them back to a battle they had long forgotten. "Am I going to die?" the prince mumbled in Aello's ear. "If you do the journey will not be a lonely one" Aello answered as they ran along the edge of a river. "Those assassins belong to a guild and I noticed a symbol painted on many of their fallen" replied Aethon. "I've seen the same symbol on the ones that fell to my mace and shield. It is the Naja I spoke of earlier" added Aello. "They will not stop until they succeed with their mission" said Aethon. The sound of cracked branches and screams from the wounded echoed from behind. "Wait" Aello loudly whispered. "What is it?" Adrastos asked as he crept beside her. "Another ambush" she answered. "What has your fate showed you?" asked Adrastos.

Aello stood silent for a few minutes as her Marid Djinn granted her foresight. After seeing the death of her comrades she gave a safe route. "There are over three dozen lying in wait. We can go around them by swimming the river to the edge of the palace and then answer with reinforcements" explained Aello. Adrastos nodded his head in agreement as the group dove into the river. A sight that a scout immediately reported to the general of the pursuing assassins. When the general received word, laughter filled the woods. "They eagerly rush to their demise! After fighting my soldiers they run three miles and challenge the rapid current of the river? They must prefer drowning over the poison of our arrows" replied the general. "It would not be wise to take the prince's personal bodyguard lightly. The king strongly advised us not to leave until we caught sight of the body" said an assassin. "Then we'll greet them at the edge of the palace. There's a bend in the river two miles from there. Send word of our movement to our spy. That will give us the time we need to assure the success of our mission" instructed the general.

Shortly before nightfall the small group had crawled from the river. "We are not alone" Aello whispered. The prince cautiously slid off her shoulders. Eyes had widened

on the face of the general and a group of assassins as they
uttered the words, "Death defying!" "Aethon and Aello clear
a path for the prince and I'll close in from behind!" Adrastos
commanded as a dozen assassins charged. Aethon withdrew
a battle axe with edges that resembled the wings of an eagle
and hacked into the rib bones of an approaching assassin.
Aello followed his swings as he plowed a path with the
carcass still attached to the edges. The sound of metal and
the cries of agony rang through the field of battle as another
group of assassins closed in from the rear. They held their
position until the prince had reached the gates. "Something's
not right. Where are the palace guards?" thought Adrastos
as three assassins loaded their crossbows.

He quickly withdrew a dagger and in one motion hurled
it through the air to kill one of the archers. He dodged
and deflected the other two arrows while the prince safely
made his way to the palace gates. Adrastos could see a smile
on the prince's face as a hooded figure stepped from the
shadows to greet him. The prince embraced him before he
extended a small scythe knife and stabbed him in the back.
Adrastos could hear the pursuing general sound the retreat
as the poison from an arrow took its toll. After finishing the
last of their attackers, Aethon and Aello joined Adrastos.
He pointed to the sight of their failure and it was at that
moment the vessels of the Marid Djinns realized their
purpose. Prevent this from happening again.

The following day of their escape word had reached
back to Brooklyn's 71st precinct. A well decorated and
distinguished homicide detective in his early thirties had
a record of solving every homicide case placed on his

desk before meeting Gall. He was ready to pour himself a cup of coffee next to the Captain's office when the door unexpectedly opened. "Detective Rodriguez, I need to see you in my office ASAP!" said Capt. Bell. "I suddenly realized why the coffee pot is next to your office" replied Det. Rodriguez. "Someone told me Bustelo was your brand. Now did you hear about the escape at the Rampton?" Capt. Bell asked as he made his way behind his desk. "I seen it on the news. Two patients are on the loose" Det. Rodriguez answered as he took a seat. "That courtyard looked like something out of Beirut. I guess it's safe to say they got their hands full" added the detective. "So do you!" replied Capt. Bell. "The Rampton is not in our jurisdiction" said Det. Rodriguez. "In case you've forgotten the Blaine murder was part of your case. As a matter of fact it's the only blemish. His brother Quinton is on the loose and you don't have to guess who'll be on the menu for the death of his brother. Another war may spark between him and the Abominables" Capt. Bell explained as he handed the detective Gall's file. "Offer him our protection and see what he'll give up" suggested the Capt. Bell. Det. Rodriguez disappointedly grabbed the file and walked out the office. The drive to Akantha's residence gave the detective more than enough time to reflect on his only unsolved case. There was no love lost the day he got the call to investigate the crime scene in Lennox Blaine's apartment. He had lost a close friend that worked in the narcotics division to the Blaine organization. His crew had little regard for law enforcement and they nearly wiped out every opposition they came across. *That was,* before they stepped on the toes of an Abonimable named Kaleb.

A rival war ensued and the detective's work load tripled. After the death of a younger Abominable named Paul he decided to campout at the hospital. Bartering for last minute confessions from the lips of a dying man proved more beneficial than working on the streets. Then came the call to investigate several homicides at Blaine's residence. When he arrived on the scene he found four officers trying to sustain Quinton. He had suffered a head injury and after seeing the coroner cart out body bags the detective recalled a bone chilling wail.

After looking over the murder scene he suspected a professional. It was as if Lennox Blaine had been placed in a body bag, thrown off the roof of the building and scooped off the ground before someone returned him to the crime scene. Any one of the four remaining Abominables could've done it, but they could barely gather enough evidence or a pair of cuffs that could pin them to the crime. All he had was a hunch based on a ton of complaints that listed injuries to victims that were left alive to pay off their debts. Conveniently none pressed charges. The detective knew it would only be a matter of time before the next retaliation so he staked out the Abominables. He harassed the youngest one and when he attempted to bring him in for questioning, the Abominable incited a riot that nearly got himself killed. The detective was fortunate enough to have a case brought up even if it wasn't for murder. During the court ordeal his suspect had befriended an elderly woman. A spiritual advisor he took up residency with. If he were to make a play, he would have to go after her thought the detective.

Detective Rodriguez barely made it up the stairs when

Akantha opened the door to welcome him. "Hello, I'm Detective Rodriguez and I was wondering if I could speak with Tibbigall Maxwell?" Det. Rodriguez greeted as he flashed his badge and approached the front door. "Gall is at work. Can I help you with anything?" said Akantha as she stepped aside and gestured for the detective to enter. "I was hoping to get the opportunity to speak with you" said Det. Rodriguez. Akantha kindly escorted him to the living room. "We can speak over a cup of coffee. I just brewed a fresh pot of Bustelo" Akantha offered as she walked over to a tray holding a coffee pot. "I'd be glad to have a cup" replied Det. Rodriguez. He slowly made his way to the couch and sat down. "This morning I had to reflect on two cases that became thorn's in my side. One case was unsolved and the other I tried to forget because it just made me sick. The first was the murder of Lennox Blaine, and the other was the murder of his younger brother's caretaker. *Have you ever endured the smell of burning flesh beaming from a Foreman grill?*" Det. Rodriguez asked in an attempt to soften Akantha. "I've been given the responsibility to care for many creatures that a lot of people would have considered monsters. Unfortunately, I've never had the privilege of using a Foreman grill to feed them" Akantha amusingly answered. "I don't think you recognize the seriousness of the matter. Some time ago I attempted to bring Tibbigall Maxwell in for questioning. Unfortunately for me, he was punished for lesser charges. Two days later my murder victim's brother made a delicacy out of his caretaker. I fear he may have the same intentions for Mr. Maxwell. If you care anything at all for the man you would convince him to come down to the station and tell us everything he knows" explained Det. Rodriguez. "Like I told you before, Gall is at work. You can leave a card. Whether or not he decides to call is his choice" replied Akantha. She stood up from her seat and gestured that the visit had come to an end. Det. Rodriguez complied with the gesture and as he lifted himself off the couch he suspiciously asked, "So what does our friend do now?" "He works for a corporate security company. Gall is an advisory on retainer. His experiences and opinion are very useful to his employer" answered Akantha.

"I understand. Please inform Mr. Maxwell of my visit and if you don't mind me asking, what's the name of this company?" Det. Rodriguez continued to question. "Styles Corporate Security" Akantha answered with a proud smile.

After their swim, Sitoel led Banter and Gall back to a safe checkpoint on the Abominable's underground route. Before the week had ended all three Marid Djinn's had safely returned to the Styles estate. They successful bonded with their vessels but as Banter and Gall dug through a stack of pancakes, they learned their vessels still needed time to bond with each other. After breakfast was served, Sitoel unexpectedly made her way downstairs wearing a *United Front of Pedestrians* shirt that complimented her figure and bared legs. Bella brought her a fresh towel as she sat at the table. Banter and Gall tried not to stare while she dried her hair. "I see you've helped yourself to my wardrobe but still refuse to comply with the color I chose for your hair" said Banter. "Copper red with my eyes and complexion would've only attracted more attention. It's bad enough I had to cut it so short, so be grateful I settled with being a blonde"

Sitoel boldly answered as she wrapped the towel around her head. "It wasn't copper red. It was ruby eruption and it was critical to our mission!" replied Banter. "I think you have some suppressed relationship issues that you need to get over. Then again, what can you expect from someone that hung a picture of the Last Supper over his bed" Sitoel amusingly replied. "You're an escaped mental patient and you're giving me a psychological evaluation" Banter snapped as Gall tumbled over with laughter. Their amusement abruptly ended after Sitoel grabbed a table knife and waved it in a threatening manner. The act immediately brought the conversation of a paintbrush to mind. "Master Styles you have a guest. She appeared just as I was taking out the trash" interrupted Bella.

Akantha entered from the hallway with an appearance that fitted the occasion. Her gray hair was straightened into a shiny silver mane that parted to cover half her face, and she wore a long chain of pearls that highlighted a white silk dress that peeked through a red Pashmina shawl. "I see my entrance is right on time" said Akantha. She opened her hand and gestured for Sitoel to hand her the knife. "What are you doing here?" Sitoel suspiciously asked. "You know Akantha?" asked Banter. "When someone comes into the caravan of a fortune teller and gives their own prediction, *you never forget the face*" answered Sitoel. "I told you your friends would help you out the darkest corner of your cell" replied Akantha as Gall jumped from his chair to greet her. "Don't wrinkle my dress!" said Akantha as Gall scooped her off the ground with a mild embrace. "You took a big risk in making this visit. My father is currently in his den" said Banter. "I wouldn't miss this opportunity for anything in the world!" replied Akantha. She suspiciously looked over Sitoel. "It would've been wiser and safer for all of us if you had waited until we've reached my corporate security building" advised Banter. "Seeing the three of you together is just a small beneficial factor of my visit. It gives the detective less of a reason to hide in wait at my domain" explained Akantha. "Detective? You told a detective to meet us here!" snapped Banter. "No. He followed me and he'll be ringing your bell any second now. There's no need to be alarmed or question my sanity. His reason for seeing us is different than you expect. I told him Gall was in your employ as an advisory" explained Akantha. "There are plenty of reasons to be alarmed and question your sanity" Banter replied before the doorbell rang. He quickly turned to Sitoel and commanded, "Go upstairs to my room and stay out of sight!"

Sitoel acknowledged with a nod and raced up the stairs as Bella answered the door. "Good morning, I'm Det. Rodriguez and I was wondering if I could ask Mr. Styles a few questions?" greeted Det. Rodriguez. "Which Mr. Styles are you referring to? Morgan or Banter?" asked Bella. "Morgan Styles" answered Det. Rodriguez. "Wait here and I'll see if he's accepting any visitors" replied Bella. Shortly afterwards she returned and escorted the detective to the den. Banter and Gall suspiciously peeked around the dining room doorway while Akantha tried to contain her excitement. For centuries handmaids had the privilege of knowing certain personal matters of the household depending on their social circle. This moment had brought her back to those days and it felt as if she had reached the climax of her favorite book. Approximately ten minutes had passed before Banter and his guests had received their invitation to the den. They could hear Morgan as Brimm stepped out the room, "Make sure he brings the old hag with him". "Your father requests you and your guest to join him in the den" said Brimm.

A broad smile appeared on Akantha's face as he escorted them back to the den. When they entered Brimm quickly made his way back to the desk and stood at ease by Morgan's side. Across from Morgan, Banter and Akantha comfortably sat in a pair of burgundy padded leather chairs centered in the middle of the room. Gall towered between them with his arms folded as the detective cautiously observed everyone's actions from the fireplace. Akantha found the irony overwhelming as she gripped the ends of her shawl and depicted the situation. Det. Rodriguez was the highest authority figure in the room. Yet still, with a fugitive franticly pacing around upstairs and a room full of people who were an accessory to the crime, he hadn't had a clue. Across from her Morgan Styles sat with one eyebrow raised high into his forehead, and a sigh informed her of his disappointment to see her alive another day. She knew he would like nothing more than to snap his fingers and have his lap dog Brimm correct the failed attempt. A man that was currently trying to ignore his sweaty palm condition. Then there was Banter, his discoveries were bringing him closer to a truth that even he didn't want to acknowledge, but bravely recognized the importance to do so. Last was Gall, who was patiently lying in wait for someone foolish enough to step over their boundaries so he could do what he does best. "I guess I'm lucky to have all of you here at the same time" said Det. Rodriguez. "My time is very precious Det. Rodriguez and my patience for uninvited guest is running thin. So please get right to the point" Morgan rudely interrupted. "Let me begin with how I started my week. I had visited Akantha's residence for the purpose of warning Mr. Maxwell about an escaped fugitive named Quinton Blaine. Due to past events I have reasons to believe he'd make an attempt on Mr. Maxwell's life". "I fail to see how or why this concern's my family?" replied Morgan. "I received some news that made a lot of people skip tea time down at the Rampton. After identifying one of the corpses that aided Quinton's escape they realized he received aid from a group of guerilla soldiers last known to be working under a faction in Columbia. They started to think that would be his next point of destination, but they discovered a pre-paid phone on one of the assailant's and tracked a number back to Styles Corp. After finding out about Gall's current employment under Styles Corporate security I assumed Quinton had spent his time and money on a plot that would either incriminate or assassinate Mr. Maxwell" explained Det. Rodriguez. "Another thing that's baffling is that the escape was worthy of an episode of a reality T.V. show and three of the assailant's mysteriously end up dead" explained the detective. "Daring Escapes. I could've been on that show!" joked Gall. "I know, which makes me wonder why Mr. Styles would even consider the idea of hiring you?" Det. Rodriguez asked as he leaned over Morgan's desk. "Let's ask Banter about that. Styles Corporate security is his branch of business now" replied Morgan. He calmly leaned back in his chair and patiently waited for Banter to stumble out the situation. "Personal bodyguards will be one of the services I offer my clients. So I've asked Mr. Maxwell to head one of my training programs. I find his insight and experience a valuable source for dealing with an element I know nothing about" explained Banter. "If Mr. Maxwell is interested in sharing any of those experiences with the 71st precinct he should come down to the station. We can arrange a deal faster than Quinton can fasten his *Kiss the Cook Apron!*" Det. Rodriguez amusingly replied. A smirk appeared on Gall's face before he childishly responded, "While you're waiting for that to happen you can hold your breath and repeatedly count to your middle finger. When you start to turn blue…" "Gall don't be rude!" interrupted Akantha. "I figured that's the way you'd feel about it. So I'll be patrolling Styles Corporations like a vulture. Thanks for your time gentleman and I'll be seeing you around" hinted the detective as he made his way to the door. "Mr. Brimm, escort our guest out. All of them!" said Morgan as he left his chair to stand by the fireplace. Before leaving Akantha approached Banter and gave instructions. "You must bring Sitoel to my residence. She still needs to learn how to channel her gift" Akantha whispered with a goodbye kiss. Banter nodded his head in agreement and waited until he heard the front door close before questioning his father, "Were you involved with that matter at the Rampton?"

"Were you?"

"No, I had to prepare for finals"

Morgan turned from the fireplace and gave Banter a

cold stare. "I'm glad to see you're still focused on matters concerning your family and business. Make sure you stay that way! Those people the detective spoke of sound dangerous and so is the company you're presently keeping. I wasn't the least bit surprised when he told me someone wanted them terminated. I suggest you make an effort to seek a more suitable employee for your training program. Your current one doesn't seem to have the promise of longevity". "I think he'll work out just fine" Banter replied as he made his way out the den.

Banter returned to his room and tapped on the door before he slowly opened it. "The detective is gone" Banter whispered before a knife unexpectedly pressed against his throat. "Good, because I don't plan on going back" Sitoel replied as she lowered the knife. "I'd appreciate it if you leave the utensils on the table" said Banter as he gripped Sitoel's wrist and forced it out of her hand. "As for the matter of you returning to a mental hospital, that is still questionable. You weren't granted amnesty. If you want to clear your name you must learn things and Akantha can teach them to you. She explains the mystical things way better than I can. You can borrow a couple of sweat suits till you find something more suitable" said Banter as he grabbed a duffle bag from his closet and tossed it on the bed. "Why can't I stay here? There's plenty of room" Sitoel asked as she toured Banter's wardrobe. "For starters my guest house is being fumigated" Banter answered as he watched Sitoel boldly dress in front of him. His imagination wondered as she slowly inched a pair of black suede sweat pants over her waist and quickly turned to catch Banter admiring from behind. "So why don't we share this room?" Sitoel asked as she gracefully jumped into the center of the bed. "I don't think my suppressed relationship issues could tolerate it. Now hurry up and pack" Banter demanded as he snatched the sheets from under Sitoel and watched her roll onto the floor. Downstairs, Mr. Brimm patiently waited for the right moment to address the news about the Rampton. "I had no idea how incompetent they would be" pleaded Brimm. "Ineptness cannot begin to describe how fortunate we are right now. The detective's theory even had Banter guessing about my involvement in the matter. In all, I guess I have Mr. Blaine to thank for my sudden turn of events. Tell me he's joined our ranks?" asked Morgan. "They say he prefers to be called *The Delicacy*. He's currently in one of our safe houses in Jersey" answered Brimm. "Wonderful, now make sure *The Delicacy* knows the benefits of working under my wing. After you handle the expenses, introduce him to our arsenal and have Mr. Price deliver the addresses of Mr. Maxwell's closest kin" instructed Morgan. "I'll handle it immediately" replied Brimm as he rubbed his hands together.

Shortly before noon Banter and Sitoel arrived at Akantha's residence. "I want you to know that I'm not going to forget how you treated me!" Sitoel threatened as she made her way up the stairs. "Gall already alerted me about your fighting skills. I'll be sure to keep an eye open the next time you have a paintbrush in hand" replied Banter. "I prefer escrima sticks" answered Sitoel. "You studied stick fighting?" Banter asked in a manner that expressed interest. "I guess you don't know everything you need to know about me" Sitoel replied before ringing the bell.

After Gall answered the door he escorted them into the living room. Akantha had just finished lighting her last fragrance candle and the scent of Persimmon flooded the room. "Have a seat and help yourself to some Persimmon tea" greeted Akantha as she poured some into a cup. "Is this really necessary?" Sitoel skeptically asked. "Your gift of foresight is very valuable, but I fear the medications you've endured have tampered with your ability to summon it. Your system must be as pure as the day when you first received your gift if you are to retrieve the carpet" explained Akantha. "At the Rampton I had two kills that carried the shadow of an eagle. Do I have a special gift?" asked Banter. "It is a sign that your Marid Djinn's have bonded. The stronger the bond becomes, the clearer the fates woven before you become" explained Akantha. "Retrieving the carpet is another matter I want to discuss with you. I appreciate you freeing me from prison but I was told I'd be given the opportunity to clear my name, and solve my sister's murder. I don't understand how that could be possible if I end up doing something that would get me sent back to prison. I'm sorry, but I don't need foresight to know how this can turn out" Sitoel answered before taking a sip of tea. "A thief with morality. You must've went to countless shows and used your gift to steal the secrets of other magician's for your own escapology acts. Now you're telling me you're worried about using it to commit another crime?" replied Banter. "There's a big difference between stealing secrets and how I received my answers!" Sitoel nervously answered before taking another sip of tea. "She's right Banter. There are greater risks and dangers involved. Sitoel's gift is the foresight of death. She learns from failed attempts. Hers and the Marid Djinn's" explained Akantha. "If it makes you feel better, what you take does not belong to Morgan Styles" added Akantha. "Then who does it belong to?" Sitoel curiously asked. "Me!" Iblis shouted from the flames of the fireplace. A loud roar echoed through the living room and it imitated the revving sound of a chopper motorcycle engine as the immense shadow of a hooded figure emerged from the fireplace. "Who are you?" Banter uttered as he grabbed him by the throat. "You do not recognize the one who spawned the being within you?" Iblis asked as Banter's Marid Djinn emerged. "Father" Banter replied in a tone that echoed a hiss. The reply had caused Iblis to release his grasp on Banter's throat, and after doing so he quickly soared across the room to address Sitoel in the same manner.

The act provoked her Marid Djinn to emerge as he slowly explained, "My Marid Djinns were spawned for the sole purpose of defiance, and feared no creature while doing so! After countless wars something uncommon began to stir inside them. Their death defying feats inspired faith, courage and loyalty. In death their vessels beaconed the light of martyr's. The course of their transference still torments me till this day!" said Iblis. He released his hold on Sitoel and slowly floated to Gall. "There still might be hope *for you*. I cannot allow them to interfere with the pact forged between me and Morgan Styles. The carpet and crown cannot leave his place of sanctuary before I receive my sacrifice!" Iblis instructed. He kept his face a blur within the black hooded robe as the other Marid Djinn's cautiously watched. "The vessels discovering the truth about their past and the selection of their fates are of great importance. You must recognize the natural course of events!" pleaded Akantha. "Do not tell me what to recognize! I'm fully aware of the course of events. Sitoel can proceed. When she reaches the sanctuary of the carpet she is not to remove them. She can summon the guardian angel and the being will tend to her need. While she's still within the walls!" instructed Iblis. "You can't expect her to complete the task successfully within that amount of time!" contested Akantha. "Why not? They are death defying" Iblis replied as he stepped into the flames of the fireplace. "Wait! Something has been troubling me and I believe you know the answer" said Banter. "Ask me what you wish and do not make haste" said Iblis. "Who killed the prince?" asked Banter. "It wasn't me" Iblis answered as he jumped into the flames of the fireplace. "I'll guess we'll never know" replied Banter. "I'm afraid you're already aware of the answer. His tongue knows no truth. Iblis has no value for time or your vessel" Akantha disappointedly mumbled as she walked over to the bookshelf to retrieve one of her sacred books. "Taking this path will only give your vessel a brief understanding of what's to come. She will see the images but she will not know how they came about or how to alter them" warned Akantha. She turned to a page with a picture of the carpet.

Displeased by Iblis's comments, Sitoel's Marid Djinn paid no mind to Akantha's warning as it angrily commanded her, "This is what we must seek out, and this is how we will go about it!" Sitoel placed the hand that bared her Marid Djinn's symbol on the page and circled the image. Akantha took a deep breath and crossed her fingers as she explained,

"During the Great War of the Heavens Iblis sent Jinn's to spy for signs of prey. A vain task because the heavens were always protected. A Jinn could never violate its border's without being fired upon by a hail of comets. So Iblis thought of another way to obtain the information he needed and it was the Angelic carpet". "See our father slay its guardian. Follow this path and you will also cast two fates to its protector!" instructed Sitoel's Marid Djinn. It showed Iblis brutally torturing an earth angel. He stabbed and bit the creature until it released its crown and ended its misery. Afterwards a vision carried her through the levels of Styles Corporate building and her mind openly received the experience. After she exited the carpets chamber, her eyes quickly opened and alerted everyone in the room. "Damn you Banter!" shouted Sitoel. "I beg your pardon?" replied Banter. "You did something that got me killed!" Sitoel answered as she slowly regained her senses. "Did you get to the carpet?" Akantha worriedly asked. "Yes, and the way I had to do it stunk" Sitoel answered as she paced around the living room to gather her thoughts. "I don't understand child? You must give me a more detailed description. Is it something that can be altered?" asked Akantha. "I don't think so. I was in a sewer and the stench helped me get past the guard dogs" answered Sitoel. "So my idea did work!" interrupted Gall. "That's not all. I've seen the carpet and it spoke to me! It started to tell me things about myself, Banter and Gall" Sitoel explained with excitement. "That doesn't make sense? You said the carpet was used to conquer kingdoms by revealing their weaknesses. Why would it tell her things about us?" asked Banter. "The carpet was woven by five earth angels.

One of which was the carpets guardian. They roamed the earth overhearing conversations and influencing people's decisions. During his defiance Iblis discovered its location and raided their temple. When the battle was over, he stole the carpet with the guardian's crown. After hanging it in his sanctuary it tormented him about his acts. It reminded him of the meaningless pursuits to gain favor in the eyes of a higher authority figure. Unable to further tolerate its presence, he quickly discovered a way to use it against man. He knew earth angels felt indebted to the service of the slain guardian and would always honor the memory of the being. They would only need to see the crown and they would willingly allow someone to partake in their conversations. The strength and power of a kingdom is based *on its people*. So after learning of their strengths and weaknesses they became easy prey for a conqueror. Especially one in league with Iblis. There was only one catch. Iblis demanded a sacrifice for its use" explained Akantha.

Banter curiously turned to Sitoel and asked, "So what did you ask it?" "I don't know? All I can remember is what I smelled and how I felt. Considering how things ended, the news wasn't all good. I also saw something horrible happen and for some reason I blamed you!" Sitoel answered as she leaned over the living room table to pour herself another cup of tea. "We can increase your chances by practicing the route to my father's safe at my security building. When I'm sure the detective isn't in the area, I'll come get you" advised Banter as he exited the living room. "Hold on, there's something I have to do too!" said Gall as he reached for his jacket and followed Banter out the door. "I will teach you how to summon the carpets guardian" said Akantha as she walked to the bookshelf to retrieve another book. "Why can't I wear the crown?" Sitoel curiously asked before taking another sip of tea. "If you use the crown you will be forced to abide by the terms Iblis made. You will have to make a sacrifice. Something he can't allow without already receiving one from Morgan. So consider yourself lucky because he would not have asked for something ordinary from you" Akantha explained as she calmly sat beside Sitoel and began her lesson.

While they practiced, Gall asked Banter for a ride to Chinatown. They slowly cruised the busy area until they had reached a cluster of grocers and fish markets on Mulberry Street. "Pull up at the fish market on your right side" Gall instructed the driver. "Is this part of your great idea?" Banter asked as they stepped out the vehicle. "Yes. I was already thinking of a plan to get into Styles Corporate building and it was through the sewer" answered Gall. "So why are we here?" asked Banter. "The owner had a problem awhile back and he hired me on retainer. He became a good friend and told me if I ever needed a favor to come and see him" Gall explained as he made his way to a beautiful Asian woman working the cash register. "Gall!" she happily shouted as she stepped from behind the register and gave him a hug. "Nice to see you again May. I was wondering if I could speak to the old man?" Gall politely requested with a mild embrace. "Sure. He's in the back with my uncles. Just follow me" May replied before signaling another employee to take her place. They quickly exited the rear of the shop and entered a back storage room. A surprised look appeared on the faces of the gentlemen sitting at the table as Gall's large frame peeked through the beads that decorated the doorway. Gall respectfully bowed his head before addressing the head of the table. *"Xiongqi Juren!"* the old man happily shouted. *"Xiongqi Juren?"* Banter curiously asked. "Giant murder weapon" answered Gall. "I need a favor. I will like all of your fish scraps" asked Gall. The old man took a pull from an opium pipe and exerted a small stream of smoke before he nodded to his daughter to comply. "You'd be pleased to know that I sold the sword. I put the ink that remained in the blade in this bottle" the old man told Gall as he lifted himself from the chair. He walked over to a combination locked cupboard behind him and removed the sealed container. "I can put it to use" replied Gall. "I can't keep scraps sitting around for too long. It'll stink up the place. When will you be back to pick it up?" May curiously asked as she gathered buckets. "I'll be back at the end of the week. I just need to find a good place for storage" Gall answered as he patted Banter on the back. "This will cover her ticket in, but how are we going to get her out?" Gall asked as they boarded the vehicle. "I'll have something figured out by the end of the week. There's still a few things I have to cover" answered Banter as he opened his laptop. "Like what?" Gall asked. He peeked at the site Banter brought up on the screen. "Her face" answered Banter. "The mask you pick better be a pretty one if you expect her to wear it" joked Gall. "I got that impression this morning at breakfast. That's why it grieves me to find a jeweler to place a few stones in the rubber necklace I've designed" replied Banter. A smirk suddenly appeared on both their faces as Banter displayed the chemical contents of the chain. "She was right. You did do something that almost got her killed!" Gall replied with an outburst of laughter.

During the course of the week Banter made things appear normal to the patrolling detective. He spent his mornings taking finals and afternoons hiring a staff for his business. His evenings were spent in the lab. There he modified Sitoel's gear and created a scale model of the boar hound's passageway. It had two routes. One to the sewer and another leading to his father's trophy vault. The last precautionary measure was another request from Gall. Two large containers of liquid Ambien.

Early Friday morning, Banter and Gall arrived at work and left a half hour before six o' clock that evening. They politely waved at Det. Rodriguez before boarding the limo and after being followed home, they waited until midnight to return to Styles Corporate Security. Gall escorted Sitoel to the lab carrying a knap sack and duffle bag. "I have to spend the whole weekend here?" asked Sitoel. "Yes, if you want to make it in and out of there alive!" said Banter. He retrieved a silver suitcase containing Sitoel's gear and handed it to her. When she opened it her eyes widened with amazement. She removed a black Venetian volto mask with rubies cut to resemble keys. Three were embedded around the left eye to resemble the tracks of a tear drop, and a clear casing with a large square pendant had a ruby key design. Three rubber chain links peaked her attention. "Is this a bonus?" Sitoel curiously asked. "You can't wear it until you're ready to infiltrate Styles Corporate. It has a safety mechanism that you need to learn. You activate it when you screw the three rubber chain links into the pendant. It'll give a nasty surprise to someone trying to snatch it off you, as a helpful reminder wear it outside your collar and keep your head raised high" advised Banter.

"Is that why the material of the mask feel's funny?"

"It's lined with a nylon cordura substarte and a proprietary polymer neoprene compound"

"Are you trying to scare me?"

Banter gently placed the necklace back into the suitcase and answered, "Don't worry it's only for your protection". After spending the entire weekend rehearsing their plan and sparring with each other, the three Marid Djinns suited up to infiltrate Styles Corporate building. A half hour before midnight a U Freight truck sat just two blocks away. It discretely covered a manhole leading to the sewer. Banter sat in the driver's seat adjusting his headset as he patched Sitoel's mini camera and transmitter into his lap top. "I have a visual. Now say something so I can test your transmitter" said Banter as he adjusted the volume on his headset. "I can't hold my breath and speak at the same time!" Sitoel snapped as she handed Gall the last bucket of fish scraps. "Perfect!" replied Banter.

When they were done unloading, Sitoel grabbed two giant spray containers and followed Gall into the sewer. Below ground they left a trail of fish scraps that lead to Styles Corporate emergency sewer exit. After simmering in a storage unit for half a week, vermin and stray cats easily followed. "I'll try to get as close as I can without being detected by the camera" said Gall. A cunning smirk appeared on his face as he sprayed Ambein on the fur of

every cat and rat that passed by. When Gall had acquired a
sufficient amount of bait, he herded them toward the door.
Seconds after a handful of strays triggered the alarm a chain
gate descended ten feet from the doorway and unlatched the
locks that restrained the boar hounds. Gall patiently waited
and observed as they stormed into the caged area devouring
whatever prey they had trapped inside.

The guards in the control room were about to place bets
before Polex entered. "What's going on here?" Polex asked as
he approached the computer console. "Some strays set off the
alarms in the sewer again" answered the dispatcher. "Send
a couple of guards to clean it up before the carcasses attract
more attention!" ordered Polex. He cautiously glanced at the
vault cameras before leaving the room. When nothing else
stirred in the cage but the hounds, the guards unlatched the
locks to their passageway. As the chain gate retracted the
boar hounds scurried through the passage and climbed the
ramps to their kennel.

The rest depended on speed as Sitoel activated an
electronic jammer for the camera and sprinted down the
tunnel. She slid under the rising gate and through the
carcasses of stray's before crawling through the boar hound's
passageway. "You have to reach it before the dogs make it
back and the guards activate the locks" advised Banter.

Sitoel picked up her pace, and when she had reached
the door to the trophy vault she switched on the electronic
jammer. Then she slowly lifted the gate and crawled into the
room. Her eyes immediately fell on the luster of the gold
crown resting on a podium in the center, and the angelic
carpet hung overhead. It was made from silk and on the end

of the warps were gold braided tassels. A surrealistic picture of four earth angels lifting a crown to a beam of light was woven in the center. "Stop daydreaming and get to a safe position!" Banter shouted through the transmitter. Sitoel ran to a blind spot in the corner beneath the camera in response.

After she deactivated the electronic jammer, she kneeled and respectfully asked the crown for permission. "Guardian, I humbly ask to partake in a conversation with the angels of the carpet. I mean them no harm. I await your permission" said Sitoel. It only took a brief moment before she got a response. "Why did you summon me? I am no longer part of this realm" a voice echoed from the podium. "I need to communicate with the angels of the carpet but I cannot wear the crown. The current owner still owes Iblis his debt" explained Sitoel. "Iblis! Morgan is in league with Iblis? Is this man an enemy to you?" the Guardian angrily asked. "That is something I need to find out" answered Sitoel.

There was a brief pause of silence and after a short while the Guardian honored Sitoel's request. "Angels of earth, please forgive my intrusion. If you can allow me a moment of your time someone would like to partake in a conversation about the current owner of the carpet" asked the Guardian. Sitoel looked on dumbfounded as the images on the carpet and the Guardian suddenly merged into life like characters. As their facial features emerged from the carpet, so did their words. They politely answered in block sequence, "Morgan Styles. Mongol Corporate Raider. Minion of Iblis. Yes we know of him. He has power and many strengths but his life will be cut short if he fails to pay Iblis and perish his enemies". "Who? What enemies?" Banter shouted through the transmitter before Sitoel repeated his words. "The Jinns. Three Marid Djinns. Banter Styles. Sitoel Carrea and Tibbigall Maxwell" answered the earth angels. "Their lying!" shouted Banter. "How can this be?" asked Sitoel. "We warned Morgan of this threat a long time ago. When he failed to meet Iblis's payment to sacrifice his first son. On the night of the planned assassination Morgan paid a woman to lure Banter into the den of a vicious gang. No one knew Banter was a Jinn. *One of three Marid Djinn's!* When Morgan discovered the truth about Banter he immediately set out to perish the others. Sitoel Carrera. The Great Secret. *One of three Marid Djinns!* Tibbigall Maxwell. Gall. *One of three Marid Djinns!*" explained the earth angels. "Why me?" Gall suspiciously asked as he entered the vehicle and adjusted his communicator. "What steps did Morgan take to rid himself of this problem?" asked Sitoel. "It began with an alliance between Morgan Styles and Lennox Blaine. For the death of Tibbigall Maxwell, Morgan Styles agreed to support Lennox Blaine's organization and their war against the Abominables. On the night of the planned assassination Lennox Blaine's henchmen waited for Tibbigall Maxwell outside a diner he frequently visited on Bay Chester. Two men entered to lure Tibbigall Maxwell outside. But a fight with Tibbigall had left them disabled. The sight angered two armed henchmen waiting in their vehicle. They rushed the attempt. Paul's soul was collected on that night. Not Tibbigall Maxwell's. So much sadness and anger. We tried to communicate with Tibbigall Maxwell to change his ways. He didn't listen. It was *Typical*. He was Tibbigall. *One of three Marid Djinn's!* He infiltrated Lennox Blaine's building in retaliation and flooded the gates of hell with the souls of Lennox Blaine's henchmen. All except for Quinton Blaine. *The Delicacy.* A cannibal. Morgan Styles war with the Abominables had ended before it began. Morgan continued his attempt to vanquish his son's Fate by diminishing the Marid Djinn's number. Virgil Price found the third Marid Djinn. Sitoel Carrea. The Great Secret. *One of three Marid Djinn's!* The attempts made to sabotage her acts were useless. She knew several ways to escape. So Morgan Styles devised a scheme that involved her sister. Nina Carrea. It included an insanely jealous wife. A mayor named Evelyn Ortega. The scene would look like a crime of passion. They had planned for Evelyn Ortega to confront Nina Carrea about her acts of adultery. Then one of Morgan's henchmen would assassinate them. Afterwards he would inform Sitoel of the meeting and the danger her sister was in. So he could assassinate her when she arrived at the location. Unknowingly, Evelyn Ortega was already a soul corrupted by power and hatred. An undisclosed affair to her political career was a bigger threat and disgrace than the act of the affair itself. So she took matters into her own hands. She murdered Nina Carrea. She buried her body a few feet from the outgrown roots of an old willow tree on her coffee plantation. On the night of Sitoel's capture Evelyn Ortega drugged her to retrieve the evidence she had discovered. The following day she returned to the coffee plantation and buried them with her sister. Hope had seemed lost for Sitoel, but Virgil Price photographed and recorded his dealings with Morgan Styles as a precautionary measure. Too many people disappeared after he was asked to investigate their whereabouts. He keeps the tapes and rolls of film under a floor board in his closet at his condo. It's on Jefferson Street in Brooklyn" answered the earth angels. The news tapped a nerve in all three Marid Djinns.

Sitoel adjusted her mask and a tear overlapped the left eyepiece. It followed the track of embedded rubies and reflected a sparkle from the light beaming off the carpet. "So much sadness and anger in your thoughts. It's not too late to change your path" advised the earth angels. "It's too late for them! Because I am Sitoel Carrea. The Great Secret. *One of three Marid Djinn's!*" Sitoel angrily replied. Overwhelmed by her emotions, Sitoel rushed out the boar hound's entry gate without activating the electronic jammer, and when she entered the sewer she was struck on the head by Polex. Shortly afterwards, he woke her up with a couple of slaps to the face. "Your blood will blend in well with the vermin and strays that cover my coveralls should you raise your hand again!" Sitoel threatened in a tone that echoed a hiss. "She's awake!" Polex excitedly shouted as Winston handcuffed both her hands to a pipe on the ceiling. "That wasn't a nice thing to do to the boar hounds. They would have given you a quicker death if you hadn't put them to sleep" said Polex. He removed his jacket and turned the camera over the door in another direction. "I guess that means you want to be alone" Winston heckled as he stepped back into the building through the emergency exit. Polex complied with a nod as he removed a small pike from his hair. He slyly placed his hand on Sitoel's thigh as her Marid Djinn weaved a fate. "Fate has woven two deaths!" Sitoel warned in a tone that carried a hiss. "I'll make sure the first one is gentle" Polex amusingly replied as he reached for the zipper on Sitoel's coveralls. He suddenly paused when he recognized the symbol Akantha had warned him of. It also resembled the key centered in Sitoels necklace. "You won't be needing this!" said Polex as he snatched the chain from her neck.

Polex quickly regretted his actions as he pulled on the pendant and activated its safety mechanism. Within seconds the locket had opened and sprayed enough liquid nitrogen to cover Polex's entire face. He slowly asphyxiated as cold burns amassed. At that moment, Sitoel elevated her legs and kicked Polex into the wall behind him. The impact forced him to fall forward, and at the same time the liquid nitrogen smothered the remaining oxygen in his body, the fall shattered his face.

The shadow of a chain link mask lifted over the torn facial features like a curtain and exposed the shattered organs to Sitoel before disappearing. Her Marid Djinn also granted her the strength to break her chains and stomp on the small pile of facial tissue beneath her. It caked into her boot soles to generate a sound that appeased her anger as she raced back to the surface. "What took you so long?" Banter shouted as he exited the vehicle. Sitoel climbed out the manhole and answered with a punch that knocked him halfway into an alley. "You gave me a liquid nitrogen chain choker!" she angrily answered. "It wasn't meant to be a chain choker" Banter defensively replied as he rose to his feet. "When you're hanging from a pipe *it's a chain choker!*" snapped Sitoel. "Enough! We know the enemy to unleash our anger on!" Gall shouted from the passenger side window. "I'm not going back home" said Banter as he made his way to the driver's seat. Gall opened the door and scooted to the middle to create a needed barrier between the two. "I need time to put a plan together. I don't want Alexander getting caught up in the middle of this!" explained Banter. "We'll have to prepare one at Akantha's. The news of the break in would have the detective covering both buildings" said Gall as his cellphone vibrated in the inner pocket of his coveralls. He immediately recognized the Abominable's number and answered it. "What's the emergency?" asked Gall. "Kaleb!" answered Matthew.

Gall sadly hung up the phone and demanded to be taken to the Abominable estate. "What's wrong?" Banter asked as he made a sharp turn onto the Manhattan Bridge. "I'll find out when we get there" Gall worriedly replied. When they arrived at the Abominable estate they found Victor and Matthew waiting outside. "You can wait for me here. I won't be long" said Gall as he stepped out of the vehicle. Victor explained as he approached, "Kaleb was missing when we arrived for work this morning. We entered the house and found this. They also left a message on the kitchen table". Victor continued as he escorted Gall into the house. Everything from the front door to Kaleb's office had been broken and riddled with bullets. Two men in fatigues laid dead as they passed through the doorway, and seven more were chopped down before they made it up the stairs by an XM8 assault rifle that Kaleb kept. When they entered the kitchen they found the head of a pig propped in the center of the table. Quinton had emptied the salt and pepper shaker to scribble a message around it, *"I'll invite you as soon as I complete the menu!"* "I figured I'd wait until you see it before I do a clean up" said Victor. "Don't clean it. Call the 71st precinct and inform Detective Rodriguez about the matter" answered Gall as he began to inspect the area. "I heard you were going corporate. Did you forget how things like this get handled?" Matthew disappointedly asked as Gall made his way out the kitchen. "I didn't forget how to handle things and neither should you! Start making phone calls. Reach out to everyone we know. If their still in the country I want to know where!" Gall instructed before he left the house.

That same morning after a quick shower and breakfast at Akantha's, the Marid Djinn's continued with their daily routine. Before noon Det. Rodriguez entered Banter's office flapping his arms like a vulture circling prey. "I told you it was going to be like this. I don't like calls at four in the morning. Especially from places I just finished patrolling. I'm sorry gentleman but I'm afraid we're going to have to take a ride down to the station" said Det. Rodriguez as he gestured for Banter and Gall to follow him out the door.

When they had arrived at the station, Banter and Gall suspiciously watched as the detective strolled into his office with a T.V. video recorder. "This morning a couple of my buddies from the 5th precinct made me aware of a break in at your father's building. A funny thing though, they say the perp only stole a guard's face. They didn't think it was related to my case, but you and I know better! Before I left to investigate I get another call from my department to assist in a matter on Early Street in the Bronx. The resident might look familiar to you" explained Det. Rodriguez as he pushed play on the tape recorder.

It was footage from the camera that hung over Kaleb's

door. The firefight must've lasted nearly an hour as the detective fast forward to the scene where fifteen soldiers stormed the room. The next scene showed them dragging Kaleb from his office in chains. Gall's anger increased as they kicked and punched Kaleb down the stairs. After they carried Kaleb out the front door, Quinton entered with a smile and an enormous pig head. "We already have officer's working the case, but you and I know how valuable time is right now. You need to tell me everything you know about the Abominables and Lennox Blaine's murder" pleaded the detective. "You're trying to get me to talk while some maniac is about to feast on my brother? You should be spending your time trying to find him!" shouted Gall. "Detective, the captain would like to see you in his office" an officer interrupted. "I'll be right back. In the meantime the both of you should consider making some new arrangements" Det. Rodriguez advised before leaving his office. The detective disappointedly shook his head as he made his way to the captain's office. "I need you to go to the Styles estate ASAP!" demanded Capt. Bell. "I already have his son and Maxwell in my office. We were just reviewing the abduction of Maxwell's brother" answered Det. Rodriguez. "Then you better be in a position to have Maxwell make a deal because there's been another kidnapping. Morgan's youngest son was just taken this afternoon. We have a dead driver and no witnesses. You need to go over there and see what you can make out of it. Don't blow this detective!" instructed Capt. Bell.

Banter and Gall were leaving the precinct when the detective returned to his office. They had just stepped out

the building when Gall received a phone call. He glanced
at the caller I.D. and immediately recognized the name
Guccio Cognome. An Italian chef that owned a ristorante
that featured him making his famous sauce in a 15,000
liter pot. "Good afternoon. *Come va?*" greeted Guccio.
"Things could be better. How's the ristorante?" answered
Gall. "Busy. Some tourists came in from out of town. My
nephew Baldo delivers fifteen to twenty plates a night to
the same address. They say they come for the fishing, but
he only sees the fast women and guns" replied Guccio.
"What kind of guns?" asked Gall. "Mp5 and RPK's. He
tells me one man in particular is interested in renting my
pot. He offered to pay extra if I leave some sauce. Something
tells me that if I give it to him it will not come back the
same. After I heard from your brother I wondered if this
information would be of value to you?" replied Guccio.
"This information is a great benefit to my brother. On his
next delivery tell Baldo to make arrangements with the man
for the pot. When you confirm the date and time call me!"
instructed Gall. "I will do this favor for you, and if this man
is dangerous *embrazzo!*" replied Guccio. "Grazie Guccio.
Ciao!" said Gall. Gall quickly hung up the phone as Det.
Rodriguez approached him. "You don't have to wait for a
driver. You and Gall can ride with me back to the Style's
estate" offered the detective. "I'm not going back to the
estate!" Banter rudely replied. "You're not interested in your
brother's kidnapping?" asked the detective. "What are you
talking about?" Banter worriedly asked.

"Alexander was abducted and I'm on my way to your
estate" answered Det. Rodriguez.

"Then what are we waiting for!" snapped Banter as they rushed to the detective's vehicle.

When they had arrived at the Styles estate, they found the front gate swarming with reporters. Banter shielded his eyes from the barrage of flashing lights as reporters rushed the car with questions about Alexander's abduction. Over a dozen guards cleared a way for the detective's vehicle after identifying him. As soon as the car had reached the front steps, Banter jumped out and rushed through the mansion doors. Three men stood guard outside the den and as Banter approached one guard unknowingly tried to search him before entering.

An impetuous act as Banter responded with a round house kick that sent the guard flying through the doors. "Where were you?" Banter shouted as Brimm withdrew his batons. "Where were you?" answered Morgan. "Are you implying that I had something to do with this?" Banter replied while Gall and Det. Rodriquez entered the room. "We should all settle down" advised the detective. "Settle down? Last night someone broke into my corporate building and killed one of my guards. Today, I return home to find out my son has been kidnapped and the only thing you can tell me is to settle down. I'll settle for you doing your job!" yelled Morgan. He walked to his bar and poured himself a glass of brandy. "I already gave my statement to the authorities handling the case. Brimm can escort you to the door!" he added. "Is that how you explain being a good father!" said Banter. "It's beneath me to explain my actions to you. Your recent decisions have left me unable to acknowledge you anyway" answered Morgan. Banter angrily clenched his fists and moved forward in a threatening manner before Gall placed his hand on his shoulder. "You don't want to display something that you'll regret later" hinted Gall. Banter immediately stopped and nodded his head in agreement before turning to the detective. "I trust you'd keep me informed?" requested Banter. "I'll let you know if I hear something. Gall, you should take time to think things over. I don't want you walking around this city with a target on your back and not know my door was open. You'd just be giving Quinton a better opportunity" advised Det. Rodriguez. "That door is still open? Well let me give you a piece of advice. Stop trying to go through the ones that aren't!" Gall boldly replied as he made his way out the house with Banter.

When they returned to Akantha's home, they found her and Sitoel watching the news. "I see Morgan Styles has made arrangements to settle his debt" said Akantha. She calmly poured Sitoel another cup of tea. "What's that supposed to mean?" asked Banter. "The boy is just a lure. Morgan would not replace him with Banter" added Gall. "You're wrong! The terms of Morgan Styles arrangement is no different than when he first used the carpet. Morgan has run short of time and the attempts on his life are a reminder of that. He will take the crown and carpet to an undisclosed location and see to Alexander's demise!" explained Akantha. "He's just a kid. I failed him" Banter disappointedly mumbled before he punched the wall. Sitoel walked over to console him. "I know what you're going through. There was a time when I felt the same way. The worst thing you can do right now is blame yourself" Sitoel advised as she gently patted Banter on his back.

A grim mood settled in Akantha's living room before a phone call brought a smile to Gall's face. He immediately identified the caller. "Buonosera my friend in need!" greeted Guccio. "Grazie, amico fidato!" Gall happily answered. "Sixteen plates were delivered to our friend tonight. We made arrangements for him to pick the pot up tomorrow after closing. I figured I'd wait till I speak to you before I include my sauce?" replied Guccio. "Fill the pot half way with sauce" answered Gall. "I will do this for you. Do you need any further assistance?" Guccio asked in a concerned tone. "No, I already have a team. Grazie!" answered Gall. "I have some good news! I have an idea on where their keeping Alexander. If you want to come along you'll have to follow my directions to the letter" said Gall. He walked over to the bookshelf to remove a silver briefcase from a hidden compartment. "That's fine by me. I just want Alexander back in one piece" replied Banter. "Then go back to that lab of yours and prep two coveralls for hunting. I don't want to carry any scent that would alert Quinton. Try lacing them with wafers and they have to be ready by tomorrow night!" instructed Gall. "What about yours?" Banter curiously asked. "Don't worry about mine. I'll smell like dinner" Gall answered as he retrieved his mask and kusari fundo chain. "So where are you headed?" asked Sitoel. "You still have your mask?" asked Gall.

"Yeah"

"Then go get it. On the way there you can ask your Fate" answered Gall.

A smirk appeared on Sitoel's face as she followed his instructions and within two hours both Marid Djinns were making their way into a Brooklyn condo from the terrace. Sitoel carefully watched as Gall easily penetrated the security system and made his way inside. "Why can't we just grab Virgil Price's evidence and leave?" asked Sitoel. "You still have a lot to learn if you plan on working with me. Why don't you just grab yourself a sandwich and relax. You might learn something before the night is over" answered Gall. They patiently waited until ten o'clock that evening. Virgil entered the apartment and strolled into the kitchen looking over a few pieces of mail before he was unexpectedly grabbed from behind. A giant hand smothered his mouth and another grabbed his right wrist as he tried to reach for his side arm. "You don't want to make matters worse. My employer has become aware of your secret recordings" said Gall. He slowly removed his hand from Virgil's mouth. "Tell Mr. Styles I only kept them as a precautionary measure. In case I ever found myself in a situation like this! If I'm missing for more than a day, all that evidence will be mailed out to the local authorities" Virgil nervously pleaded. "Does that mean I won't be able to find all that stuff in your little special hiding spot in the closet?" replied Gall. A look of despair appeared on Virgil's face as he questioned, "If you know that much and I'm still alive, there must be something else he wants?"

"Tomorrow night he would like you to take that evidence down to the 71st precinct and leave it for Detective Rodriguez"

"Why, and what does he expect me to do after that?"

Gall maneuvered his arms to place Virgil in a sleeper hold before making another request. "My employer will be leaving his normal way of life to start another. I suggest you do the same after you complete your task. We took a couple of recordings and the package labeled Carrea" said Gall. "The one with the tapes and pictures of Mr. Ortega with the gypsy woman? You don't work for Morgan!" Virgil groggily uttered before his sleep. "Now what?" Sitoel asked as she tucked the envelope of evidence in her jacket. "Now we prepare for our dinner date!" answered Gall.

The following evening, just before closing a few men from Guccio's staff had just finished loading his pot onto a flatbed truck. Two soldiers lazily watched from the driver's seat inside as he approached. "Where is my payment!" demanded Guccio. "What are you complaining about?" asked the solider. "Give him the envelope already" said the driver. The solider quickly handed Guccio a large padded envelope and waited for him to check the count. After sorting through a large stack of bills Guccio nodded to the driver and sang, *"Suelta Mi Mano"*.

A half a block away from the ristorante Banter and Sitoel tailed the truck. The drive lasted two hours before the truck slowly cruised along the Maurice River in Heislerville, New Jersey. "I left you something under your seat" said Banter. Sitoel reached under her chair to retrieve a small jewelry box that contained a chain with a ruby pendant. "How did you manage to pick the pocket of a jacket with all those bells?" Banter asked as the truck in front came to a halt. "They held the event in an old tavern. The ceiling had weak support beams and after I failed they hung me directly over the coat rack as a lesson. The beam broke after my death and knocked over the rack. The purse fell out of the pocket and that's when I found out where it was. So the following day I strengthened the beam in the ceiling. When it was ready, I entered the tavern with a rope and a boastful challenge" explained Sitoel. "Clever. You picked the inside pocket while you hung from the ceiling" replied Banter. He placed the car in park and went to the trunk to remove a suitcase that contained a small inflatable boat with his rifle. After inspecting the contents of her jewelry box Sitoel jumped out the car and grabbed Banter's hand. She pulled him close for a kiss on the cheek before Banter pushed her off. "Don't miss!" he snapped in a tone that echoed a hiss.

The flatbed continued onto a driveway leading to the lighthouse. "My pot has arrived!" Quinton cheerfully shouted as the trailer backed up to a large grill base in front of the oil house. "Clams Posillipo is on *The Delicacy's* menu tonight. So don't clam up. The recipe say's I'd have to discard the ones that don't open!" Quinton taunted as he poked Kaleb with a table fork. "Bon appetit cannibal. When my brother's find you it'll be the last meal you'd ever enjoy" threatened Kaleb. "I'll remember those words every time I belch" Quinton replied before leaving the room to assist with the grill's fire.

A few miles away, a Marid Djinn masked herself and loaded two Skorpion VZ pistols as she jogged through the grassy fields surrounding the lighthouse. On the opposite end, another Marid Djinn anchored his boat and slowly crept ashore. After he positioned himself on a ridge that covered his rifle's range to the lighthouse, he quickly scanned the perimeter for signs of Alexander. He adjusted the rifle's optic lens and seen three men carrying crates filled with clams out the front door. Quinton followed with a bottle of wine. They happily greeted the two soldiers as they rolled the pot off the flat bed. Banter continued to roam past two floors with windows before he disappointedly set his sights on the tower. After the pot had been placed on the grill, a solider quickly lighted the wood and charcoal pieces beneath. "Cheers!" saluted Quinton. He guzzled down half the bottle and demanded, "Bring down the rest of the meat!" Three soldier's made their way back to the house before a signal shot interrupted them. Before anyone could react, Sitoel switched her guns to full auto and unleashed a fate.

Her lips curved within the outline of her mask to blow a kiss while she discharged shells that pancaked against the ribcage of the soldiers and sent shattered fragments through their coronary artery. "That was for Nina!" Sitoel shouted as blood stains from the bullet wounds strangely formed the imprint of her lips and sealed their fate with a kiss. Quinton quickly threw the other two in the line of fire as he ducked and ran back to the house. "You want to cancel *The Delicacy!*" Quinton shouted as he entered the house and retrieved one of the RPK's leaning against the window. He immediately received his answer as Sitoel continued to fire from a brush of trees in front of the house. When he couldn't pick up a scent, Quinton nervously broke a few boards that sealed a first floor window and started a fire fight. Under the cover of darkness Sitoel ran to different areas to keep Quinton distracted.

A successful tactic that provoked Quinton to seek

higher ground. He nervously emptied two magazines before he grabbed another loaded rifle and rushed to the second floor. Outside, a string of bubbles reached the surface of Guccio's sauce as Gall emerged with his Venetian mask and his hair ponytailed in Bushido fashion. "You want to cancel *The Delicacy!*" was the repeated cry that fueled him as he tossed a grappling hook to the rim of the pot to climb out. When Gall had reached the top, he leapt onto the roof of the oil house and disrobed. After removing his soaked jumper, Gall cautiously made his way to the house in a tee shirt and boxers. He slowly unraveled the kursari fundo chain wrapped around his forearm as he recited the verses from a *Warriors Creed* in his head. He steadily climbed the stairs while regulating his breath control as he closed in on his mark. "You think you can cancel *The Delicacy!* You think you've won? You forget one thing. I still have a guest to serve!" Quinton shouted after emptying his last clip. He withdrew a butcher knife from his back pocket and began to pleasure himself with thoughts of carving Kaleb into pieces before his death or capture.

As he rushed through the doorway Gall skillfully wrapped the wrist holding the knife and embraced him. "How?" Quinton uttered as Gall twisted his arm behind his back. "Right now I'm the only one in a position to ask questions" said Gall as he tightened his hold around Quinton's neck. "Where are the rest of your men?" asked Gall. "They went back to Columbia" answered Quinton. "With the boy?" Gall continued to question. "Yes. His father has a base out there for private rituals" said Quinton.

"Where?"

"I don't know! I was just along for the ride. I was supposed to finish you when you came for your brother"

"What did you do to my brother?"

Quinton struggled to speak over Gall's forearm, "You got here before I had a chance to do anything". "Then your fate is not mine" Gall disappointedly responded as he applied enough pressure to put Quinton to sleep. When he was done he carried Quinton's body to the tower. When he reached the top, he gently placed Quinton on the floor and greeted Kaleb. "I would've expected a bigger fight from an Abominable" joked Gall. "Unchain me and I'll show you what I had planned for the ones coming to cook me!" replied Kaleb. "In due time" said Gall as he headed back down stairs. When he stepped outside, Sitoel asked with the echo of a hiss, "Are you ready?" "Yes" Gall answered as he made a defensive stance. Sitoel quickly withdrew a pair of escrima sticks and attacked. Gall withstood the blows for fifteen minutes and snapped at the first drop of blood. "Enough!" he shouted with a hiss.

Sitoel immediately stopped and watched as he headed to the oil house to retrieve a few necessary items. When he was finished, he returned back to the tower. "What kind of rescue is this? You can play lighthouse keeper on your own time!" Kaleb complained as Gall placed a lighted lantern in the frensal frame of the tower. He positioned the optic lens to create a path of light that beamed over the Maurice River. "Are you crazy? Do you want to invite the locals to a crime scene?" contested Kaleb. "Guccio made a request" replied Gall as he picked Quinton up and positioned him in front of the lens so he could cast a shadow on the water.

When he was done, he returned downstairs. "Wait until your back on the main road before you make the call and don't turn on your lights before you've reached it!" Gall instructed as he tossed Sitoel onto the roof of the oil house. "I know!" Sitoel replied before removing one of her gloves to display her Marid Djinn's symbol. After doing so, she reached out and hauled Gall to the roof. He retrieved the rope from his grappling hook and tied it around his ankles. He left himself enough rope to keep his head above the sauce before leaping back into the pot. "Put out the fire on your way out!" instructed Gall.

Sitoel obediently followed instructions and within half an hour authorities arrived on the scene. Gall could hear an officer radio for assistance as a squad car pulled up to the pot. The shadow on the water immediately gained their attention. "There's someone in the tower!" the officer shouted. The driver withdrew a megaphone from the rear seat as they exited with their guns drawn. "This is the New Jersey State Police Department. I want you to come out of there with your hands placed over your head!" instructed the officer. Gall crossed his fingers and patiently waited as the officer gave another warning. When there was no response, Gall had doubted his judgment. It was at that moment a Marid Djinn reflected on the shadow casted on the water to complete a fate that was woven with the utmost delicacy. Within seconds a muffled shot raced over the heads of the patrol unit and discarded *The Delicacy* as if he was a bad clam. Kaleb amusingly whispered as the corpse fell to his feet, "Gall you crazy dog!"

Within an hour several emergency response units and

news teams had arrived on the scene. A helicopter circled the air with a high beam for ground support as medical technicians pulled Gall from the pot and tended to his wounds. "You say there was a boy and woman with you?" an officer questioned as Gall covered his head with a towel. "Yes, my brother and I were taken prisoner by the same soldiers that abducted Morgan Styles son. There was a woman with us. I didn't recognize her but she kept mumbling about being the Great Secret. I also remember hearing something about a base in Columbia. I believe that's where the soldiers were taking them. You have to get this information to Detective Rodriguez in the 71st precinct before it's too late!" Gall explained in a concerned tone. "Where's my brother?" Kaleb shouted as medical technicians struggled to keep him on a stretcher. "I think it would be best for you to ride with him. I can catch up with you at the hospital" suggested the officer. "I think that would be best" Gall coyly answered.

Before noon Detective Rodriguez disappointedly made his way to Capt. Bell's office. "Why haven't you answered your pages? I've been looking all over for you. Where have you been?" shouted the captain. "I've been trying to close a case. Last night someone left a blackmail packet for me. One of Morgan Styles employee's is a turncoat. Inside was enough evidence to connect Morgan Styles to crimes of blackmail, extortion, embezzlement, price fixing, kidnapping, conspiracy to commit murder and murder in at least a dozen cases. A couple of them involving Tibbigall Maxwell. I ran down to the courthouse to get a warrant for Morgan's arrest this morning but by the time I had reached the estate he was gone. The maid said he had made

flight arrangements. So I went to his private airstrip and
discovered his jet landed in Columbia. I just finished placing
his warrant in the NCIC index" explained the detective.
"Mr. Maxwell might be pleased to hear that. They pulled
him from a pot of sauce this morning. *The Delicacy* was
about to cook Gall and his brother in Guccio's famous sauce
with some clams before a unit from the New Jersey State
Police showed up. They responded to an anonymous call
about a firefight at the East Point Lighthouse. They found
bodies on the scene and a sniper opened fire on them. He
fled the scene after Quinton's death. They found the rifle
and ballistics matched it to the one used in the Rampton
escape. I'm guessing our sniper guy is a cleanup man for
Morgan Styles turncoat". "Things must've went south
with the Blaine organization" commented Det. Rodriguez.
"He probably sent him out when he caught word about a
turncoat. The only thing that puzzles me is why he would
kidnap his son and a woman?" asked the Captain.

"Another prisoner?"

"Gall left a statement that said she was being held
prisoner. He overheard her say she was *The Great Secret*".

Det. Rodriguez took a brief moment to ponder on the
name and made a connection. "Sitoel Carrea! There was
information involving her and her sister in that packet" Det.
Rodriguez replied as he leapt from his seat and rushed out
the office. "Where are you going?" shouted the Captain. "To
close a case!" answered Det. Rodriguez. On the other side of
town Gall returned to Akantha's residence with a hospital
identification bracelet on his wrist. "Alexander?" Banter
worriedly asked as he rushed out the living room. "They took

him to Columbia. Your father has a base there" answered
Gall. "When I was looking over the files we took from
Virgil Price I seen information about a base in Columbia.
He sent intel to an outpost on Malpelo Island" said Sitoel.
"Those coordinates should give us a lead to Alexander!"
replied Banter. "I can charter a plane from an old friend
that flies that air space regularly. He'll gladly drop us off
for a reasonable fee" added Gall. "A ceremony must take
place before the sacrifice. It will last the course of a day and
then shortly before midnight Morgan must offer Alexander
to Iblis. If you intend to save your brother, you must do it
before then!" advised Akantha. Banter acknowledged with
a nod as Sitoel handed him the information. "We can pick
a few things up at my corporate security building before
we leave" said Banter. "I have everything I need right here"
replied Gall as he approached a large wooden grandfather
clock with a metal cabinet implanted in the base. A devilish
grin appeared on Gall's face as he eagerly typed in the four
digit combination. "My war chest!" Gall excitedly mumbled
as he removed two large metal suitcases.

Within a few hours the three Marid Djinns arrived at
New York Skyports Incorporated. A shiny black limo made
its way to a hanger that harbored a jet black Catalina sea
plane with words printed on the side. *"Slippery When Wet!"*
was the company logo and a caution sign was painted on the
tail fin. Gall stepped out the car to greet the pilot and his son.
A middle aged African American man named Gilroy Todou
happily embraced Gall as he approached. "Make sure you let
him know this plane does not take off unless he can hold the
cross for more than fifteen minutes!" Gilroy's son shouted

from the passenger door. "What's wrong with Tobias?" Gall
suspiciously asked. "I know we owe you our lives, but Tobias
has a different recollection of that experience. He was just a
kid when he seen the other side of you. When those natives
dumped us in that crocodile pit we thought we had spent
our last day on earth. Then your eyes became as black and
emotionless as that predator. We saw you brake the jaw and
spine bones of a 29ft. croc and to be honest with you, we
both needed diapers afterwards. Tobias never could forget
that day and when he became of age he devoted his life to
Christianity. The only reason he isn't sitting in a church
right now is because this is a family business. After my sight
went bad he became the only pilot. I've always appreciated
your family's business. I hope you can understand" pleaded
Gilroy. "I understand friend. Now help me load these cases"
replied Gall as Banter and Sitoel boarded. When they were
done, Gall boarded and Gilroy handed him a large Celtic
cross that hung over the pilot's cockpit. Gall placed the cross
in the center of his chest and amusingly replied in a voice
that imitated a vampire's, "I cannot shape shift and fly to
Columbia. Will you please take me?" "I'll be delighted to
take you. They have beautiful women. Beaches" replied
Tobias. "Malpelo Island" interrupted Gall. "*Shark infested
waters!* I should've known this would be one of those trips!"
said Tobias. He disappointedly snatched his cross from Gall
and sat at the cock pit. "The three of you must be closer than
three clicks if you plan on doing a human torpedo into those
waters" said Tobias as he started the ignition. "Three clicks?"
Banter curiously asked. "My father grew up with two older
brothers and they were very close. He used to tell me stories

about how they grew up during the civil rights era. He said during those times they had to be armed and as tight as three clicks. Out in the country a trespasser would hear the same sound if they approached their house with unpleasant intentions. A click from a double barrel shotgun at the front door, one from the right side of the porch and another from the bushes planted on the left side of the house" explained Tobias as the plane took off into the air. "Don't worry, I can tell you from experience that my sharks will recognize a Marid Djinn!" Gall replied as he removed the bottle the old man handed him in Chinatown.

Already on the shores of Malpelo Island, Morgan Styles discretely watched as Winston dragged Alexander into a room and threw him into a steel cage that hung in the far corner. After Alexander had been locked inside, Winston pulled a lever by the door that slowly lowered several beams with water jugs tied to them. "You're going to be in a lot of trouble when my father and Banter come for me!" Alexander angrily shouted. "I hate to disappoint you, but your father won't! As for your brother, I can't wait for him and that crazy girlfriend of his to show their face again. We have a score to settle" Winston replied before slamming the door. "Your design displays a lot of effort but will it guarantee results?" Morgan asked Brimm. "Your debt will be paid by either son before the end of the feast" answered Brimm. "I hope your prediction factors in the abilities of all three Marid Djinns. I cannot afford any mistakes!" Morgan nervously replied. "There's no need to worry. The three Marid Djinn's were not the only creature's spawned by Iblis!" answered Brimm. He removed his shirt to display the emblem of a deadly *Naja*.

Shortly before sunrise the Marid Djinns had reached their destination. They soared through the Mosquetero peaks and discretely launched three large metal cases close to shore. "I'll call to let you know when it'll be safe for you to come back and pick me up!" said Gall as Banter and Sitoel suited up. "Just you? What about them?" Tobias curiously asked. "I complied with your father's wishes and obeyed your rules for being a passenger, but now you must remember mine" replied Gall. Tobias nodded his head in agreement as he quickly recalled Galls strict rules about asking questions about cargo and client confidentiality. "Good luck!" Tobias shouted as Banter and Sitoel jumped from the planes folsum. "Happy hunting!" he added as Gall masked himself and leapt into the open sky. Under a black hooded cloak, Iblis discretely watched their dive from the highest peaks on the island and eagerly mumbled, "My children have arrived!"

Everything was now in place for a final confrontation. Gall dived into the water and emptied the contents of the bottle into the sea. He quickly finger painted sharks, and the liquid inked Great Whites into the sea. When Banter and Sitoel swam to Gall's position their eyes resembled those of their surrounding predators. Banter cautiously withdrew his hunting knife while one of Gall's sharks circled them. "Put that away and grab one" Gall instructed in a tone that carried a hiss. "You'll have to explain before I trust one of them" replied Banter. "Me too!" added Sitoel. "You should know by now that we're not the only beings with special gifts. That liquid came from the sword of Lu Dongbin. One of the Eight Immortals. He used the ink to draw pictures with his sword and those pictures have the ability to come to life" explained Gall. "We're really going to have to sit and talk about the places you've been when this is over" replied Banter. They grabbed the dorcal fin of the nearest shark and it carried them to shore.

The morning sunrise had cast a reflection on the silver cases and it served as a beacon when they reached the shore. Gall quickly knelt down to unlock one and eagerly withdrew two AA-12 shotguns. Banter and Sitoel joined him as he loaded two clips and strapped on a gun belt that held Tommy gun cartridges. "I call them a twist of fate!" said Gall. He cradled two cartridges that contained a blend of high explosive, fragmentation and armor piercing ammo. Banter unlocked his case and withdrew an algae camouflaged blanket. Underneath was a M-110 sniper rifle and two customized electric tonfa batons. He took a deep breath as Sitoel approached and whispered a foresight in his ear. "Are you certain it was him?" Banter asked while he armed himself. "After all that we've been through, you pick now to doubt me?" Sitoel angrily replied before removing two camouflaged blankets. She tossed one to Gall before strapping on a gun belt that contained two 61 VZ Skorpion's and a pair of escrima sticks. "His fate is sealed" replied Banter. "I'll join you as soon as I deliver the other half of mine!" Sitoel shouted as she ran to a secluded location between the reefs.

Banter and Gall cautiously advanced on an abandon navy garrison and laid undercover until their pass of entry arrived. A private charter boat importing food from the main land had reached the shores shortly before noon. Winston stood on the sundeck admiring the sea when he noticed a school of sharks still close to shore. "Bring up the prisoner's!" commanded Winston. A group of soldiers quickly retrieved two officers and Det. Rodriguez from the deck below and pushed them onto the plank of the vessel. "Did you think your arrival in Columbia would go unnoticed? Mr. Styles is a powerful man with great reach. That also includes political parties" said Winston. He removed the pikes hidden in his hair and instructed the soldier's, "Leave the detective on board. He'll be our entertainment on land. The other two can walk the plank". Winston poked the hands and legs of the officers so their blood would attract the sharks as they tried to swim. "I swear you'll pay for this. We're officers of the law!" Det. Rodriguez shouted as his escorts were tossed overboard. "We have no laws out here!" replied Winston. After docking their boat, the soldiers' quickly unloaded their cargo and returned to lay an ambush for the Marid Djinn's. Winston positioned soldiers on the steep reefs and returned to the sundeck to admire the scenery. He indulged his fantasies as a pirate of the high seas before the silhouette of a beautiful nude swimmer cultivated him. A crooked grin formed on his lips as he knelt down to retrieve a shoge hook. "Ahoy, come aboard! These are shark infested waters!" Winston shouted as he slid down the ladder's poles and ran to the ship's rail.

Like a seductress luring a man into her clutches, a Marid Djinn manifested its power of attraction for mischief and death. An outburst of laughter echoed over shore when Winston discovered his projection was merely a blanket of algae. He angrily speared his hook into the debris as if he was harpooning a whale and carelessly reeled it to the vessel. While removing it from the water two sharks unexpectedly jumped fromn underneath and snagged him in. Winston nervously tried to unravel the end of the chain knotted around his wrist as the sharks dragged him a mile into sea. When they had reached the desired location, they released Winston and circled. The sharks kept him at bay while Sitoel swam underwater to gather the loose end of the chain. She quickly reeled up the slack as she swam to the surface for air. A quiet stir crept from behind Winston and within seconds several chain links had been looped around his face. Sitoel pulled him deeper into the water while traces of blood seeped through the links and tightened her grip for a *woolding fate*.

It carried a scent through the salt water that excited the circling sharks. Before her feet had touched the ocean floor, Winston's eyes had bulged out of their sockets and through the chain links. The technique for the pirate's torture made his fractured skull an irresistible lure for her new found friends. While they feasted, a shark boldly parted the school of predators and quickly escorted Sitoel back to the surface. "Neither one had any manners. One brother couldn't keep his hands to himself, and the other couldn't stop staring!" Sitoel snapped with a hiss as she rode the dorsal fin back to shore.

Two levels underneath Malpelo's fauna sanctuary, Morgan Styles monitored the Marid Djinn's movements from a security camera. "I want a squad to open fire as soon as they exit the elevator!" Morgan commanded a general standing by his side. The general saluted and quickly moved to execute his orders before a stream of smoke caught his attention. It formed a ring around the general's neck and crushed his larynx as Iblis materialized into his hooded robe. "What's the meaning of this?" demanded Morgan. "I will not tolerate any further interruptions! Now my payment and entertainment will come through the hands of *Fates*. I even arranged a place for the meddling detective!" he answered as he leaned to speak through the intercom. "All soldiers will immediately leave their post and report to the arena.

You will clear all passageways and avoid any contact with the intruders. Anyone disobeying this order will suffer dire consequences!" Iblis instructed in a voice that mimicked Morgan Styles. "I can still make payment!" replied Morgan. "For that reason you still breathe. Now go to the arena. After I summon a formidable opponent for my son, I'll join you on the balcony" Iblis instructed before leaving the room in a mist of smoke. "An invitation?" Gall curiously mumbled as a group of soldier's left their position from behind the reefs and entered the barracks. "It's not like my father to give out invites. Especially when he knows what we came here to do" answered Banter. "It makes sense to me" Sitoel interrupted as she approached and twisted her hair into a tight pony tail. "The fates I saw took place underground!" she added before she boldly approached the center barracks. She guided them through two levels beneath the sanctuary and cautiously exited an elevator that lighted a passageway through an underground sea cave. Two large steel doors opened as they approached and revealed a large arena hidden within. Sitoel pointed out another opening in a neighboring sea cave. "Alexander is being held in that one" said Sitoel. "You have to outsmart the speed of a snake to survive" she advised. "I'll keep them busy while you free him" said Gall as he boldly entered the passage to the arena. "As for you, a drink can spare you a lot of heartache!" Sitoel hinted as she followed Gall through the doorway.

A sinister grin appeared on Iblis's face as two of his Marid Djinn's descended the stairs to the arena and pointed their guns toward anything that moved. "Wait for me here" Gall instructed as he jumped into a pool of water covering the arena floor. A large wooden pillar stood in the center and it had Det. Rodriguez tied to it. A cloaked Iblis stood on top of the pillar with bright red eyes piercing from under his hood. "Your weapons, skills and gift of bone breaking have gained you a lot of notoriety. I wonder how you will fair against a creature that has the ability to mend every bone you break?" asked Iblis. "I'll answer that after I break them!" Gall answered as he loaded his special cartridges. "We shall see" replied Iblis. An outburst of laughter filled the arena after Iblis snapped his fingers and summoned the legendary Kappa of Shinto mythology. The three foot river imp extended his limbs from a turtle shell and kneeled before Iblis while soldiers continued to laugh. "You dare mock me!" shouted Iblis. He jumped into the water and kneeled down to pour three handfuls into a depression that rested in the center of the Kappa's head. Then he stirred the strength giving fluid to ignite a transformation that turned the creature into a 7ft. monster. One worthy of Gall's attention. "Enjoy!" Iblis blurted as he leapt onto the rail of a balcony.

In the opposite passageway, Brimm greeted Banter with his hands raised toward the ceiling. "No need for that rifle here. You'll never get the key to that cage if you shoot me" said Brimm. He slowly removed his shirt and sunglasses as Banter cautiously walked to a corner in the room and rested his rifle against the wall. "Now give me the key!" demanded Banter. "You'll have to earn that piece of information, and if you look around you'll know how" answered Brimm. Banter cautiously watched as the pupil's in his eyes and skin transformed into the physical features of a cobra. His fingernails extended like fangs as his palms secreted a neurotoxin. *"Naja!"* Banter shouted in a tone that carried a hiss. His Marid Djinn immediately familiarized the creature from his past. Banter removed the batons strapped to his back while Brimm made use of his physical attributes. He displayed the speed of a cobra as he raced around the perimeter and pushed the water jugs hanging from the beams. An effort that started a chain reaction throughout the room.

In the arena, Det. Rodriguez recited every verse he could remember from his bible as a Kappa and armed Gall circled the pillar. "Are you going to cower behind him all day?" teased Gall. The Kappa answered with a loud screech and dove underwater. Before Gall could set his sights on a target, the creature surfaced from behind and tossed him into the arena walls. Before Gall could regain his bearings, the Kappa quickly swam to his position and tossed him to the opposite end. "Enough!" Gall angrily responded as he turned and unleashed a line of fire.

A heap grenade had the biggest effect as a string of bubbles surfaced from the Kappa's turtle shaped shell. When the Kappa surfaced it brought a sparkle to the Marid Djinn's eye. He switched his rate of fire to full auto and pounded through the creature's shell. A cry of agony echoed from inside as incendiary rounds and pieces of shrapnel pushed the Kappa into a corner and tore his shell apart.

Meanwhile, Brimm continued to toy with Banter. "Was it skill or your Marid Djinn that always managed to break my record?" Brimm asked as he kicked a water jug in Banter's direction. Banter quickly crossed his arms to shield himself from the blow and left himself open for a leg sweep. The fall peaked the anger of his Marid Djinn. Banter quickly regained his bearings and maneuvered to the center of the room. "I hope your keeping count!" Banter shouted with the echo of a hiss. He cracked two neighboring water jugs with one blow to create a steady leak, and they swung side to side to leave the marking of an X on the floor. "So how many hits will it take for you to escape my trap?" taunted Brimm.

He rubbed his hands together so the neurotoxin could coat his fingernails and maneuvered through the swinging jugs for a lethal strike. When he reached the center of the X, the Marid Djinn kicked a water jug through the center of the mark. "One!" answered the Marid Djinn as he followed with a baton. Brimm dodged the water jug only to feel the impact of the blow. While he struggled to return to his feet the Marid Djinn struck him again to render him unconscious. "I knew you'd beat him!" shouted Alexander. "Did you see what he did with the key?" Banter asked as he kneeled down and searched Brimm's pockets. "He swallowed it" answered Alexander.

In the arena, a small mist of smoke rose from Gall's gun barrels after emptying his cartridges. The crowd booed as the Kappa laid lifeless, but the sound of bones snapping back into place quickly regained their attention. The soldier's watched in awe as the Kappa slowly extended his arms through the torn pieces of his shell. It was at that moment a Marid Djinn emerged to weave a fate to break mind, body and spirit. When the Kappa had extended its neck, the Marid Djinn raced to his position and embraced him. The creature barely put up a struggle before he snapped his neck.

He proceeded to inflict fractures throughout the Kappa's body with submission holds. Leaving nothing to chance, he slammed the creature into the water and sat on its back. After placing it in a chin lock, he pulled its head back to its torso and drank the strength giving fluid that rested in the depression of its head. "Brilliant!" shouted Iblis.

In the opposite room Banter had hung Brimm in the place of a broken water jug. He turned on the power in his baton and revived Brimm with two slight touches. "Curse you and your Marid Djinn. I'll never give up the key!" scowled Brimm. Banter acknowledged the response by pushing a baton through the front waist line of Brimm's pants. "Pay attention Alexander. At first this may seem harmless" said Banter as he briefly paused to hit a neighboring water jug. A study flow of water gushed from the bottle as Banter threatened, "But when I activate the baton and swing him in the direction of the flowing water". "Alright!" shouted Brimm. His neck made a wave like motion and within seconds he spewed out the key.

After Gall quenched his thirst a growl echoed through the arena. He increased his hold on the creature while it's strength giving fluid flowed through his veins. As he increased in size and strength, his kusari fundo slowly unraveled from around his right forearm. He quickly gripped the chain and looped it around the Kappa's neck as it snapped back in place. *Then, he broke it again!* Before it could mend its bones the Marid Djinn broke its legs and tied the blunt ends of the chain around its ankles. It was a bind that caused the Kappa to repeatedly snap its neck and legs every time they snapped back in place. "*The Gall!* Who amongst you will embrace him!" boasted Iblis. Gall scooped up the Kappa and boldly threw it into the crowd of soldiers. The sight of the creature's struggle amplified their fear and the soldiers stampeded out of the arena.

In the neighboring cavern, Banter freed Alexander from his cage. "Wait for me outside" Banter requested as he walked to the corner of the room and retrieved his rifle. Alexander slowly walked out the room and briefly paused at the doorway. "Go!" snapped Banter. "OK!" Alexander disappointedly replied. Banter patiently waited for the sound of running footsteps as he scoped his targets and activated the baton in Brimm's pants. When Alexander had gained distance, he slowly made his way to the doorway and fired rounds into each water jug. Brimm nervously struggled to free himself as large puddles of water amassed on the floor. "Don't slither!" warned Banter as he withdrew a baton from his back pouch. He activated it and tossed it high into the air before firing a final round through Brimm's rope. The man snake met a timely fate as the baton simultaneously followed him to the floor. A smoke screen filled the room and screams carried the charred scent of flesh as Banter left the scene with a smile.

A look of concern suddenly appeared on his face as he looked down the passageway for Alexander. His view had been blocked by a platoon of soldier's running franticly from the arena before a familiar cry quickly caught his attention. "Dad!" Alexander shouted as Morgan picked him up and carried him into the balcony stairwell. Banter raced with increased speed and withdrew his knife before entering the balcony. "Battles, wars and assassinations. None were more memorable to me than those that casted the shadow of betrayal!" said Iblis as father and son cautiously looked upon each other. *"You too Brutus?"* Banter angrily replied. *"You too child?"* corrected Morgan.

Alexander nervously watched as Banter's knife slowly slid through his hand and the tip of his fingers locked on the point. While Morgan debated his next course of action, Gall quickly freed Det. Rodriguez and joined Sitoel on the arena staircase. "Do not make haste!" advised Iblis as he pointed into the center of the arena. The pool of water quickly expanded and flooded the entire level. A devilish grin appeared on the face of Iblis as a school of sharks circled beneath the balcony. "Forgive me son" mumbled Morgan. He picked Alexander up to toss him over the rail but before he could finish the task, Banter threw his knife into Morgan's shoulder blade. Morgan was forced to release his hold on Alexander and they both fell over the rail.

Banter raced to the edge to help his father and brother as they clung to the edge. "You can only save one. Choose wisely!" taunted Iblis. Banter extended a hand to each. "I can save them both!" pleaded Banter. The response only ignited Iblis's anger and he grabbed the arm with the symbol he placed on his Marid Djinn long ago. It generated a pain that caused Banter's arm to go numb. "Don't let go!" cried Alexander. "I can't hold on" Banter uttered as Morgan slid from his grip and fell into the school of sharks beneath. Iblis snapped his fingers and the crown returned to his possession with the carpet. A broad smile appeared on his face as he gave Banter a final decree. "What was his, is now yours. Tell Gall his increased size won't be permanent but he now possesses bone mending ability, and it will help when he increases his size again. He merely has to consume water to loosen the strength giving fluid that now coats his skeletal frame. As for Sitoel, under your employ she'll continue to see fates. *And they will be often!*" Iblis shouted before he dove into the pool of blood and feasting predators. A tear trickled down Alexander's face as he tried to make sense of it. "Banter, he was going to throw me in" said Alexander. "Don't say it! In fact, after today don't even think about it" replied Banter as he hauled his brother to safety.

As Sitoel exited the arena she curiously asked Det. Rodriguez, "Does this leave us on a good note?" "I'm going to close my case with this being part of Morgan's occult practices and satanic rituals. No one will believe anything else. Unfortunately you'll still have to be kept in custody till we straighten your story out. Now I have to get to the control room and notify the authorities about those soldiers" explained the detective. Gall used his new strength and size to punch openings in the caverns until he made his way out. He continued down to the shore while Tobias flew overhead. The aircraft made an abrupt landing after catching sight of Gall. "What did they feed you down there? *Or what did you eat?*" Tobias nervously asked with a cross in hand as Gall swam to the aircraft. "Did you forget the conversation we had earlier!" replied Gall. "Fair enough, but I still need to know where we're going?" asked Tobias. "Spain" Gall answered while he fastened himself to the plane's bow. "Spain. Beautiful women. Great drinks and tapas" Tobias excitedly replied. "For the running of the bull!" interrupted Gall. "It's a little early for...*I should've known!"* Tobias disappointedly answered as he started the ignition.

The following week Banter changed his new found wealth and business. Styles Corporate and Styles Corporate Security had merged into the Three Click's Protective Services to avoid the scandal the name had carried. Inside the executive suite Gall stood beside Banter as he conveyed to a team of lawyers on the speaker phone. "So she'll be joining us soon?" asked Banter. "Yes sir. We were also fortunate enough to have obtained a confession from Mrs. Ortega and her husband. Authorities said she owned up to Sitoel's crime before they even had the opportunity to apprehend her for the murders of Nina Carrea and Felipe Vega. A gas attendant that worked near their coffee plantation" answered the attorney. Banter suspiciously looked at Gall as he shied away to the fireplace. "That will be all then" replied Banter. "Do you care to comment on Sitoel's fortunate turn of events?" Banter amusingly asked as he packed his briefcase. "You know my policy" said Gall as he removed Sitoel's ring from his pocket. They left the office and made their way to the elevator. When the doors opened Akantha unexpectedly walked out with a young woman. A seductive red silk dress complemented her petite figure and highlighted a pale complexion. The dull grey color of her pupils mysteriously pierced through her red hair as she parted a few strands that hung over the bridge of her face. The only thing that wasn't offset about her appearance was the ice blue attaché case she was carrying. "I apologize for this abrupt visit but your services are greatly needed" said Akantha as she greeted Banter with a peck on the cheek. "I can always make time for you" replied Banter as he gazed upon the woman's bright red hair. It had the effect of a bad omen from a past experience. "Her name is Sound and she is Vrykolakas" explained Akantha as she stepped aside to introduce the woman. "Keres!" Gall disappointingly blurted. "I don't understand?" asked Banter. "Keres are like cousins to the Jinn's" replied Gall. "Family?" Banter curiously asked. "More like distant servants. In war, when the Fates were done the Keres were given the task of clearing the battlefield of the dead. A sweet deal until they got greedy. Suddenly a corpse wasn't as fulfilling as a wounded soldier. You can just imagine what happened to an innocent bystander shortly after that!" explained Gall. "I am Sound! Chief Protector in the House of Sumpter. In my life time I served no such creature, less he cared to feast upon his own entrails!" Sound angrily responded as her fangs became visible. "I know what you are...*but what am I!*" snapped Gall. His Marid Djinn emerged with the echo of a hiss as a kusari fundo slowly unraveled down his sleeve. "That will be enough" interrupted Akantha. "Regardless of your manners, my employer is willing to pay you five hundred thousand dollars to personally guard and escort the transportation of an artifact. He will pay half now and you'll receive the rest upon delivery" Sound explained as she opened the briefcase and displayed the money. "Before I accept any assignment, I have to know who your employer is and what we are protecting" replied Banter. "Then I must tell you another story..." answered Akantha.

Three Marid Djinn's in:
Reign of Fate

A week before this very night Banter Styles received a final decree from Iblis. A word of mouth that seemed to put an end to all his problems. Unfortunately, it didn't include the supernatural ones. After resolving his personal issues a whole new world opened its doors. Proof of that was a vampire named Sound. She boldly displayed her fangs to Gall after requesting their services. "Sound is a soldier in peril. She was given the task of stopping the course of Ragnarok" explained Akantha. "Ragnarok?" Banter curiously replied. "We call it the Reign of Fate" added Sound. "It depicted the end of the Norse gods. I thought it was already prevented when Fenrisulfr the wolf was tricked into bondage?" Banter asked as he escorted Akantha and Sound back into his office. "The bondage you speak of is a fetter. Metaphorically known as a wolfstrap. I have recovered the original and my Governor has given me the task of retrieving another" Sound explained as she placed the attaché case on Banter's desk. "I had a special interest in mythology since elementary school. If my knowledge of Norse mythology serves me correct, you don't need the Marid Djinn's. You must seek out the Dwarves of Svartalfaheim" Banter amusingly replied with an outburst of laughter. "This is no joking matter. My tolerance for these men has come to an end!" snapped Sound. "You must look past Banter's foolish understanding of your mission. Please allow me to explain" pleaded Akantha. "A warning had been given before they used the wolfstrap to bond the monstrous wolf Fenrisulfr. It was to be made certain that no one entangle themselves with the creature during the time of binding or they would fall victim to being bonded to the creature forever. Unfortunately, this warning was ignored. Fenrisulfr had sensed the magic of the strap and the only way Tyr could convince him to wear it was to place his hand in the wolf's mouth during the time of binding. He successfully binded Fenrisulfr, but Tyr lost his hand as a consequence. The imprisonment of Fenrisulfr was thought to have prevented Ragnarok before the magic of the strap took its toll. Tyr's devoured hand had allowed the monstrous wolf to take on human form. *Fenrisulfr became the first Lycan!* Confused by his current state and the powers it granted him, Fenrisulfr escaped his imprisonment and sought one of the Fate's to explain his place in Ragnarok. During that time a bond had been formed between them and before his demise the Fate had given him two sons" explained Akantha. "Hati and Skoll! More commonly known to their Lycan buccaneers as Enemy and Lord Treachery" interrupted Sound. "So you need the straps to confine his son's" replied Banter. "That still doesn't explain why Sound, the chief protector to the house of Sumpter expects the aid of Marid Djinns?" questioned Gall. "The capture of a Maird Djinn's offspring is no simple task. One of the main reasons why the joining of two creatures of this caliber are forbidden. The abomination can be powerful enough to alter events or recreate them. During our pursuit they assumed the identities of two buccaneers named Fancios L'Ollonais and Roche Braziliano. We became aware when Francios ravaged the impenetrable fort of Maracaibo and held Gibraltar for ransom with Lycan abilities. Around this time his brother started to display the same sadistic traits with a pair of claws and it compromised their secret. We discovered a connection between the two when Roche bought a ship from Francios. We obtained this manifest at the cost of several lives and the capture of my apprentice. It is the only intel we have of their crew and pack" Sound explained before she handed it to Banter. He quickly unraveled the scroll and read:

Lycan Buccaneers
Ship Manifest

Ship: Deaf Dum Dead

Colors: Two monstrous wolf heads with bloody fangs feeding off two bloody cross swords. Screaming skeletal head centered above all.

Captain: Lord Treachery

Known pack/crew: Po Paws, Sycamore Wellington, Ninety-six Nine, Collard Legends,

Purge Moonshine, Blush, Cilantro
Faye, Bloody Bartholomew Smyte.

1ˢᵗ Mate: Enemy

Known pack/crew: Unchained Gauge, Motley Yukyur Graves, Blackmarket Ginyel, Obnoxious Koss, Pryur Body, Bopo Lava, Grit Blast and Muzzle Blast.

2ⁿᵈ Mate: Montbars "The Destroyer"

Known pack/crew: Agilroy Finalgates, Timber Orslope, Tiki Sangre, Malicious Merck, Morbid Medley, Souvenir Bloodstream Bally, Prison Levelfield and Rega Palazzo.

Sound worriedly walked over to the office window while she continued to explain, "I have a close bond with my apprentice. We were at a level of sharing thoughts and emotions. Those animals tortured him until I revealed every rescue and attack. Now the connection we share only creates another near death experience. I never informed the Governor about my weakness and I could not refuse this mission because of the obligation to my title". "So here you are with two hundred and fifty thousand dollars" said Banter as he withdrew a stack of bills from her attaché case. "So where do we get the second strap?" asked Gall. "When I recovered the original strap I also uncovered the secret to make another" answered Sound. "You solved the dwarves riddle?" asked Banter. "It wasn't too difficult after discovering the strap had been made from skin. Solving the riddle informed us of who we should seek out for the hide. *The sound of a cat's footfall, the beard of a woman, the roots of a mountain, the sinews of a bear, the breath of a fish and the spittle of a bird.* In turn describe the traits and characteristics of a dwarf from Svartalfaheimr. Earth, deathliness, rock, technology, forging and luck. We were able to make contact with a dwarf for the hide. He resides beneath the Adirondack Mountains and offered us the hide we needed in exchange for a gift" answered Sound. "What dwarf would be so eager to offer his hide?" Gall suspiciously asked. "A live one wouldn't. The hide we bought belongs to a dead dwarf. One that has been hung for a crime. All we have to do is collect it and return it back to the house of Sumpter" answered Sound. "First of all, there is no we. Your very presence puts the job and my team in jeopardy. Tell the dwarf that Gall and I will make the exchange. We'll place the corpse in your hands when we return" instructed Banter as he carried the first half of his payment to the office safe.

He quickly secured his earnings and offered his hand to seal the arrangement. "We'll leave the day after tomorrow. I need time to prepare our gear and weaponry" replied Banter as he escorted Sound and Akantha to the elevator. "I have some liquid Aconitum that I use to coat my red beard eagle spear. It can be useful" offered Sound. "*Wolf's Bane.* I guess I can put it to some use. You can have it delivered to my estate tomorrow night" said Banter. After exiting the elevator Akantha kindly pulled Banter aside and advised him, "It is wise to wait. Be sure to give Sitoel my love when she arrives". "When she arrives? I wasn't going to offer her a position in the company until I return" replied Banter. "My dear boy, you possess so much knowledge but still have much to learn about the intentions of others" Akantha amusingly replied as Gall escorted her out the building.

The following day, Banter returned to work at the corporate security lab with Gall. After spending the previous night studying and searching the internet about the weaknesses of werewolves, Banter customized a weapon. "A whale gun?" Gall disappointedly replied as Banter displayed its features. "A shoulder gun to be precise. The harpoons come with two types of explosive projectiles. This one is a fragmentation harpoon. The shrapnel will inject silver pieces into the hide and internally sever the organs of any prey. The other harpoon is an incendiary projectile. A thernite reaction will immediately take place upon impact" explained Banter. "Death from within!" Gall excitedly replied as he anxiously snatched the harpoon from Banter. "This is the first time I created something to deal with a mythical creature. In case something unexpectedly arouses I figured we can rely on these" said Banter as he walked over to a steel cabinet and removed two customized Venetian mask. A broad smile appeared on Gall's face as he recollected the first time he used its neuro disruptor. After handing it to Gall, Banter adjusted his sonic disruptor and neatly packed it in a cushioned steel briefcase. "I'll lace our coveralls with hunting wafers" said Banter as he walked over to a clothing rack. "You are a born general. I'm proud to fight by your side" boasted Gall.

Later that evening Banter returned to his estate and was rudely greeted by a visitor. As he opened the door, Sound rushed from behind and tossed him through the doorway. Banter flew across the hall and unexpectedly landed in front of Alexander's feet. "Banter brought home a warrior princess!" Alexander excitedly shouted. "Master Styles this behavior is highly irregular" Bella commented as she placed her hand over Alexander's eyes. Banter angrily rolled over to find Sound standing in the doorway. She was wearing an open faced brigandine with a long leather spiked skirt and high heel leather boots. "What's the meaning of this?" Banter demanded as he lifted himself and straightened his suit. "It doesn't sit well with me to be left out. I still have skills and abilities that can be useful for this mission" pleaded Sound. "I took some time out to do research on those abilities. You have strengths, but you also have flaws. Especially in a terrain where you can't cross running water! Your Wolf's Bane is a better offer. Did you bring it?" replied Banter. "If you invite me in, I can give it to you" said Sound as she shamefully lowered her head to the harsh comments. "You may enter" invited Banter. Sound grabbed her red beard eagle spear and entered with a small container. "Bella, retire Alexander for the evening and hold off any further disturbances" instructed Banter. He grabbed the container and gestured for Sound to follow him upstairs. "Master Styles there's something you should be aware of" Bella tried to explain. "Not now!" replied Banter.

Banter escorted Sound into his room and to his surprise found another unexpected visitor laying on his bed. Her blonde hair overlapped from between two bed pillows that conveniently hid her face, and a sleek muscular frame bulged under the satin sheets that complimented her figure. A seductive setting regardless of the Last Supper painting that hung over head. "Who are you and how did you get here?" Banter suspiciously asked as he approached the foot of his bed. "I expected a warmer greeting than that. You act as if I've never been here before" said Sitoel as she raised her face from the pillows. "I see you have company. Who is she?" Sitoel intriguingly asked. She quickly fastened the cover sheets over her frame and left Banter with a loss of words while Sound introduced herself. "I am Sound. Chief Protector to the House of Sumpter" answered Sound. "And I am very amused" Sitoel rudely replied as she glanced over Sound's attire. "You have to forgive Sitoel. She was recently released from a mental hospital. You might have heard of *The Great Secret*" explained Banter. "I've heard of a woman called *Sit-o-well*. How ironic to find a gypsy resting peacefully under a picture that depicts a betrayal of Christ. Many people were asked but only a gypsy was foolish enough to accept the task of making the nails for his crucifixion. Tell me gypsy, do your women still use their brassieres for pocketbooks?" Sound asked in a distasteful tone. "Allow me to correct your misinterpretations. I am *See-too-hel*, and I don't need a Marid Djinn to see your fate!" Sitoel angrily responded as she withdrew a pair of jointed iron sticks from under the pillow. "That will be enough for now!" Banter quickly interrupted as both women clenched their weapons and approached each other. "Sound is a client and jealousy doesn't suit you well" Banter advised as he stepped between the two and escorted Sound out the room. "Don't flatter yourself. I'm angry because I still use my brassiere for a pocketbook!" Sitoel shouted as she gathered her clothes.

When she was done getting dressed, Sitoel joined Banter and Sound in the dining room. She curiously glanced over a map of the Adirondacks as she approached the table.

"Sound hired us to extract an artifact from the Adirondack Mountains" said Banter. "Us? Is that an invitation?" Sitoel excitedly asked. "I was planning to offer you a position when I returned, but now that you're here you can join us. Tobias will drop you over this abandoned site" explained Banter as he pointed out a highlighted area on the map. Sitoel leaned over the table and read the lettering, "Adirondack Iron Works". "You'll follow this trailhead and make an exchange at the blast furnace. After retrieving the artifact you will meet us back at my cabin on Saranac Lake" instructed Banter. "Why so far away?" asked Sound. "Far away is the best place to be with *Enemy and Treachery* in pursuit of you. You'd be an irresistible prey for a predator and after your display downstairs, I'm now convinced you'd be a perfect distraction" answered Banter. "Bait? You're bringing me along for bait!" Sound angrily replied. "I figured that would be the best place to display your superior skills. Be sure to keep every detail of its location in your thoughts when you make contact with your apprentice" Banter instructed with a smirk that showed redemption. "In case you were wondering, that's the reason why I keep a pair of jointed iron sticks under the pillow. If you need me, you know where to find me" said Sitoel as she grabbed her backpack and headed toward the guest house.

At ten o'clock the following morning a cargo van labeled Three Clicks Protective Services entered a private hanger at JFK airport. As Gilroy Todou looked over the maintenance logs to his aircraft his son eagerly rushed to greet his passengers. "The Adirondack Mountains is a great place to visit this time of year. The camping, fresh air and canoeing are excellent choices if you're…" Tobias quickly paused as a cold chill began to run up his spine. "I should've known!" he angrily shouted to his father as Gall unloaded Sound's coffin from the rear of the van. "Was it made to order?" joked Gilroy. "No one said anything about a coffin!" Tobias protested as he approached Gall with a clip board displaying the passenger log. "I beg to differ my young friend. Her name is right there" replied Gall. He pointed out Sound's name before he lifted her coffin onto his shoulders.

While Tobias looked over the boarding log, a blood curdling scream from inside the coffin sent another chill up his spine. "No! Please stop. You're killing him!" echoed from the coffin as Sound tossed around in a dormant state. "She's still alive!" Tobias nervously whispered to his father. "I've known Gall a long time. If she's still alive, we can look past this. It's the ones you don't hear from again that'll make you want to pray for him" Gilroy explained as Gall slid the coffin under the belly of the plane. "Open up the torpedo doors!" Gall shouted as Banter and Sitoel gathered their luggage. Gilroy shrugged his shoulders as Tobias disapprovingly nodded his head. "I'm not loading anything until I tape a cross to her doors!" demanded Tobias. He rushed aboard his aircraft to retrieve his holy relic before loading the coffin.

During the flight Sound's connection with her apprentice created more tension between the passengers. "You must be possessed with stupidity if you think I'm going to torpedo a coffin into Saranac Lake!" complained Tobias. "I'm just joking. I needed a good laugh to take my mind off that screaming" replied Gall. "Fortunately we don't have to worry about being discrete on this trip. Sitoel will be the only jumper" explained Banter as he handed out the team's communicators. After adjusting her headset, Sitoel quickly withdrew a thin aluminum briefcase from under her seat. "So what's in the briefcase?" she curiously asked before a loud transmission raced through her communicator. "That's between the contact and the client. Do not go snooping around!" Banter yelled through the microphone before Sitoel angrily snatched off her headset. "I trust you'll be able to manage until you meet your contact?" asked Banter. "I'm no stranger to the outdoors. I traveled to many countries with my kumpania and we weren't guest in any hotels. I can hold my own until the contact arrives" Sitoel boldly answered as she placed the briefcase back under her seat.

When the group arrived at the Adirondack Airport, Gall and Banter loaded their cargo into a rental van. They traveled eight miles to the Styles vacationing home on upper Saranac Lake. The only pathway leading to it was a long narrow staircase that stretched from the road to the front yard. After unloading their cargo, both men immediately put their plan into action. They sorted through the surrounding brush for a good position to lay an ambush and dug a small trench. The position gave a clear view of the perimeter, and after moving all the furniture into the neighboring boathouse they baited Sound's coffin. "You went through a lot of trouble to protect the Kere" said Gall as he placed the coffin in the center of the rear floating dock. "She still owes half a payment" Banter replied as he exited the house with two sandwiches.

Back aboard the aircraft, Sitoel parachuted a wooden

crate over the saw mill area of the Iron Works before preparing herself for a dive. "Be on time. You don't get a lot of chances with a parcel pickup cord!" warned Tobias as he circled the area for a clearing. Sitoel acknowledged with a nod and quickly dove from the plane as he passed over a small lake that amassed from the flooded mines beneath. Her arrival had not gone unnoticed as a black bear curiously watched on its borders. When Sitoel swam to the surface she kindly greeted the animal. "Don't worry. I won't be intruding for long!" she shouted as she swam to the opposite end of the bear. She stepped out of the water and approached the mill where her crate had landed. After removing a few items, she broke off a few pieces of wood for a campfire. It wasn't long before the reflection of the flames on the briefcase quickly overwhelmed her curiosity. "I won't! I wouldn't! I shouldn't…*but I will!*" Sitoel humorlessly taunted herself as she opened the briefcase and inspected its content's. Her eyes widened with amazement as she gently removed two raspberry laced cropped camisoles.

Later that evening, at the house on Saranac Lake. Sound's casket door flew open and she stepped out with her spear in hand. "I'm in the mood to slay many Lycans!" Sound shouted as she licked her fangs. She cautiously approached the rear double glass doors and lightly tapped the glass to gain Banter's attention. "You can join us" invited Banter. Sound accepted the invitation and returned to her coffin to remove a champagne bottle filled with blood. When she entered the house she boldly stated, "I prefer to dine alone". "Suit yourself. We won't fret over a Kere!" Gall replied as she entered the livingroom. They curiously watched as Sound placed her spearhead into the flames of the fireplace and removed a small bottle of wolf bane from her brigadine. She quickly emptied the contents of the bottle onto the head of the spear and watched until it reddened.

To lace the tip was part of her warrior ritual, and she ended it with a drink of blood. While the blade cooled, Sound removed the cork to the bottle and guzzled without pause. Her eyes darkened in color and her fangs extended as she relentlessly funneled the last drop to moisten her lips. "I'm looking forward to this display" Gall whispered to Banter as he grabbed his mask and another sandwich from the counter. "Me too!" Banter replied as Sound smashed the empty bottle into the fireplace and postured herself for meditation.

The group waited until midnight before a series of howls interrupted the still of the night. Banter and Gall closely watched through a pair of binoculars from the trench as Sound rose to her feet to peek out the frame of an open window. "Six in the pack tonight and Enemy is among them!" Sound warned as she perked her nostrils through the air to gain the scent of her pursuers. Banter and Gall's Marid Djinn's quickly emerged as six Lycans charged down the hill and leapt into the front yard. They were as tall as Gall and bared all the physical attributes of a wolf. They walked upright and their fists bulged into paws while they extended claws as sharp as a cutlass sword. One Lycan quickly displayed that ability as he hacked off a tree limb and instructed the others to circle the house. When they were in position, he threw the tree limb through the window. "Coiling snake!" Sound shouted as she grabbed her spear and made a coiling motion to deflect the object. She returned to a defensive stance as a Lycan boldly entered the house and followed the attack. "Dragon snaps its tail!" Sound shouted as she charged and slapped the forehead of the Lycan with the spearhead. The blade had left a slit that immediately leaked blood and poison into his eyes. As the Lycan franticly stumbled through the room she applied her finishing move. "Piercing fang!" Sound shouted as she charged with speed and precision. After thrusting her spear into his chest area, Sound retrieved her weapon from his back and taunted the others while shaking the blood off in a contemptuous manner. An act that provoked two more Lycans to charge through the house and attack. "Now!" Banter loudly whispered to Gall. They slowly turned their disruptor's to maximum and watched the three Lycans waiting on the perimeter whimper in agony before Gall took the first shot. An incendiary projectile that pierced the hide of the closest Lycan and unleashed a fate of *divine fire*.

While in a formation that resembled the front and rear line of colonial minutemen, a Marid Djinn weaved *a star spangled fate*. Banter fired a fragmentation projectile while Gall reloaded his weapon. The shot impacted both Lycans and imploded a fate that erupted a sparkled coat of blood from the eyes, nose and ears of both Lycans. After witnessing the fates, the remaining Lycan mustered its strength and charged at the Marid Djinn's. As Gall aimed his rifle a spear pierced its back and impaled it to a neighboring tree. "The battle is won!" Sound boldly yelled from the porch with two Lycan carcasses laying by her coffin. "Which one is Enemy?" Banter asked before a shadowy figure standing on the road platform interrupted. "Sound, my brother sends his regards and suggested you take this corpse instead of our hides!" shouted Enemy. "Eon?" Sound nervously blurted. Enemy waved his lifeless body in the air as Sound raced for the staircase. Within seconds from reaching the top step Enemy tossed Eon's body into the air. An act that only gave Sound the option to catch the body or pursue. "Take the shot!" Sound angrily shouted to Gall as she raced back down the stairs to catch her apprentice. Before Gall could set his sights on a target, Enemy had disappeared. Banter approached Sound to offer his assistance but discovered the body in her arms had already been made a corpse. A fist shaped hole in the place of Eon's heart was the signature mark used by the Lycan buccaneers.

Banter sadly watched as a tear of blood trickled down Sound's cheek while she cradled Eon. "He said take this corpse instead. If I were you I'd inform your Great Secret of the danger that awaits her" Sound sadly mumbled. "You gave up her location? Didn't I instruct you on what information to give them!" Banter shouted as he adjusted the communicator hidden within his hood. "I couldn't help it. Eon was also my lover" Sound defensively replied. "Sitoel, what is your current status?" shouted Banter. "*Grimm!* I just handed a little person two expensive pieces of lingerie" Sitoel answered as a dwarf struggled to pry open the briefcase. "Did they deceive me?" the dwarf asked as he unsheathed his blade. "No, but I could've picked a better color" Sitoel amusingly answered as she unlocked the latches and revealed its contents. "It's the texture, not the color that will please my princess. Nothing underground can match it. I will take you to the body now" the dwarf replied as he closed the briefcase and whistled to an awaiting ride. "Body? What body? I'm here to pick up an artifact!" contested Sitoel. "If it helps, the *artifact* has been dead for some time" interrupted Banter.

"Curse you Banter! When I get off this mountain…"

"If you don't hurry you won't make it off that mountain. You have some unfriendlies headed your way and they mean business. Gall and I will be there shortly. Over and out!"

Sitoel angrily turned off her communicator as two black bears approached from the brush. "Don't worry. The body is not far from here" said the dwarf as he mounted a black bear and gestured for Sitoel to do the same. After doing so they raced to a hidden location in the woods. "It appears that we are in the same predicament. I can't help but to ask if it's for the same reasons?" asked the dwarf. "Reasons? There is only one explanation for me being here and that's foolish" replied Sitoel. "I can assure you that foolish is a common ingredient in both of our pots. I am just one of many suitors vying for the hand of the princess. They will offer quartz and stones forged into necklaces and homes but as sure as my name is Victorhelm, I will gain it!" recited Victorhelm. "Are you foolish to be so sure of yourself?" Sitoel amusingly asked. "No, I'm certain of what she desire's most. I'm only foolish because I chose to barter the body of a fellow dwarf to compensate for it" Victorhelm answered as they approached the outskirts of a blog. "Here lies Audhild. A dwarf well on his way to becoming a dark elf before his hanging" said Victorhelm. He jumped off the back of his black bear and began rummaging through a pile of leaves. "Dark elf?"

Sitoel suspiciously asked as she removed a small flash light from her pocket. "Beings that have no other purpose but to cause malice or grief. They offer their services as mercenaries and trackers. One tracked down Audhild and issued his sentence" explained Victorhelm. He briefly paused to pull on a vine that was hidden under a pile of leaves.

At the end of the vine was a well preserved corpse wrapped in deer's skin. "I'll be missed if I don't return soon. My friends here will help you back to the mines" said Victorhelm as he mounted the corpse on Sitoel's black bear and removed the briefcase. "Thank you, and good luck with the princess" replied Sitoel as she kneeled to give Victorhelm a kiss on the cheek. "Farewell!" Victorhelm shouted as he returned into the darkness of the forest. After the bears brought Sitoel safely back to her campsite, she inflated a neon lighted raft and placed the corpse in its center. Then she paddled back into the center of the flooded mines. A broad smile appeared on her face as the sound of Tobias's aircraft approached. She fired a signal flare as he circled the area and lighted small lanterns to make the pickup mark visible. "There she is. Lower the hooks!" Tobias shouted as he flew to her position. Gall successfully aligned the hooks for the pickup and as the straps retracted the raft, Sitoel's Marid Djinn emerged. A howl of reckoning soared over the woods and quickly gained everyone's attention. "Hurry!" Sitoel shouted in a tone that echoed a hiss.

As the raft flew from the water, two monstrous wolves leapt from the woods and raced down from opposite ends of a connecting sandbar. Within seconds they had reached the hovering vessel and clawed a gigantic hole through the bottom that caused the corpse to tumble back into the water. To avoid the same fall, Sitoel quickly grabbed a hold of the dwindling straps. "Sitoel's in trouble!" Gall shouted as he handed Banter his shoulder gun. Banter quickly grabbed the weapon and sturdied himself to get a lock on a target, but couldn't risk the possibility of hitting Sitoel. "Why didn't you take the shot?" Sound angrily shouted as Banter lowered his gun and aided Sitoel onto the plane. "I didn't have one!" snapped Banter. "I never seen lions like that before. They were black with spiked manes?" Sitoel questioned as she tried to catch her breath. "They're not lion's. They're monstrous wolves and nothing like the ones we faced at the house" said Gall as he locked the belly doors and returned to his seat. "Lord Treachery and Enemy have the ability to be men, Lycan and monstrous wolf. Right now they're the least of your concerns. My Governor will want to hold court after I report the loss of the corpse and two failed kill shots. I suggest we all be in attendance when he arrives!" Sound worriedly explained as she leaned back into her seat. "I should've known" Tobias worriedly mumbled as he headed back to the Adirondack airport.

A clean up and sweep of the area took place when the Marid Djinn's had returned to the cabin. After burying the dead Lycans, Sound phoned her Governor and sadly returned to her coffin. At her request Banter and Gall placed Eon's body on the dock the following morning. When Sound awakened that evening she swept his ashes into the lake. "A storm is coming!" Gall loudly whispered as he started the fireplace. "I can sense it too" said Banter. He leaned back in a recliner and stared at the ceiling before

Sitoel calmly strolled into the room with a sandwich and a glass of wine. "Does anyone care to shed some light on our situation, or do I always have to be the last one to find out?" Sitoel asked as she made her way to the couch. "Sound was given the task to prevent Ragnarok. The final destiny of the Norse gods. We needed to retrieve the corpse so she could manufacture another belt to capture the two wolves that attacked you earlier" explained Banter. "That's only what's known to us. I believe the Kere is still keeping things about her mission a secret" said Gall. "Like what?" asked Banter. "She's an assassin. I'm starting to believe she wants the wolves dead, not captured. Her response for us not taking those shots made that evident" explained Gall. "Did it ever occur to you that the loss of a loved one could've provoked the outburst" replied Sitoel. "Yeah, but I prefer to believe the contract. That strap was made to bind the jaws of Fenrisulfr forever, *and his last meal was a hand*" answered Gall. "We weren't hired to be assassins" replied Banter. "I suggest you give her Governor that same answer when he arrives" Gall advised as he headed for the staircase.

Later that evening, two jet planes entered a hangar in the Adirondack Airport. Tobias curiously watched as both pilots stared out the window in a trance. When the jets came to a halt, the passenger doors opened and ten soldiers in black fatigues, armed with sword's and automatic rifles raced out the doors of both planes. Tobias ducked under the dashboard and peeked at a man descending the staircase of the plane with a bald head and lava colored eyes. His facial features were young but he carried the demeanor of an elderly business man as he buttoned the jacket to a Canali shadow striped suit and adjusted a burgundy tie. "Get the dwarf and bring him back to the cabin on the lake" he commanded. "No failure. No delay!" a group leader shouted as the soldiers raced from the hangar. The second group followed the man as Tobias picked up a communicator and phoned Banter. "Why are you calling me?" Banter groggily answered. "A group of soldiers entered the hangar and left out of here faster than a shadow could follow. I think their headed your way" answered Tobias. Banter leapt from the couch and retrieved a glock from the kitchen draw and peaked out the kitchen window. "Thanks for the warning, but they're already here" said Banter. He watched as Sound escorted the group to the rear door. "You may enter" invited Banter. When they entered the house, Sound introduced the man that boldly led his soldiers into the living room. "This is my Governor" said Sound. "There are three people in your group?" the Governor asked while he stared at Sitoel. "Gall is upstairs" answered Banter. The Governor pointed to the ceiling and three soldiers raced upstairs to retrieve Gall. Overwhelmed by the sight in front of him, the Governor leaned over the couch to brush two strands of hair from Sitoel's forehead and unexpectedly found the point of a jointed iron stick under his chin. "Your invitation came with boundaries" Sitoel warned in a tone that carried a hiss. The sound of two bodies collapsing on the floor upstairs followed as Gall made his way downstairs with his kusari fundo chain wrapped around the neck of a soldier. "These Keres forgot their place!" Gall snapped as he tossed the soldier over the rail. "Now that we've familiarized ourselves with each other. Let's discuss the matter of my property" replied the Governor. He cautiously moved from Sitoel's reach and adjusted his tie as the second group of soldiers approached the front door with Victorhelm in hand. "Everyone here has received payment for a task and I have nothing to show for it" said the Govenor. He opened the door and a soldier tossed Victorhelm inside. "You must retrieve another corpse" demanded the Govenor. "Do you think our graveyards are filled with dwarves hung for their crimes? Corpses like that don't grow on trees. You need one that is undergoing a transformation to dark elf and I can't go around digging up graves unnoticed!" explained Victorhelm. "So the task will be harder than you expected. Complete it or a dwarf will surely hang from a tree of mine, and even then you will not be alone. I will also include a maid and boy, a spiritual advisor, a few Abominables, and a gypsy traveling through Spain with her *kumpania!*" threatened the Governor.

Banter, Sitoel and Gall looked at each other while they weighed their options. After evaluating their situation Gall lowered his head and advised, "We can't be everywhere". "I'm glad we're in agreement, and with a new agreement comes new terms. Retrieve the corpse. As a precautionary measure I will take the dwarf and female Fate. Sound can fill her spot and guide you back to the house of Sumpter when the corpse is recovered" explained the Governor. "I'm not going anywhere!" Sitoel contested as she leapt from the couch and stood beside Banter. She eagerly awaited a response before Banter lowered his head and unexpectedly replied, "It's for the best". "I trust she'll join us shortly" said the Governor as he exited the house with his soldiers. "Wait! There's something you don't understand. If I don't return they'll send someone for me!" Victorhelm pleaded as the guards dragged him from the house. Sitoel gave Banter a cold stare as she pushed aside a few guards and gave Gall a hug. After saying goodbye to Gall, she stepped outside and a soldier carried her into the night. "I told you a storm was coming" said Gall as he patted Banter on the shoulder and returned to his room. Banter responded with a nod and waited until Sound returned to her coffin before writing Gall a small note to find in the morning.

As the Governor boarded his aircraft with Sitoel and Victorhelm, a hunting party of dwarves returned to the hidden passages of the Adirondack mine pits without their prince. "You dare to return without my son!" shouted the High Chief. "We searched everywhere and found nothing but an abandoned camp with broken pieces of wood. It carried the writing of the forbidden cities. We believe it to be linked to Victorhelm. The dogs also picked up the scent of death" explained the soldier. "The scent of a dwarf?" the High Chief worriedly asked.

"Yes"

"Victorhelm?"

"We're not sure"

The answer immediately sparked the High Chief's rage and he demanded, "A week before my son bares gifts for Gasliemir's daughter and you can't tell me if he's alive or dead? Take all your findings and a pound of iron ore to the pit of Mount Marcy. There you will give them to the dark elf Rottenvein. Tell him to seek out my son. If he's alive, he must return him to me. If he is dead, tell him to quench my thirst for revenge with a wrath so oblivious that Odin would seek out his services!" commanded the High Chief.

The following morning, Gall woke up for breakfast and found a note telling him to meet Banter by the road. He left the house and climbed the staircase to find Banter waiting in a van. "What's this all about?" Gall suspiciously asked as he boarded the vehicle. "Sound's mental ability!" answered Banter. He quickly pulled off and continued to drive to a store a few miles down and parked the van to explain, "There was only one other time I heard the word kumpania and that was when Sitoel spoke of her tribe in Spain. I also thought about Bella and Alexander. During that time, what was on your mind?" "I see your point and it's probably the only reason why the Governor left her with us. Luckily we're not at a total disadvantage. She's not the only one with superior probing skills. Sitoel slipped this to me right before she left" replied Gall. A broad smile appeared on his face as he removed the Governor's wallet from his pocket. "I think they might be keeping her here" said Gall as he handed Banter a shipping receipt. He quickly glanced over a piece of paper that displayed a crate addressed to Mount Rose Cemetery in York Pennsylvania. "In my line of work there would only be two options. You can either packup everything you love and go on the run. Or you can go after the bosses. I always picked number two. You can keep Sound busy while I get answers from the cemetery" explained Gall.

"Easier said than done" replied Banter. "Not if you see Akantha. I'm sure she'll have a solution to our eavesdropping problem. In the meantime you should keep Sound locked in the company vault". A smirk appeared on Banter's face as he turned the van around and asked, "And what will be my excuse when she wakes up?" "Tell her we did it as a precautionary measure" Gall amusingly replied as they returned to the cabin to prepare for their departure.

Later that afternoon, Banter and Gall parted ways at the Adirondack Airport. Tobias flew Banter and Sound to JFK where a security team waited to deliver her coffin to the corporate vault. While Gall was in route to Mount Rose Cemetery, Banter eagerly sought Akantha. He barely made it to the top step before she opened the door and asked, "Why are you alone?" "We ran into some trouble during our stay in the Adirondacks" Banter disappointedly answered as Akantha escorted him into the living room. She calmly poured two cups of perisonne tea and waited for Banter to explain.

Banter gave a detailed explanation of the events that took place and when he was done, Akantha responded with an unexpected reaction. "How foolish of you! Even after I had advised you to be weary of the intentions of others, you still parted ways with the ones that matter most!" Akantha angrily shouted. "Are you saying we were wrong to think about the safety of our families?" Banter defensively replied. "No, the fault lies in overlooking the *Fates!*" answered Akantha. She took a few sips of tea and asked, "Were you not even curious as to which *Fate* mothered the offspring of Fenrisulfr?" "The thought did cross my mind. It had to be Sitoel's" replied Banter.

"You've obviously failed to realize that a Marid Djinn is neither male nor female"

"Sitoel's Fate is not the mother? Then that would mean that it's either me or"

"*Gall!* Gall's Marid Djinn mothered the offspring of Fenris. If his hunch about Sound being an assassin is correct and his Marid Djinn discovers the plot to kill the offspring true, the retaliation will be disastrous!"

The news sunk Banter deeper into his seat. "That's why he was so eager to go" replied Banter. "Your decision to allow Sitoel to leave with the Governor is another cause for concern. Rumors say he has a lust for mortal women and uses it to find ways to create supernatural beings like his personal guards" said Akantha. "I didn't have much of a choice. I couldn't do anything about the loss of the corpse and Sound's mental ability left us at a disadvantage" replied Banter. "What's done is done. I cannot change the course of events, but I can remedy the problem of Sound's mental ability. I can give you two sacred objects. Pendants that were constantly prayed over by monks that belonged to the Sacred Order of the Dragon" siad Akantha. She walked over to retrieve two pendants with emblems of sacred bells and trumpets from her safe. After handing them over to Banter she curiously asked, "Now that you have managed to separate yourself from your team. What do you intend to do?" "Make better bullets!" Banter answered as he raced from Akantha's residence.

That same afternoon Gall arrived at Mount Rose Cemetery. He discretely roamed the grounds until he came upon an abandoned cathedral. The familiar scent of death caught his attention as he circled the perimeter. He was no stranger to the smell, especially while in a cemetery, but this scent also carried the smell of fresh blood. He cautiously peeked through the windows and discovered a row of coffins lined around the alter. Blood splatter on the walls and benches meant the vampires resting inside had accommodated their appetites there on multiple occasions. With no guards and two hours of daylight still on his side, Gall boldly entered. He silently thought to himself about their purpose of being there as he slowly made his way down the aisle and approached a pit in the front of the altar. It was designed to raise and lower caskets from the crematory below, but a bright spectrum of light alerted Gall to other intentions. "A death trap!" Gall mumbled as he looked over an iron cage resting on a bed of large spikes.

He quickly rose to his feet and raced down stairs to the crematory entrance for a better look. As he entered the lower level the smell of death grew stronger and he discovered the shaft wasn't the only thing the vampires rebuilt to serve their purpose. They had repaired the crematory oven to dispose of the carcasses they fed on. While Gall sorted through the large piles of ashes he discovered the original wolfstrap. "They wanted it to end here!" Gall angrily mumbled. Overwhelmed by rage, Gall removed his mask to fit another. With no further thought he fastened the strap around his waist and unleashed another beast within. A growl roared from the oven while the sight of the deathtrap shredded memories of a Marid Djinn raising two cubs. His bone mending ability eased most of the pain of his transformation, but his flesh still ached as Gall embraced the physical attributes of a monstrous wolf.

A grey mane amassed on his frame and the spiked

edges glittered as if he had been scorched by the heavens for chasing the moon. When it was over, a howl of reckoning riddled the cathedral and the possessed monstrous wolf raced to the altar. It was at that moment a Marid Djinn emerged to weave a fate that gained recognition throughout the underworld for unwarranted exposure. Gall approached the coffins and emerged into the Lycan stage of his transformation. As he walked upright, his front paws bulged into fists and extended claws that resembled the cutting edge of a cutlass sword. When the transformation was complete, the possessed Lycan savagely pounded the latches on the coffins to prevent any means of escape. When he was done, he used his claws to carve a hole in the head area of each coffin. Then the possessed Lycan created a horrific master piece that filled the cathedral with screams. When the last victim had been claimed Gall returned to his human form to admire the aftermath. A scene that boldly displayed five Colombian neckties.

After Banter's visit with Akantha, he returned to his lab to design a projectile that would accommodate his M-110 sniper rifle. He had just handed a lab technician the specifications for incendiary and fragmentation ammo when he received a call from his chief of security.

"Mr. Styles, we have a problem of great concern at the corporate building" said the guard. "Is this about the coffin I had sent to the vault?" asked Banter. "That's not the problem sir" replied the guard.

"Then what is?"

"The boar hounds are dead"

"I'm on my way"

When Banter arrived at his corporate building he found his chief security officer and staff sergeant waiting in the lobby. "The boar hounds?" Banter suspiciously asked. "We had received an alarm from the sub entry level. The boar hounds were released. We also sent a couple of guards to do a sweep of the area but found nothing. When the guards returned to their post, they looked at the monitor and discovered the dogs were dead" explained the staff sergeant. He escorted Banter to the security room and leaned over the desk to play what the camera had recorded. Flashing lights and the release of a chain link fence indicated an intruder, but nothing showed up on camera. Banter suspiciously looked over the film and turned on the camera to the vault where Sound's coffin had been placed. Her casket doors were open and she angrily stood a few feet from it as Banter zoomed in with the lens. A smirk appeared on his face when she caught sense of him watching. In response, she displayed her fangs and threw her spear into the center of the lens. Banter quickly thought of an explanation to give to his security staff but before he could say a word his chief officer interrupted, "No need for an explanation Mr. Styles. You've retained the same staff that worked for your father. We'll take care of the vault tape and notify the ASPCA as soon as you leave". Banter gratefully responded with a nod and turned a switch to unlock Sound's vault door. "Whatever the ASPCA find put it in a report and leave it at the lobby desk. I'll follow up on it in the morning" instructed Banter. He hurried to the next level to meet Sound as she pushed her way past the guards. "What's the meaning of this?" she shouted. Banter grabbed her by the forearm and hurried her up the ramp to the ground floor. "It was a precautionary measure" Banter defensively replied. He escorted her through the main entrance and into his limo. "Something is wrong? Does it pertain to our search?" asked Sound. "I should be asking you those questions!" shouted Banter.

"What are you insinuating?"

"A pack of guard dogs were found dead while you were on the premises. You might have turned into a mist of smoke for a quick meal?"

"How dare you accuse me. I'd never feast on an animal!"

Banter sunk back into his seat and nervously mumbled, "I don't know the full extent of your abilities?" "Well allow me to show you" replied Sound. She stared into Banter's eyes while her pupil's gave a peculiar luster and uttered a whisper that asked about his whereabouts before she suddenly stopped to cover her ears. "You possess a sacred pendant and you doubt me!" snapped Sound. A smirk appeared on Banter's face as he withdrew the pendants tucked within his shirt. "I guess that puts an end to your snooping" Banter boasted as he brandished a pendant displaying the trumpets of Jericho. "Pull over!" Sound demanded the driver. The driver obeyed the request and nervously pulled into a vacant lot. When the car came to a stop, Sound looked at Banter with dark grey eyes and blurted, *"Touche!"*

Before Banter could interpret her intentions, Sound leapt from the back seat and attacked the driver. She viciously fed on him until his skin paled and ended her meal by snapping his neck. As his lifeless body collapsed on the steering wheel, Sound stepped out of the car and jumped in the driver's seat. "I'll be your new driver. Now we don't have to keep secrets about where we've been" said Sound as she pushed the previous employee to the passenger side. "Suit yourself, and after you clean up your mess this limo will be your coffin. My guest house is being fumigated!" Banter angrily replied before Sound drove out the lot.

The following day Banter reported to work before noon. To his surprise everyone was standing outside and the corporate building had been sealed off. The sidewalk was flooded with local authorities, press and workers of the Central Control for Disease and Prevention. He ordered the cab driver to park at the side entrance of the building and found a familiar face waiting for him. "I always had a hunch I'd see you again" greeted Det. Rodriguez. "Aren't you out of your jurisdiction?" Banter asked as he stepped out of the cab. "I transferred after I returned from Malpelo Island. I wanted to keep a close eye on your team. So is there any information you would like to voluntarily disclose for my investigation?" asked the detective. "I haven't a clue about what happened. I recently returned back from a trip in the Adirondacks" answered Banter.

"The Adirondacks? You might want to get yourself checked while the CDC is still here" said Det. Rodriguez.

"Checked?"

"Do you know anything about Naegleria Fowleri?'

"It's a brain eating amoeba"

Detective Rodriguez removed a small notepad from his coat pocket and read his details to further explain, "It was found in your guard dogs. The crime lab said the offbeat thing about these amoebas were their size and appetites.

They believe someone nurtured them under geothermal conditions, but can't explain the nonstop attack on the canine's system". "And you came down here to investigate that?" questioned Banter. "That and the strange writing printed on the sewer wall" said Det. Rodriguez. He handed Banter a photo from the folder he was carrying. "Underneath that writing someone hammered a large iron nail through a broken piece of a crate that had your company logo on it. The writing is a rune casting that says *Thurisaz*. It means what opposed you. That message came with a brain eating amoeba" explained the detective.

"What opposed you?" mumbled Banter. "That's right. I guess the perp can't get one over on you. So maybe I shouldn't be too worried about it being a death threat. After you get yourself checked out and catch up on things around the workplace, give me a call" replied Det. Rodriguez as he retrieved the photo from Banter and made his way to his car.

After checking with the CDC, Banter returned to the estate and found a tall hooded figure, barefooted with torn coveralls by his gate. He cautiously withdrew his glock as he rolled the window down and advised the cab driver to slowly enter the driveway. "You're in the wrong place if you're looking for a homeless shelter" Banter yelled from the window. "I don't show up for work one morning and you presume I'm homeless" Gall amusingly replied as he removed his hood. "Hurry up and get inside!" Banter loudly whispered as he quickly opened the door and instructed the driver to continue driving. "What's wrong?" Gall curiously asked as Banter withdrew the sacred silver pendants over his shirt. "Sound is in the garage. I brought her here after the guards informed me about the death of the guard dogs. Someone or something was crafty enough to let amoebas do their dirty work. They even left me a warning on the way out" explained Banter. "It could be the Keres. I ran into a few of them yesterday and it didn't end well" replied Gall. "Then one of these could have been of some use to you" said Banter as he removed one of the small chain pendants and tossed it to Gall. "Silver no longer agrees with me" Gall replied as he ignored the toss and allowed the pendant to fall to the floor. "You've been bit?" Banter nervously asked. "I'm not a vampire" answered Gall. "*Whew!* You had me worried for a second" replied Banter. "I chose what was behind door number two" said Gall. He unbuckled his coveralls and revealed the wolfstrap on his waistline. "You took the original fetter!" replied Banter. "In order to find the corpse, we have to find the den. I can easily do that as a Lycan" said Gall. "So the tales are true then. Anyone who wears it can become a wolf?" Banter asked as he looked over the fetter. "They can become that and more, if the one wearing it is a Marid Djinn" answered Gall. "What about Sound? She can no longer read my thoughts but she'll still question your absence" asked Banter. "Lead her to believe I've been captured by the Lycans. I'm sure she'll investigate the matter in the cathedral and the missing fetter. When she does they'll find my mask in the crematory oven. Sound will assume that the brother's discovered the location from her and left behind another corpse for the fetter" explained Gall. "That's a big assumption and the risk of her believing it is even bigger" replied Banter. "You can persuade her. She won't be able to detect your deceit while you're wearing the pendants" said Gall. "There's something else Akantha mentioned that I'm concerned about" Banter tried to ask before Gall opened the door. "There's no need to worry. You'll be able to find me as soon as I fall in with a pack. Just follow the trail!" interrupted Gall.

On the Governor's estate in Ballestrino Italy, Sitoel and Victorhelm tried to familiarize their surroundings in the House of Sumpter. The estate was at the top of a hill and beneath it lied an abandoned village. "Minions of the Govenor tour the grounds with guard dogs during the day" noted Victorhelm. He stared out the cellar window while standing on Sitoel's shoulders. "Things don't get any better at night. I caught a woman peeping through the cell window. I tried to speak but she was acting snobbish" said Sitoel. "Was she a beautiful ebony haired damsel with beach sand skin and slanted eyes?" Victorhelm curiously asked. "Yes, did you see her too?" asked Sitoel. "She's headed this way with three other women!" answered Victorhelm. Sitoel gently placed him on the floor as the women kneeled down and crowded around the window. "There she is. The new mistress of the house!" the woman angrily shouted. "You're not vampires" replied Sitoel. "Are you saying we're no better than a *Fate?* Our children are the Damphirs that personally guard the Governor. They have proven to be far more worthy than any offspring a Fate can offer. All you have proven to be is a problem" answered the woman. "A problem that will soon be terminated!" commented another. "I don't understand what this is about, but I'm not having any children!" replied Sitoel. "That will be wise of you. If you were to have a child they would be hunted down by the gods and disposed of" replied the woman. Sitoel angrily warned in a tone that carried a hiss, "You should choose your words more carefully?" "Tell us how it feels to learn that childbearing will only result in their death?" the woman heckled as she pointed down to Sitoel. "It would feel like this!" Sitoel shouted as she leapt up to the window and reached out for a handful of hair. When it was within her grasp, she pulled it until she fell back to the ground. Everyone watched with a stunned expression as the head of the woman smashed into the bars in front of her. Two bar studded indentures traced down the bridge of her face and blood dripped from the bald patches of her scalp after Sitoel released her hold. "We might be spending our final moments within these walls when word of that reaches the Governor" Victorhelm worriedly replied as the woman's companions picked her up and carried her back into the house. "Speak for yourself. I still see fates!" Sitoel responded as she angrily punched a hole through a barrel of ale.

That night, Banter and Sound snuck into the sewers to do their own investigation. "Are you sure you're telling me everything?" Sound asked as she looked over the rune symbols written on the wall. "Yes! Gall went for a walk in the Adirondacks and didn't come back. When I returned my guard dogs were viciously killed and on the way out I received this warning. Gall was right about your mental ability. When it doesn't serve your purpose it becomes a curse instead of a blessing. Now I got to look over my shoulder for Lycans! Just how much information were you and Eon relaying before his death?" accused Banter. "How dare you blame these happenings on me or Eon!" replied

Sound. "You know I'm right. Everything you've learned or known before Eon's death has been compromised!" Banter purposely ranted.

He continued to press until an expected outcome took place. Sound began to doubt herself, and it provoked a race to the nearest pay phone. She quickly placed a call to a groundskeeper in Mount Rose Cemetery. A minion that served a group of assassins by gathering homeless victims and returning them to the cemetery for feeding. "I wish to speak to Natis" Sound nervously asked. "I'm not allowed to go to the other side of the cemetery for any reason other than feeding" replied the groundskeeper. "Then go out and summon one of the others quenching their thirst!" demanded Sound. "I haven't seen anyone cross over to feed for about two days now. Their last delivery is still roaming around the perimeter and it's starting to look bad. If they don't come to eat soon I'll have to chase them away!" explained the groundskeeper. Sound briefly fell into a daze as the receiver dropped from her hand. After Banter climbed out of the sewer, he cautiously approached with two fingers crossed on one hand and the other placed on the blunt handle of a silver hunting knife tucked in his back waistline. "Do we have to bother with planning our next move?" asked Banter. "We must go to Pennsylvania to check on another matter!" Sound angrily answered as she hurried to the driver side of the limo. A cunning smirk appeared on Banter's face as he released the grip on his knife and replied, "Whatever you say".

Gall had spent the entire day traveling from borough to borough before he finally picked up the scent of blood and raw meat. The trail started from the neighboring alley of a meat market and ended at an abandoned Sedgewick Avenue train station. Overshadowed by the Major Deegan Expressway and a passing Metrorail, Gall stumbled on a pack of Lycans. Three feasted on raw meat while resting on a decrepit platform. Two others sparred in the center of a dust cloud while Gall quietly crept to their borders and discovered a slight difference in their appearance. These Lycans wore a protective vest over their chest. "Word travels fast" Gall mumbled as he transformed into his monstrous wolf state. A growl quickly alerted the others to his presence as he boldly entered their circle in search of the Alpha.

The pack cautiously huddled together while their nostrils flared to identify the approaching monstrous wolf. Snarls and growls amassed before the pack displayed their fangs in a threatening manner. Within seconds of a passing train, Gall had attacked the closest Lycan and locked his jaws around his throat. "Wait!" pleaded the Alpha as he quickly returned to his human form. "We only threatened to attack because of your appearance. We only know of two monstrous wolves, and neither one would be foolish enough to roam in the open freely. Are you a descendant of Fenrisulfr?" the Alpha asked as the others patiently waited for an answer.

Gall returned to his human form and extended a hand to lift the Alpha off the ground. "That I am. Can you direct me to my brothers?" Gall asked as they escorted him back to the platform. "Our laws forbid any Lycan to hold court with Enemy or Lord Treachery without their consent. We can send word for a meeting, and if they acknowledge your request we'll lead you there after our mission" explained the Alpha. "Mission?" Gall curiously asked. "You came upon your brother's during a troubling time. We are at war with the Norse gods. Lord Treachery has placed a bounty on Heimdall's horns" answered the Alpha. "A bounty on a god?" Gall asked with interest. "The monstrous wolves have decided to make their stand in the Adirondacks and the bounty is a direct retaliation for the information he provided Odin. It was the cause of his actions that brought an untimely demise upon Fenrisulfr. Every Lycan in existence is in route to collect. A victory will also bring the reward of buccaneer status. You're welcomed to join our pack and partake in the hunt" explained the Alpha. He pulled on a meat hook that was pinned in the leg of a lamb and feasted while Gall continued to question, "I will join your pack, but how do you intend to catch a being like Heimdall?" "We'll figure that out when we get to the Adirondack Mountains. Now familiarize yourself with your brothers and enjoy the feast. It could be your last!" replied the Alpha as the pack changed into their Lycan state and immediately sank their fangs into their meal.

The following evening, Sound and Banter arrived at Mount Rose Cemetery. Sound barged into the groundskeeper's office and pinned him up against the wall with the handle of her spear placed under his chin. She slowly lifted him up to the ceiling and asked, "Where are they?" "They're in the abandoned cathedral" answered the groundskeeper. "And you haven't been there for the past couple of days?" Sound continued to question. "Past couple of days? I haven't been there since they arrived! I already told you that over the phone. Their rules are strict. I leave them alone and bring the food. In return, they leave the money. Except this time they haven't eaten or left anything within the past couple of days. I swear!" answered the groundskeeper. Sound quickly released the man and raced to the abandoned cathedral with Banter close behind. She marched up the stairs and repeatedly called out the name Natis and kicked open the doors.

Banter carefully watched as she proceeded to the resting coffins and fell to her knees. "This is an outrage! A desecration! To violate and defile someone's…" "Home?" Banter interrupted. He slowly approached and placed his hand on her shoulder. "I can still hear their screams. This was done by Lycans and I swear the consequences for their actions will be severe!" Sound angrily yelled as she rose to her feet and stormed back down the aisle. "Tantrums are not going to help any" Banter commented. "This is not a tantrum!" replied Sound. She knocked over a few benches in search of clues while Banter headed for the crematory. As he exited the cathedral, his Marid Djinn suddenly emerged. "Watch out!" Sound shouted as she tackled him down the stairs. Banter lifted his face from the ground and quickly withdrew his knife as three sharp edged boomerangs soared overhead. "Stay behind the tombstone" Sound advised as she pursued one of the boomerangs. She quickly raced through the graveyard and leapt into the air to grab it when her assailant unexpectedly grabbed her ankle. An act that caused Sound to bump her head against a large cross tombstone in front of her. As she fell into a daze she heard a raspy voice warn, "Release Victorhelm!"

Banter cautiously peeked his head over a tombstone before another boomerang forced him to take cover. "This will be the final warning before my wrath!" he threatened as a boomerang sliced through a tombstone in front of Banter. "The wrath of who?" Banter asked as dodged the broken piece. "The wrath of Rottenvein!" Rottenvein shouted before disappearing into the night. Shortly afterwards, Banter aided Sound back to the steps of the crematory. She quickly pushed him aside and ran to the oven. "Your anger is a little late for combat" said Banter. "He only bested me because I expected to find a Lycan!" Sound snapped as she crawled into the oven. She searched inside and disappointedly removed Gall's mask before returning to Banter. "The original fetter is gone and I believe Gall is among the ashes. They left his mask as a message" said Sound. "Are you sure?" Banter worriedly asked. "The sound of a Lycan breaking bones and flesh apart still carries. He was lucky to be dead before they burned him alive" Sound explained as she handed the mask back to Banter. He lowered his head and faked an emotional sob while Sound consoled him. "We have suffered losses but we will avenge our comrades" promised Sound. "You said you knew who attacked us earlier?" asked Banter. "I know of their kind. He was bald and had an iron patch covering his right eye. His face was colly marked and there's no mistaking the craftsmanship of his weapon" answered Sound. Sound removed a boomerang from her brigadine and displayed it to Banter. "He's a dark elf!" Sound blurted as Banter looked over the weapon. "Werewolves and dark elves. It's starting to get to the point where I have to make a special bullet every time I leave the house" replied Banter.

That same evening in the house of Sumpter, an argument between the house wives and the Governor was suddenly interrupted by an unexpected visitor. In a tone that rattled the shingles on the roof a stranger shouted the name, "Loki!" The front doors flew off the hinges as he boldly entered the house. The black hood of his robe covered all his facial features and made his long white beard appear as if it was only hanging from a shadow. A long boar spear rested in a sling on his shoulders and it was the only thing his body exposed. "Loki, come out of your darkness and acknowledge my presence!" demanded the stranger. "I was under the impression that our identities were to remain secret" the Governor replied as he descended the stairs with his personal bodyguards. "If your henchmen act quickly, you can avoid living in secrecy" said the stranger. "I only cower because of your actions mighty Odin" replied the Govenor. He snapped his fingers and gestured for the guards to remove the broken doors from the staircase. "I can sense your futile efforts to provoke me with your words. Do not forget your vote to put an end to the monstrous wolves. It was just as beneficial to your existence. So heed my demands before the urge of striking you down overwhelms me. Heimdall has found the den of Hati and Skoll. Send your assassin to deal with the matter immediately" instructed Odin. "We have yet to obtain another fetter that can aid us in the task" replied the Govenor. "Then send your personal guards to aid her! Do not make haste or fail me in this matter. Mimir has forseen the fall of Heimdall" said Odin. "That severed head also predicted your fall, but still you stand here before me" replied the Govenor. "Do not toy with me Loki. Heed my words if you value your existence in this realm!" demanded Odin. His words funneled a rage that unleashed a small stream of smoke from the Govenor's nostrils, and his eyes fueled a bright lava colored light that chased the shadow on Odin's face. A light that came to an abrupt stop when it reached a sinister smile. "You will deliver the carcasses of Hati and Skoll, *or take their place!*" Odin whispered in a tone that echoed promise and authority before leaving the house. "Damphir's gather your weapons from the arsenal!" commanded the Govenor. The Damphir's obeyed the command and returned in a line of formation with incredible speed. "Retrieve the information from Heimdall and join Sound for the kill" he instructed. "No failure! No delay!" the Damphir's shouted as they raced from the house.

Gall's pack was the first to arrive at the Adirondack Mountains. During their journey Gall familiarized himself with his brothers. Their Alpha Pekoe introduced them as Zulo, Graphite, Frenzy, Tales and Lanka. In camp Gall disappointedly flared his nostrils while analyzing the young and impetous pack. To be so eager to rush into battle against the Norse gods without a plan labeled their lives short lived. He spent a brief moment fretting the consequences before he quickly devised a scheme of his own. The bounty Lord Treachery placed on Heimdalls horns seemed more like a plot of strategy than revenge. Heimdall served the Norse gods as an early warning system. He diligently attended to the task with ears that could hear a blade of grass grow and sight that covered every corner of the earth. To be rid of him would create a window of opportunity for the pack. "This is it!" shouted Pekoe as the pack looked up from the base of

Mount Marcy. In the middle of the night they followed a secret trail of claw marks while scaling the southwest slope to a town called Newcomb. "Enemy left word that Heimdall roams these grounds in his animal form. A ram with gold horns. Let the hunt begin!" instructed Pekoe. The pack howled in response and transformed into their Lycan state. As they branched out, Gall cautiously strayed from the pack to hunt on his own. The closest Gall ever came to a god was Akantha. She constantly boasted about caring for them and while in their company, she picked up Ambrosia. The Greek gods could not resist its smell or flavor. Nor could they resist the memories it carried. With that in mind, Gall sought something with the same effect on a Norse god. So he broke into the nearest tavern and retrieved two large oak barrels of mead and carried them to Lake Tear of the Clouds. There an excavated glacier created the mist and environment that made Gall's fur and mane virtually undetectable. He poured a trail of mead through the trees and brushes. When he was done, he emptied a barrel on the outskirts of the lake and propped the other barrel just a few feet away. Then Gall dug a hole and camouflaged himself within a dirt bed. While in hiding, Gall regulated his breathing and silently recited the verses to a Warriors Creed.

Shortly before sunrise Heimdall responded to the sight of broken mead barrels and followed the misplaced scent of mead. He charged down from the peak of Mount Marcy and picked up the trail leading to Lake Tear of the Clouds. When the barrels were within sight, Heimdall lowered his head and eagerly charged down the path with the intention of breaking a barrel to quench his thirst. He salivated at the thought of gulping his way through a puddle before *Fate unexpectedly extended its hand.* The claws of the possessed Lycan pierced the throat of the charging ram and dissected the creature from the neck to its tail. As the torn carcass slid to the base of the barrels the possessed Lycan jumped from the cover of blood and organs to unleash a howl of reckoning. Gall boasted with sarcasm as he hacked off the horns and allowed his bone mending ability to snap the minor fractures in his wrist back into place. "I am Gall!" he greeted.

Later that evening, Banter, Sound and the Damphirs arrived at Mount Marcy to retrieve the information from Heimdall. They began a search that started from the bottom of the peak, and before midnight found Heimdall's carcass at Lake Tear of the Clouds. "This will not end well for us. We must hurry before it attracts attention" said Sound. The Damphirs quickly made a raft and placed Heimdall's carcass on it for a Viking burial. "What did you mean when you said this will not end well for us?" Banter curiously asked as Sound set the raft on fire. "A Norse god has fallen! Once Heimdall passes the gates of Valhalla the fear of Ragnarok will once again be upon the lips of the Norse gods. Odin will not take his death lightly. He'll send someone out to seek justice and pass sentence for our failures!" answered Sound. "Who will he send?" asked Banter. "Ponder on the thought of being Odin for a moment. Who would you send to avenge Heimdall and enforce your hand?" replied Sound. Banter sacredly answered, "I would call Loki or". Before Banter could finish his sentence the siren of a patrol car unexpectedly arrived on the scene and forced them into the woods. In the Hall of Valaskjalf, on a high seat that displayed the entire universe and outer worldly realms Odin finished Banter's sentence, *"I would call Thor!"*

Odin mournfully shouted at the sight of Heimdall entering the gates of Valhalla, "Thor! Heimdall has fallen. Thor answer my call!" Thor raced to the Hall of Valaskjalf on his chariot in response. He slowly approached his father while vengeful tears accumulated around the soles of his feet. The weight of his armor rippled small waves through the puddles and shattered against the base of the high seat when Thor kneeled before Odin. "Bid me your will father!" Thor angrily asked as he gripped the handle on his Mjollnir. "Heimdall was a son to me and as much a brother to you. Do not show the slightest bit of mercy when you avenge his death and rest my worries of Ragnarok. Loki has failed me in this matter. When you are done, return him to Asgard for sentencing. Let nothing or no one stand in your way!" commanded Odin. Thor obediently acknowledged his father by rising his Mjollnir and boarded his chariot in route to Midgard.

That same night in Highfalls Gorge, Gall's Lycan pack earned an unexpected visit. A broad smile appeared on Pekoe's face as he stood up to greet the approaching stranger. "We almost mistook you for an easy meal" said Pekoe as Enemy entered the campsite with a protective vest and dredlock's covering his face. He ponytailed his hair to expose the hardened features while looking over Gall's appearance. A bold act that made Gall aware of centuries of hate for the Norse gods, but to Gall appearances meant nothing. He looked directly into the eyes of his long time

Enemy to familiarize him with the beast within. "This is our new brother and slayer of Heimdall. Brother Gall!" Pekoe boasted as Enemy flared his nostrils to gain a familiar scent.

Gall cautiously removed the pouch wrapped around his waist and handed it to Enemy. After he inspected the contents, Enemy addressed Pekoe. "Tell me Pekoe. If he belongs to your pack, *and if he is your brother?* Where is his vest!" snapped Enemy. He grabbed Peko's neck with his free hand and tossed him into a neighboring brush. "Don't be alarmed by my brother's actions. His concern earned the love of his followers and the respect of the Lycan buccaneers" a voice explained from the shadow of a neighboring tree. Gall assumed it belonged to Lord Treachery but couldn't understand why he chose to remain hidden. "My name is Gall and I'd like to collect my bounty" requested Gall. "The horns are authentic brother!" shouted Enemy. "We must drink and celebrate Lycan for tomorrow is not promised to you. Odin will surely send his top enforcer to seek out your immediate demise" said Enemy. He tossed the bag of horns to the lurking shadow and a heavier one was tossed back to him. "Join me for a drink?" Enemy invited as he handed Gall his reward. Gall's eyes widened with interest as he opened the bag and gazed upon rare gold escudo coins. "As you should be grateful for my brother's concern, it will also be wise of you not to refuse his invitation" advised the lurking shadow. *"Here's to you and here's to me. Friends till the end we will always be, but in the event that we should disagree. It will only be me!"* Enemy warned as he gestured for a toast. *"Live respected. Die regretted!"* Gall warned as he returned the gesture. "You may very well earn a place in our pack. The honor bestowed upon you will be great because we only hunt with each other" said Enemy as the Lycans cheered and headed for the nearest tavern.

After Odin's departure from the house of Sumpter Loki summoned the Norse god Freyr. "Heimdall has fallen and because of your failure Odin has unleashed Thor. If you do not meet your fate in Ragnarok, Odin will surely make you wish you had after he issues your sentence. So tell me Loki, why do you summon me at a time when you should be preparing your rite of passage into Valhalla?" asked Freyr. "I need not worry of a fate during Ragnarok because I have a dwarf to make a fetter below me. As for Odin, he'll either meet his fate during Ragnarok or at the hands of my newborn son!" Loki excitedly replied as he pondered on the thought. Freyr responded with an outburst of laughter, "New born? How much mead have you consumed to believe that a Damphir could best Odin or a Fate?" "I did not summon you for your opinion or humor. I summoned you for your assistance in persuading the vessel of a female Fate into mortal pleasures. I have one in my possession. She can give me a newborn far more powerful than Hati or Skoll could ever be!" explained Loki. "Have you not learned from Fenrisulfr? His offspring was an abomination. Cursed to be hunted down like their father. Do you believe Odin would allow another creature so powerful to exist?" Freyr ambiguously questioned. "Odin will not know! Heimdall has fallen and Ragnarok has taken a course with no order. If you do not aid me in seducing the female Fate you too will have to prepare a rite of passage" answered Loki. "There is

168   JUAN BERRY

only one way to persuade a female Fate into mortal pleasure, you must become the one her vessel desires. I can aid you in an enchantment of illusion. In the mountain region of the Svartalfaheim dwarves grows a plant that possesses the vitality to overcome cold climates. The dwarf shrubs are known to many mortals as Diapensia and its oils are a key ingredient to the solution of your problem. Fortunately for you, a wedding ceremony is about to take place in that region. As Governor of the dwarfs' realm it would be unbefitting of me not to attend, but what am I to do with Hati and Skoll roaming about?" asked Freyr. "My assassin and personal guards will guard your stay while Thor tends to Hati and Skoll. In turn you will prepare the solution I need to seduce the female Fate" requested Loki. "Agreed!" Freyr excitedly replied. "I'll send word of your arrival and have them meet you on the highest peak" instructed Loki.

After fleeing Heimdall's Viking burial, Banter and Sound returned to the house on Saranac Lake with the Damphirs. Banter had just started to relax on the living room recliner when the team leader alerted Sound to an urgent phone call on a cell phone. Banter spent a brief moment sorting his thoughts and guessing the importance of the call when his Marid Djinn unexpectedly emerged. "Your services are no longer needed!" Sound shouted as each soldier tossed a grenade through the cabin windows. Banter quickly leapt from his chair and raced with increased speed for the rear double glass doors before the impact of the detonation blew his body into the center of the lake. He slipped in and out of consciousness as his Marid Djinn swam effortlessly through the debris. When he crawled on the shore he made an attempt to familiarize the distorted image of an approaching man. "Thank you" Banter gratefully mumbled while the man picked him up and tossed him onto his shoulders. "Do not thank me. Your life has not been spared. If you do not lead me to Victorhelm, I will place you in a fire that won't spit you out!" Rottenvein replied as he carried Banter back to his lair.

Early the following morning, Thor arrived at the Adirondacks in the cover of a thick fog. It hovered over Lake Tear of the Clouds until he came upon the spot where Heimdall had been slayed. The cold vapors surrounding the area had frozen a patch of moistened soil and it retained Heimdall's blood. As the fog slowly parted Thor removed his Mjollnir from his waistline. He stepped down from his chariot and smashed the blunt end into the patch of Heimdall's blood. Then he withdrew a pouch containing rune stones from his belt and casted them over the dirt. "Lead me to your slayer!" demanded Thor. Within seconds Heimdall's blood had flowed onto the blunt end of the Mjollnir and formed a runic compass. When the casting was complete, the blood on the blunt end beaconed a bright red glare that highlighted a route to Gall.

It only took a brief moment for Thor to reach the vicinity of Lake Champlain. The fog that camouflaged his chariot amassed over the condemned Crown Point Bridge as a pack of Lycans prepared for battle. Thunder and lightning flashes crackled through the clouds as Thor summoned the powers of his Mjollnir. "Attack!" Pekoe shouted as the pack transformed into their Lycan states. Zulo, Tales and Lanka charged through the closed barricades of the bridge and scurried up the steel beams in response. When they had reached the top, they extended their claws and foolishly leapt to Thor's chariot. "Murderous dogs do not belong on my plain!" Thor shouted as three lightning bolts smashed the Lycans into the bridges platform. They whimpered in agony as the study flow of electrical currents shattered their vest and disintegrated their carcasses. After witnessing the demise of their brothers, Graphite and Frenzy climbed the Crown Point Lighthouse with the same intentions. They eagerly waited in the tower and taunted the approaching fog with howls before Thor's Mjollnir fired from its mist and struck them down into the pit of the tower. When the Mjollnir returned to Thor's hand, he summoned a lightning bolt to finish the deed. The impact created a mythical flame and the charred carcasses beaconed a light within the lighthouse. Pekoe was the last in sight and he sadly looked over the lake before Thor delivered a final blow. The impact of the lightning bolt crackled the pavement and a passing wind scattered Pekoe's ashes on the lake.

When there was no Lycan in sight, the fog that carried Thor's chariot slowly sank to ground level. He stepped down and kneeled on the outskirts of the lake to wash Heimdall's blood from his Mjollnir. When he was done, Thor suspiciously watched the blood float to a stream of bubbles in the center of the lake where Gall surfaced. "I see your cowering has ended slayer. It will not bring you victory today!" said Thor. "Cower? You misjudge my intentions" replied Gall. "I misjudged nothing. I need only make my actions clear by sentencing a slayer to a watery grave!" Thor angrily shouted as he raised his Mjollnir. Gall quickly dived back underwater as a monstrous wolf unexpectedly charged at Thor from behind. The impact placed Thor in the center of the lake where Gall's plot began to unravel.

In the waters of Lake Champlain Gall knew it would have been ill fated for Thor to summon lightning, and to weild the Mjollnir he needed a pair of iron gloves called Jarngreipr. To possess the strength to wear the iron gloves, Thor had to wear an iron belt called the Megingjora. It was at that moment a Marid Djinn emerged to weave a *placid fate.* Thor hurled his Mjollnir at Gall and removed his belt to keep from sinking. Gall embraced the blow of the Mjollnir and used the bone mending of his ribs to keep it in his clutches. It brought a stunned expression to Thor's face as Gall returned to his position on the blunt end of the mythical hammer. When Thor extended his hand to grab the handle, Gall pulled him in and embraced him. The vibration of bones breaking kept a study stream of air flowing from Thor's mouth as Gall quickly inflicted his rib cage and two humerus bones with fractures. Thor recklessly swung his hammer and struggled to hold the weight of the Jarngrepir until water filled his lungs. When they had reached the bottom of the murky waters, Gall advanced to a sleeper hold position and constricted his arms until Thor was freed from the weight of the Mjollnir. After applying more pressure Gall returned to the surface alone. As he crawled ashore, Thor's body drifted to the surface without his armor. Enemy shouted with sarcasm as he pulled Gall from the water, "Now you've done it Lycan! You can't even begin to imagine the deaths that Odin would cast upon you when he sees his son pass the gates of Valhalla!" "Do you know any cheers without death threats?" Gall amusingly asked as he slowly rose to his feet. "Let us drink!" invited Enemy. "Surely, but first I have to see an old friend" replied Gall. "Wherever you go I will follow. From this day on you belong to my pack, and will join the ranks of the Lycan buccaneers. Worthy to be called brother. Brother Gall!" Enemy replied in a tone that expressed authority. Gall bowed his head to acknowledge the honor bestowed upon him as they made their way to Akantha's residence.

In a cavern west of Mount Marcy, Banter slowly awakened and found himself hanging upside down over a pit. "The humans called her Jolly" said Rottenvein as he sliced two pieces off a roasting moose and tossed it into the pit. "What do you call her?" Banter asked as a hungry black bear growled below. "Angry. Just like I trained her to be. Now tell me where Victorhelm is!" Rottenvein demanded as he placed his knife on Banter's rope. "You should've chose a better prisoner. The soldiers that tried to kill me are the only ones that can answer that question" replied Banter. "You lie! Your symbol was found in our woods. You traveled and fought alongside the blood drinkers!" shouted Rottenvein. "Because Victorhelm wasn't their only prisoner! We had an agreement with the soldiers to retrieve the corpse of a dwarf to make a fetter. The same one made to contain Fenrisulfr. Victorhelm delivered a corpse but it was taken from us. The soldiers took Victorhelm and my friend prisoner for the failed delivery. They claimed they would release them as soon as we returned the corpse. I don't know what went wrong after that" explained Banter.

The black bear below growled for more meat while

Rottenvein analyzed the truth in Banter's words. "There's only one corpse Victorhelm could've taken without the High Chief or anyone finding out about it. I kept it well preserved in a blog, not far from your camp" replied Rottenvein as he sheathed his knife and grabbed a pouch containing his boomerangs. "Where are you going?" Banter suspiciously asked. Rottenvein looked over two glass jars containing Nagleria Fowleri. "Dead or alive I can find the corpse. Pray for your sake that the blood drinker is still willing to barter for it!" Rottenvein answered as he raced from the underground dwelling.

Later that evening, Gall and Enemy arrived at Akantha's residence. "I prefer to stay out in the open" said Enemy as he cautiously stood watch from the steps. "I understand. My visit won't be long" replied Gall. He climbed the staircase, and like he expected Akantha opened the door to greet him. "You look troubled?" Akantha asked as she peeked around Gall and gazed at Enemy. "You know me like a son" Gall replied as he greeted her with a mild embrace. "Does it pertain to what you have around your waist?" Akantha continued to question as she poked at the hidden fetter. "I'm troubled about the deaths of the Norse gods" answered Gall. He followed Akantha into the living room where the familiar scent of her candles lightened the mood for a cup of tea. "You're starting to get a sense of the road your about to travel. Tell me what took place and I'll try to give you a better understanding of what's to come" replied Akantha. "I have slain Heimdall and Thor. During the time of their death I was surrounded by light. I'm starting to wonder if that'll change when I face a darker god like

Loki?" Gall curiously asked. "My dear Gall, you are truly an exceptional being. This is why your Marid Djinn chose you. You fear you have crossed a border between good and evil, but the battles that were predicted to take place in Ragnarok were not between good and evil. In that manner neither side prevailed" Akantha began to explain before a roar that mimicked the sound of a revving chopper motorcycle engine interrupted. "The end of the Norse gods will be decided by *fates!* Their actions to prevent their demise is the very thing that has brought about their end and I quote, *"Worry never robs tomorrow of its sorrow. It only saps today of it's joy"* said Iblis as he emerged from the fireplace with a sinister laugh. He slowly approached Gall while a stream of smoke latched onto his body and shadowed it like a hooded robe. "Things weigh differently on their side of the fence, and you haven't determined on which side of the fence you truly belong because your Marid Djinn knows he can be judged for his actions. The obstacles yours overcame allowed it to make a transference. It is that feeling that confuses you, but you are still Tibbigall" explained Akantha. "What she should say is your thoughts and actions are still *Typical!*" corrected Iblis. "I understand your worries Gall, but you must keep in mind that you are your own person" advised Akantha. "Lay your troubles in the wind. You have just achieved Lycan buccaneer status and I can tell you from personal experience that you will not find a better ally. Your new found abilities and Marid Djinn will continue to aid you in your times of need. They will come in handy for the army you are about to face" said Iblis. "How do you know so much about my Lycan buccaneer status and the army I will face?" Gall suspiciously asked. "I am allied with Odin" answered Iblis. He dived back into the fireplace with an outburst of laughter as Gall turned to Akantha with a puzzled expression. "Does that mean I must face him?" asked Gall. "The greatest trick Iblis ever pulled was to convince the world that he didn't exist" replied Akantha. "You mean the greatest trick the devil ever pulled" corrected Gall. "They are the same" explained Akantha.

That same night in Asgard, Odin's allies assembled outside the Hall of Valaskjalf for a ride known throughout folklore and legend as the Wild Hunt. On the high seat Odin looked upon other realms until two Valkrys interrupted a mournful state. "Thor has passed the gates of Valhalla!" the Valkry shouted. Shortly afterwards Odin's Gungnir pinned it on a wall. A fiery tear trickled down his cheek and glittered off his armor in a blaze as he leapt from his high seat to retrieve it. The remaining Valkry could only bow at the sight as Odin grabbed the handle of the spear and kept the impaled corpse on its tip. He boldly exited the hall to command an awaiting army as a Berserker handed him the reins to his horse Sleipnir. Blood thirsty roars echoed through the hall as Odin slowly approached his front line.

As Odin shook off the carcass of the Valkry his generals saluted him. King Arthur raised Excalibur as Odin passed. Next in line was King Nuada, he saluted with a silver hand and arm that never relinquished his sword. After him Gwynn Ap Nudd of the Welsh underworld saluted with a sword that when unsheathed forced his opponents to obey his demands. Beside him was Gwydion the magician, he gracefully removed a pointed hat and acknowledged Odin with a bow. Odin continued down the line where Herne the Hunter was the next to salute with a mythical pair of antlers on his head. Last in line, wearing a black hooded cloak that only displayed the red luster of his eyes was Iblis. He tried to contain his laughter as Odin grunted and looked to an army of two hundred Berserkers. "Any mortal, beast or god that interferes with the hunt shall not be spared. Let all who gaze upon us meet their demise!" Odin commanded. He mounted Sleipnir and raised his hand to give a description of their prey. "Mimir has told me of the pestilence that has slain your gods. He is a Lycan that calls himself Gall. You will bring him back to me alive!" Odin demanded as they marched to Midgard.

Following the hunch of a hard nose detective, Det. Rodriguez investigated Banter's unusual flight pattern to the Adirondacks. He arrived at the Sheriff's Station that following morning and explained his presence as an ongoing investigation of a potential suspect to his case. After looking through recent reports his trail ended in the county coroner's office. "Our John Doe suffered from severe spinal injuries. Multiple fractures of the ribs, arms and oxygen deprivation to the lungs and brain" the medical examiner explained as he pointed over Thor's body. "All this was done underwater?" Det. Rodriguez asked as he looked over the blue discoloration of Thor's skin. "Yes, and he put up one hell of a struggle" answered the medical examiner. "Does it have anything to do with your case?" a man asked as he boldly charged through the lab doors. The detective had seen his face pictured on several campaign posters around town, *"Vote for Sheriff Jean Desmond. An*

Avalanche of Protection!" The photo pictured his features perfectly. A fit middle aged man with a tan complexion and pyramidal moustache. He quickly licked his palms to slick back two frizzy strands of hair as he approached the table. "I'm still trying to determine that" Det. Rodriguez answered as he continued to examine the file. "There was no I.D. on him and nothing came back on the fingerprints?" Det. Rodriguez curiously asked. "That's correct. We thought he might've belong to one of the colonial war reenactments, but there was no feedback on the photo we posted" the sheriff explained while he retrieved a bag containing Thor's garments. "Why would you think that? These garments aren't Colonial French or British. They relate more to a barbarian or viking theme" Det. Rodriguez replied as he looked over the contents of the bag. "One of our deputies reported a disturbance relating to a Viking burial. He said he seen a couple fleeing the scene after setting a raft and ram on fire. They also stole two barrels of mead" said the sheriff. "Ram? Are they common in these parts?" Det. Rodriguez continued to question. "Can't say that I ever seen one while camping out" answered the sheriff. "Can you give me an escort over there?" requested Det. Rodriguez. "I'm a little busy with this campaign going on, but I can have the patrolling deputy meet you out there when he starts his shift tonight. I'll leave word for him to meet you on Mount Marcy. Just find your way to Lake Tear of the Clouds and he'll join you around 10 p.m." instructed the sheriff. "I'll be there" Det. Rodriguez replied as the sheriff scribbled the directions on a piece of paper and handed it to him.

That same evening the Norse god Freyr arrived on the

peaks of Mount Marcy. Sound and the Damphirs warmly greeted him as he exited a thick fog. "Are you the assassin Loki summoned?" Freyr asked as he cautiously looked over his surroundings. "Yes, and for your protection I would like you to dock the Skidbladnir and stay safely aboard it while the Damphirs search for the Diapensia needed for my Governor's love potion" instructed Sound. "Love potion? The solution I devise is no love potion. It's merely an enchantment of illusion. For him to obtain what he seeks the Marid Djinn must be present. This is no simple task, the Marid Djinn only emerges when its vessel is threatened. In this state it will only allow the man her vessel truly desires to be near. I can aid your Governor in overcoming that obstacle, but my solution is only an illusion. His appearance will pass, but he still must assume this man's character. If he fails, he would've only have created his own fate" explained Freyr. "But the man you speak of has met his demise. I assumed we had no further use of his services. There is no character to learn from!" Sound worriedly replied. "Then your Governor has become successful in two of three steps. The sight will emerge the Marid Djinn and the last assure his fate!" Freyr explained as they descended the mountain.

After touring two bars in the city, Gall and Enemy returned to the Champlain Bridge. Before crossing Enemy immediately picked up a scent and pulled Gall aside to point out a neighboring barricade. "Make sure your vest is fastened tight brother. Odin has brought his ghost riders and a second advantage could mean the difference between life and death!" Enemy advised while Berserkers exited a fog resting on the waters of Lake Champlain. Herne the Hunter had signaled three to guard the bridge before returning to Odin's side. "Herne take King Arthur and seek out my son's body. It must be returned for a proper burial. The rest of you will follow me!" Odin shouted as the fog proceeded to Fort Crown Point. The Berserkers left to guard the bridge took on an animal form for a disguise. They discretely kept watch as a small pack of wolves. "These wolves should be of no threat to us?" said Gall as he peeked around a steel railing on the opposite end. "Do not be fooled. Those wolves are Berserkers. They possess the ability to become wolf or bear because of the pelts they wear. It enhances their fighting skills. The three before you will fight like six. They also have a high tolerance for metal and fire. I tested that theory on many occasions. A claw is but a scratch to them. You have to dig deep if you want to make an impression" explained Enemy. "What's their breaking point for fire?" asked Gall. "Ash!" Enemy blurted as he removed a grinding stone from his pocket. "We can swim around them" suggested Gall. "In freezing waters! That swim is approximately 700 meters. Then there's the risk of catching a cramp while being pursued by Berserkers" Enemy replied with sarcasm. "You're right. Where's the excitement in that?" Gall mumbled. "I'll give you a lift across. When we're within range make your attack fast and lethal!" Enemy instructed as he transformed into his monstrous wolf state. Gall quickly leapt onto his back as he jumped out of hiding.

Under the cover of his black fur, Enemy raced through the darkness of night and over the bridge with such speed that it made Gall appear as if he was just a reckless motorcyclist ignoring the barricades. When the Berserker's finally recognized the approaching Enemy it was too late. The duo had already gained ground and the advantage. Gall quickly jumped off Enemy's back and pounced on an unsuspecting Berserker before he could change into his human form. Within seconds the Marid Djinn had constricted a fast and lethal fate. After spewing a few internal organs, Gall gently placed the canine on the side of the road. Leaving behind a fate that resembled road kill.

Enemy took a different approach. While in his monstrous wolf state he smacked both Berserkers with his paws to provoke a battle on foot. The taunt forced the Berserkers to return to their human form while Enemy transformed into a Lycan state. Gall studied from a distance as he displayed the Lycan buccaneers signature move. The Berserkers withdrew their swords and fiercely charged at Enemy. He made their first strike their last mistake as he deflected their blades and clawed over their eyes to blind them. While in a dazed state, Enemy followed with a one inch punch technique over the coronary artery. Superhuman speed and strength immediately stopped the beating of their hearts and when the bodies collapsed on their knees, Enemy signed off with a flawless spear hand to the chest. A howl of reckoning roared through the area as he simultaneously removed the still hearts on his claws.

A smirk appeared on Gall's face, and his right eyebrow raised into his forehead while watching Enemy execute the technique but the howl didn't go unnoticed. Other Berserkers patrolling the area sounded a horn and alerted Odin's hunting party to their presence. Enemy angrily returned to his human form and unexpectedly scolded Gall,

"Now you've done it Lycan! Did I have to tell you to be silent? Now in order to avoid capture I'll have to carry you back to our lair. It's the only way you can keep up without me having to worry about you!" A broad smile appeared on Gall's face as Enemy transformed into his monstrous wolf state. *Then Gall transformed into his.* "So the message Pekoe sent is true. You are of our bloodline!" said Enemy. "At least you don't have to worry about cramps" Gall boasted as he took the lead.

On Mount Marcy Det. Rodriguez walked along the outskirts of Lake Tear of the Clouds until the patrolling deputy arrived. A burly middle aged man with lamb chop sideburns approached the detective with a flashlight and folder in hand. "I take it that you're the big shot city detective investigating the homicide down at Crown Point?" he asked. "I'm the detective investigating a case in Manhattan. I've followed a lead down here that may point me to the potential suspect. Can you show me your findings?" Det. Rodriguez politely asked as he looked over a name tag that read C. Ellwood. "Right this way" replied Dep. Ellwood. He escorted Det. Rodriguez to a place a half a mile from where he stood and handed him a folder containing his report. "There were two barrels of mead propped right there and a few yards into the lake was a roasted ram" Dep. Ellwood pointed out. "What about this? I don't see anything in your report about it?" Det. Rodriguez questioned as he looked over the stones from Thor's rune casting. "That's because it wasn't there at the time!" answered Dep. Ellwood. Before Det. Rodriguez could question further a call on the radio interrupted, "Clovis! Clovis Ellwood are you still assisting that city detective?" asked the dispatcher. "He's standing right in front of me. Why'd you ask?" Dep. Ellwood amusingly replied. "We have a ten 55 and a ten 91D at the Crown Point Bridge and the sheriff wants the both of you to respond" answered the dispatcher. "We have to get going and pronto!" Dep. Ellwood shouted as he raced back to the car. Det. Rodriguez quickly scooped up the rune stones and followed. "What's the problem?" he suspiciously asked as they hurried back to the main road. "We have more murders on the bridge!" answered Dep. Ellwood.

The ride down to Crown Point was the same as the ride up for the detective. The neighboring towns were filled with campaign posters and his thoughts were still troubled about Gall. He never thought solving his only unsolved case would bring more sleepless nights, but who can sleep after seeing Gall at work. The bruises and fractures on the John Doe's body were similar to the ones he discovered in the Blaine case. A discovery that placed him at a crossroad. Gall had saved his life from a mythical creature, but no one knew before this time the detective had seen other's before!

The sheriff arrived at the bridge shortly after they did. He angrily stepped out of his car in civilian clothing and licked his palms to slick back two frizzy strands of hair as they approached the scene. "Can you tell me what was written on those posters you've seen while touring our town?" the sheriff calmly asked as they ducked under the crime scene tape. "Vote for Sheriff Jean Desmond. An Avalanche of Protection" Det. Rodriguez answered as he looked over the fist shape holes in the chest of the corpses. "An avalanche of protection! How can I guarantee that with an accumulating body count, home explosions and animals that end up butchered or missing?" asked the sheriff. "Missing? An animal's been reported missing?" Det. Rodriguez asked as he looked over a dead wolf. "Somebody took Jolly. She was the sheriff's campaign mascot. Did him a favor if you ask me. That bear ain't take kindly to nobody" replied Dep. Ellwood. "I want the name of your suspect now!" demanded the sheriff. "I don't have a name and we might be dealing with more than one killer. We have a connection with these rune stones and these two have garments like the John Doe in the morgue" answered Det. Rodriguez. "So we're dealing with some type of occult?" asked the sheriff. "Maybe?" replied Det. Rodriguez. "Don't hold out on me!" snapped the sheriff. "What are you implying?" asked Det. Rodriguez. "I did some investigating of my own detective. I heard about your only unsolved case and how you miraculously happened to solve it when the suspect you were supposed to apprehend mysteriously disappeared off the face of the earth" answered the sheriff. "He did not disappear off the face of the earth!" Det. Rodriguez defensively replied. "Drowned or eaten by sharks. No one could actually attest to that but a group of looney cases with records as long as my arm" said the sheriff. "If you have something to say don't beat around the bush!" Det. Rodriguez replied. "Take it easy! I'm just pointing out that you've dealt with sadistic cases like this before and I like how you handled it. Like the man that was found burnt to a crisp with an electric billy club sticking out of his pants. I really need this matter closed before things get further out of hand" the sheriff whispered as he escorted the detective back to his car. "*You mean* before the election slips away from you" quipped Det. Rodriguez. "*I mean,* before I ship your keester back to the city with a few reprimands! Now if you intend to stay in our little town I suggest you do as the Romans do. Deputy Ellwood will continue to assist your investigation. I expect a daily report on my desk and don't doddle with progress!" advised the sheriff. "I guess this means we're partners. Give me the address to your place and I'll be by to pick you up at the start of shift" instructed Dep. Ellwood. "We're not partners Clovis, and I'll meet you at the station before your start of shift" replied Det. Rodriguez.

A little before sunrise the next morning, a thick fog filled with Berserkers had chased Enemy and Gall up one of the graphite cliffs at Highfalls Gorge. Within a few feet from being hit by a spear the sun casted a ray on its handle. "Fortunately for us, ghost riders cannot ride past sunrise" said Enemy as he changed back into his human form and gazed at their mysterious disappearance. They jumped down to ground level and entered a secret passageway beneath. Gall's eyes widened with amazement as they journeyed through the timeless caverns filled with whispers of wars. When they came upon two giant steel doors a Lycan leapt from hiding to greet them. "Bloody Bartholomew Smyte! After spending the night with Odin's ghost riders poking my spine your ugly face can bring a smile to mine!" Enemy greeted as an enormous Lycan with a disfigured face changed into his human form. "Brother Gall, allow me to introduce you to a true buccaneer. We have sailed and collected plenty of bounty in our time" introduced Enemy. "So what brings about this visit?" Gall asked as he extended his hand to the Lycan buccaneer. "Lord Treachery has been

informed of Odin's presence and Freyr's. For this reason he
has summoned the packs of Gibraltar and Maracaibo. Not
everyone has arrived yet, the others are still making their
way without detection" Bloody Bartholomew explained as
he pushed the steel doors open. Inside, a pack of Lycan
buccaneers prepared for battle. They suited themselves with
protective vests and black fatigues before saluting Enemy.
"You say Freyr has also joined Odins ranks?" asked Enemy.
"His vessel is docked on the waters of Mirror Lake. He
is under the protection of Sound and her soldiers. Lord
Treachery instructed that upon your arrival we'd see them
to Davey Jones!" Bloody Bartholomew explained. "Sound
has returned to our borders. Two birds with one stone. This
is truly a special occasion. We will fill our mugs with mead
for tonight we sail the Deaf Dum Dead!" Enemy shouted as
he raised his hand to gesture a toast. "Allow me to introduce
you to some of our crew" he added as he patted Gall on the
shoulder and lead him deeper into the cavern.

Every landing that bared a lit torch had a Lycan
buccaneer. "Po Paws!" Enemy happily blurted as he
embraced a Lycan buccaneer that was carving two large
arrows. He briefly paused while Enemy introduced him to
Gall. "This Lycan buccaneer saved my brother's life" said
Enemy as Po Paws leaned his arrows against the cavern
wall. "Cut into little pieces, burned and ashes thrown in the
wind is what I told all who searched for him. After I was
able to convince them that sociopath bit me!" explained Po
Paws. "I never tire from hearing that story" Enemy replied
with an outburst of laughter as he proceeded to the next
level. There Gall seen two Lycan buccaneers looting the

chariot that Thor had rode in on, while another slaughtered the goats. These two are the youngest of our crew. Our captain found them conjoined at birth. Their chances for survival were little to none before he took the discovery as a symbol of our brotherhood. He guided them into the waters of a Lycan buccaneer and the healing factor aided their surgical separation. They were inducted into the crew as Grit and Muzzle Blast" Enemy explained as two Lycan buccaneers approached with patches of their face still in human form. "And what have you learned while under the tutelage of the Deaf Dum Dead?" Enemy asked as they stood before them. "Grit Blast! Muzzle Blast!" they simultaneously answered. Enemy proudly patted them on the shoulder before proceeding. "Still trying to best Cilantro Faye's ikejime technique is Motley Yuckyur Graves" Enemy introduced as the Lycan buccaneer positioned his claw over the hind part of a goat's brain. "A claw is a delicate matter. If not used properly, you can leave a scar for life" whispered Motley. "Motley likes to loot his prey and tries to find ways to bury it in a live one. The day after their demise, he tracks them down to collect. He's our best tracker next to Po Paws" said Enemy as he purposely patted Motley on the shoulder to alter the incision.

A study flow of curses followed them to the next landing as Enemy quickly warned Gall. "This may appear shocking to you. It always is when people first feast their eyes on it" said Enemy. A Lycan buccaneer slowly approached while singing the words to the Reaperbahn as he extended a paw. *"The apple is gone but there's always the core"* he greeted while jingling tongues and fingers with bells tied to his

wristbands. "It's shocking because it sounds good!" Gall
replied as he slapped his paw. "Morbid Medley is the name.
I can't take credit for the tongues. Iblis gave them to me"
said Morbid Medley. "Funny how the littlest things seem
to annoy him" added Enemy. "Annoy him?" Gall curiously
asked. "It's a trick for Iblis to remove the tongue from what
he deems is a problem and place it in the center of his palm.
He wiggles it around and pretends it talks back like a puppet.
It never utters a word but the message speaks volumes for
whoever he is torturing" explained Enemy. "I can hear the
last thing they said before Iblis removed them" boasted
Morbid Medley. "What did that tongue say before Iblis cut
it out?" Gall asked as he pointed one out. "Stop punching
me!" Morbid Medley answered before they proceeded to
the next landing. "Bopo Lava and Timber Orslope!" Enemy
happily shouted as two Lycan buccaneer's approached.
"Every hole, crack and crevice will spew the blood and
flesh of a Berserker" said Bopo Lava as he brandished a
customized flame thrower that adjusted to his frame. "I'm
prepared to bite the cannon smoke. I only fear the delay!"
added Timber Orslope. "I'm Gall" Gall greeted as their
nostrils flared around him. Enemy proudly patted them
on the shoulder as they proceeded to the dock. "I'd love to
introduce you to the femme fatales of our pack but they're
working the taverns for Berserkers in search of mead. Which
reminds me, never follow a woman named Tiki into the
woods. Refuse any invitation to a room rented by a woman
named Pryur Body, and pray you pick up a Lycan scent
before you dine with Blush!" advised Enemy. "Now have you
ever feasted your eyes on such a beautiful vessel!" he boasted

as Gall admirably looked over the Deaf Dum Dead. "I can't say that I have" Gall answered as Enemy transformed into his Lycan state and unleashed a howl of reckoning.

A few minutes before midnight the pack was hiding along the outskirts of the Skidbladnir. The Damphirs had returned with the last batch of Diapensia and Freyr quickly added it to the contents of a heated kettle while Sound descended from the deck. "You called for me?" Sound asked as she looked over a table containing Freyr's herbal ingredients. Two glass bottles filled with a pearl white cream substance resting on the end immediately caught her attention. "Even the appearance is alluring" Sound mumbled as she knelt down and stared at it. "There are three glass bottles on the table. You may take the two that are already filled and give them to your Governor. I will keep the third jar for myself" instructed Freyr as he slowly stirred the next batch. "Why would a god of your stature need the substance?" Sound suspiciously asked as she carefully packed the glass bottles in a hay filled pouch. "As Govenor of the dwarfs' realm I'm obligated to attend the High Chief's ceremony. His son is a potential suitor for the princess. Custom deems it necessary for every suitor along her path to bestow gifts upon her until she makes her decision. I favor the High Chief's son Victorhelm and will see to it that her path ends here tonight. I will include this solution to his list of gifts. I have already informed your Governor of the event and retained the protection of his personal guard as payment for my services. Instruct him to apply the substance every time he deals with the female Fate. It will grant him the illusion to deceive them both, but anything more than that

I cannot guarantee" advised Freyr. Sound responded with a nod before she raced from below deck to an awaiting jet. "Curses!" Enemy angrily blurted as his nostrils flared in the passing wind. "Sound has more lives than a cat!" he added as he cautiously timed the Damphirs passing patrols.

Behind Enemy and Gall gathered the ruthless and bloodthirsty buccaneers that stormed Maracaibo and Gibraltar. Two more joined the ranks while Enemy and Gall watched from the trees of the neighboring woods. "Unchained Gauge and Obnoxious Koss approach" a Lycan buccaneer signaled. "Were you not taught how to leave a proper trail?" Unchained Gauge scolded as he crawled to Enemy's side. "Did you not find me?" Enemy answered with sarcasm. "Not a simple task after returning to the cavern with Thor's goats and chariot" replied Unchained Gauge. "If we're ever forced into hiding their ability to rejuvenate can help us avoid any obnoxious cost during war" added Obnoxious Koss. "Aye" Enemy blurted as a thick fog amassed around the ship. It provided the perfect cover as Enemy hand signaled Bloody Bartholomew Smyte to advance on the vessel and relieve it of its anchor's. After seeing the signal, the Lycan buccaneer raced from the woods with four Lycans and dove into the lake's waters.

While under the cover of a lake that reflected the darkness of a midnight sky, Bloody Bartholomew Smyte's pack made their way to the anchors and quickly hacked at the steel chained links descending from the ships bow. Unfortunately for the pack, the blows carried a vibration that was immediately picked up by the guards. Within seconds twenty Ak-47 assault rifles with suppressors had opened fire on Bloody Batholomew Smyte's pack. The muffled sound of tin tapping answered as an onslaught of silver bullets rippled from the ship's deck and into the water like raindrops in a thunderstorm. While their attention was focused on the water, Enemy signaled the pack to advance on the drifting vessel. A dust storm accompanied the fast and lethal advance while the Damphirs reloaded and repeated their attack. The repetition blanketed the sound of claws scurrying up the starboard side of the ship and gave the Lycan bucaneer's the position to place a claw at every throat facing overboard. Those that were quick enough to face death felt the jaws of their attacker puncturing their arteries until the flow of blood carried them to another existence. "We must hurry before our ship sets sail!" Enemy shouted as he transformed into his monstrous wolf state and raced for the ship. A devilish grin appeared on Gall's face as he transformed into his Lycan state to reenact the life of a buccaneer. He raced out to the vessel and jumped onto the starboard side as a trail of body parts drifted along the waves. When he climbed onto the deck he found the Lycan buccaneers tearing the remaining Damphirs apart. They slit throats and tossed severed carcasses overboard where Bopo Lava set them aflame.

Enemy returned to his human form and boldly stood under the center mast while Grit and Muzzle Blast dragged Freyr onto the deck. "Mangy dogs! Unhand me!" Freyr shouted as they laid him at Enemy's feet. "Obnoxious Koss tally our loses" requested Enemy. "Our Bloody Bartholomew Smyte and four Lycans under his tutelage have joined Davy Jones. It grieves me to say that after the death of twenty Damphir's and two Norse gods the price paid was obnoxious!" answered Obnoxious Koss. Then we must make the death of the third Norse god memorable" replied Enemy. "You will not have the opportunity to speak willingly once I begin, so I advise you to answer my questions accordingly" Enemy warned as the Lycan buccaneers began to bind all the rope they could find on deck. "I am Freyr. I don't respond to mere barking!" Freyr valiantly shouted as Enemy tied a rope to his right wrist. "Fortunately for you, pain is a universal language" said Enemy as he handed Unchained Gauge the other end of the rope. He quickly jumped overboard and swam under the ship's belly to toss the loose end back to a hand on deck. After Enemy retrieved the loose end, he bonded Freyr's other wrist and tossed him overboard. A tug of war ensued, and as they pulled Freyr from side to side his back scraped against the sharp barnacles pinned on the ship's belly. Every turn was accompanied by a thick stream of blood that flowed from his body and when it surfaced, Enemy ordered the Lycan buccaneers to lift him to the rails. "Do you understand my barking now?" Enemy asked as he began his interrogation. "Tell us where Sound has gone and when will she return?" demanded Enemy. "Sound has left with a solution to be rid of you and your kind forever!" Freyr angrily shouted as he tried to catch his breath. "Tell me all you know of this plot or lose all the flesh from your bones" replied Enemy. "Loki is their Governor. He has captured a female Fate and asked me to create a solution to seduce her. When he is done with her, a being more powerful than either of you will come to existence!" answered Freyr. The news quickly gained Galls attention and a Marid Djinn

angrily emerged to weave a fate for *the same song and dance*.
"You lie! Odin will not allow another like me or my brother
to exist. Especially at his expense!" replied Enemy. "Loki
does not need his permission. Especially at his expense!
Ragnarok has begun and every Norse god it foretold to fall
will fall. For this reason I've supported Loki's scheme. If
you do not believe me, check for yourself. I still have some
below. Apply it and see if you do not take the form of what
your woman desires most" explained Freyr. "I have no need
for such a thing. I am already what she desires. *I am Enemy!*
I shall make other uses for this weapon you've developed
and your vessel" Enemy replied as Gall pushed the Lycan
buccaneers aside and pulled Freyr aboard.

The Marid Djinn embraced the Norse god's neck and
raised Freyr's feet from the deck while constricting his arms.
The hold was as tight as a noose, and served the same purpose
while Gall constricted his muscles around his collar bone.
"This world already has a being more powerful. As Govenor
to a realm filled with festivities for virility and prosperity
you will tell all those that join you in Valhalla that no being
can boogie harder than Gall!" the Marid Djinn whispered in
Freyr's ear while he danced the Hemphen Jig to an echoed
hiss. After spending the entire night patrolling the area of
Crown Point, Deputy Ellwood and Det. Rodriguez ended
their shift with an argument. "A body is missing from the
morgue and no one heard or saw a thing? Were you on duty?"
asked Det. Rodriguez. "I'm tired of your accusations. I don't
have to validate my police work! You're no saint so don't get
all pesty with me. How can a city homicide detective solve
all his cases anyway? You should have your own sitcom"

replied Dep. Ellwood. "You think all my cases were just handed to me? The case your sheriff spoke of would've been my first unsolved case. A crime lord's organization had been exterminated and I was about to pick up the suspect. An enforcer from a rival crew named Tibbigall Maxwell. As soon as the officers in my precinct heard the name they started a pool. No one could pin a case to him and he certainly wasn't the type to give a confession. So I knew I had my work cut out for me. I was kind of looking forward to it, but that same day Gall was brought in on an entirely different charge. I thought I missed my opportunity but as fate would have it, the case got reopened. During the course of it he saved my life. I discovered something that day and I wish I hadn't" explained the detective as they stepped out the patrol vehicle and entered the station. "I sure hope you boys ain't tired because the sheriff wants you both to head right back out!" the dispatcher shouted before alerting other patrolling officers to respond to Mirror lake. "How many this time?" asked Dep. Ellwood. "A local resident at Mirror Lake reported five floaters surrounded by a pool of ashes and a strange boat. Sheriff warned everybody that if this kept up the town council would start a curfew" answered the dispatcher. "I'll let him know you're on your way up there" she added as the two made their way back out the station.

While forces continued to stir in the Adirondacks, another cause and effect was about to take place in the House of Sumpter. The following evening Sound curiously watched as her Governor applied Freyr's solution to his body. "Tell me all that you've learned of the female Fate" he requested. "When we first met she was lying in Banter's bed. The bond between them is strong and she obeys his requests. There's no doubt in my mind his face is the one she'll see when you enter" answered Sound. "Then you will escort her to the living room and make sure her weapon is visible before you inform her of his death" instructed the Governor. "You want to arm her?" Sound worriedly asked. "I must make sure her Marid Djinn is present and a confrontation will assure my results. Now go!" demanded the Govenor.

Sound raced from the room while her Governor continued to apply Freyr's solution. He walked over to a surveillance monitor in his bedroom and eagerly watched as Sound placed Sitoel's jointed iron sticks on the fireplace mantle. Then she positioned the blade of her spear into the flames of the fire place before leaving with a bottle of blood. She quickly guzzled its content's as she proceeded to Sitoel's cell. "Awake and ready yourself *Sit-o-well*. My Governor requests your presence!" Sound shouted as she tossed the empty bottle and extended her fangs. "It's about time you showed up. I can't wait to give Banter a piece of my mind. Is he up there?" Sitoel asked as she rudely pushed Sound aside and headed for the staircase. "I'll answer that question when we get there" replied Sound. She shoved Victorhelm back into the cell and locked it.

When they reached the living room Sitoel suspiciously looked over her surroundings. "So where's Banter and what happened to Victorhelm?" she continued to question as Sound walked by. "Regrettably you are alone" Sound answered as she licked the tip of her fangs and withdrew her spear from the fireplace. "I don't understand. Didn't you get the corpse?" asked Sitoel. Sound turned her back to her and walked to a corner window. "My dear *Sit-o-well,* Gall has met his demise in the hands of the Lycans. His ashes are resting in a cathedral's crematory oven. As for the corpse, we will make one out of Victorhelm" replied Sound. "Where's Banter?" Sitoel suspiciously asked. "Banter was with me when he met his demise, and it was by my hand that he died. Or should I say the hand of twenty Damphirs as they tossed their grenades into his cabin" answered Sound.

Sound cautiously watched Sitoel's actions through the reflection in the window. "Liar!" Sitoel angrily blurted. "Am I?" replied Sound. A brief pause caused her to squint her eyes as a cold chill crept up her spine. "Now I understand" Sitoel answered as her eyes lustered a vision of death. "Do you?" Sound suspiciously asked as she turned to face her adversary. She looked upon Sitoel's face while an alluring dark green color smothered her pupil's. She quickly scooped up her jointed iron sticks and unleashed its hidden weapon. Like a blind man's folding cane Sitoel removed the rings that connected the iron sticks, and unraveled the chain links hidden within. Extending the weapon into a four section short staff. "I understand your fate!" Sitoel shouted as she flogged her weapon. "Coiling snake!" Sound shouted as she motioned the spear to deflect the backlash. "Dragon snaps it's tail!" Sound continued to shout as she halted the attack and became the aggressor. She retaliated with a series of stabs to force Sitoel back into a corner for her signature move before her Marid Djinn suddenly emerged to weave a fate that broke the *Sound barrier.* "Piercing fang!" Sound shouted as she aimed the heated blade to leave a scar. Sitoel dodged the strike and retailiated with a sweeping kick. As Sound fell back the Marid Djinn quickly positioned the sharp dart edges of her sticks to break the fall. *"Marid Djinn with sound business mind!"* Sitoel shouted in a tone that carried a hiss. Sound screeched in agony as the dart edges pierced her back and exited her chest with pieces of her coronary artery impaled on the tip. "For the last time, it's *See-too-hel!*" said the Marid Djinn as ashes accumulated at her feet. She released her weapon and slowly walked to the window while an unexpected rain storm accompanied a stream of tears. They rolled off her face and rattled the window pane like her emotions. "Both of you were like family to me. How could you be so careless?" whispered Sitoel. She sadly looked into the yard and dried her eyes before the reflection of a shadow gained her attention.

Sitoel quickly turned to face Loki's new appearance. "How dare you play a trick like that on me. Sound said she killed you!" Sitoel angrily shouted as she rushed to retrieve her weapon from the floor. "Take it easy! I wanted Sound to believe that so I could follow her here" Loki defensively replied. He rushed to embrace her while the dark green luster of her eyes confirmed the presence of her Marid Djinn. "The only thing I could think about was you. I missed you so much. During your imprisonment I realized how much you meant to me" said Loki as he slowly pulled Sitoel to a neighboring couch. He gently sat her down and leaned her back into the cushions of the sofa while the flames of the fireplace increased. After he wiped away tears that fluttered joy and anger, Loki leaned her back for a kiss. He had hoped the increase flames of the fireplace would blanket a nervous trickle of sweat caused by a Marid Djinn with a weapon in hand, but it only gave an unexpected warning.

Loki immediately stopped his pursuit when Sitoel placed the dart end of her stick under his chin and recited a phrase she learned while under psychological evaluation, *"He that has eyes to see and ears to hear may convince himself that no mortal can keep a secret. If his lips are silent, he chatters with his fingertips. Betrayal oozes out of him at every pore!"* "Banter wouldn't sweat if you carried a weapon?" asked Loki. "After putting me in this predicament, he'd expect it!" snapped Sitoel. She tapped Loki's chin and left an indentured scar that pushed him off the couch. In retaliation Loki angrily commanded, "Go to Hel!"

A roar that mimicked the revving sound of a chopper motorcycle engine followed, and a thick smoke screen funneled from the flames of the fireplace. "Did you think it would be that easy!" interrupted Iblis. Loki's eyes widened with uncertainty as Iblis stepped out of the center of the smoke cloud with a female prisoner. Her flesh colored hair was fashionably pinned like a princess, and resembled the tail of a rattlesnake. The rage in her eyes gleamed like sapphire and the luster highlighted her beauty as Iblis pressed his blade against her skin. "Father?" the Marid Djinn and Hel simultaneously blurted as their captors looked upon each other. "Is she worth that much to you? To remove Hel from her realm?" Loki asked as he rushed to grab Sitoel and pulled her in front of him. "Her equivalency matches the very one my blade has become acquainted with" answered Iblis. "State your purpose. I have other matters of grave concern to attend to" Loki disappointedly replied. "The time has come for us to make preparations for a new underworld" said Iblis. "Your request is foolish! Odin has yet to fall and after summoning his ghost riders the remaining monstrous wolves will either meet their demise by his hand or my fetters. There was only one other way to change that outcome before you intruded, and Hel was about to solve that problem for me!" explained Loki. "You are the one who has intruded! Your idea is late. A being like the one you hope to create already exist. He's already slain three of the Norse gods" replied Iblis. "Then it was you who brought about Ragnarok! Your diabolical scheming has reached new heights" said Loki. "No need for compliments. Wait until after I've assumed kingship of your realms. Now we must come to terms with the conditions and the battlefield!" replied Iblis. "When Odin falls you will meet me in Vigrid as foretold. There your three warriors will face me, Hel and Jormungandr. Only then will we come to terms and now that you are aware of these matters, release my daughter!" demanded Loki. Both fathers released their prisoners and when Hel passed Sitoel she angrily responded, "When we face each other on the battlefield I'll rip flesh from bone and blanket my armor with your hide. After I pluck the eyeballs out of your empty skull I'll place them in the skull pendant of my war chain just to give your soul a never ending sight of my wrath!" "It sounds like you're a big fan of my work!" Sitoel snapped with a hiss as her eyes darkened in color. "I have no further use of this residency" interrupted Loki. He jumped out the window and transformed into a black horn scaled dragon. After spitting in the direction of Sitoel and Iblis, Hel jumped out the window and mounted him. "What now?" Sitoel asked as they witnessed their departure. "I will return you to the Adirondacks. Retrieve your weaponry and Victorhelm as well. If he does not fill the void of his absence the High Chief may wage war against the Lycans" replied Iblis.

The following day Lord Treachery joined his Lycan buccaneers at their underground lair in Highfalls Gorge. Gall and Enemy made their way through the crowd to greet their brother and discovered two unexpected visitors. "What's the meaning of this?" Gall suspiciously asked as a broad smile appeared on Akantha's face. "Her attendance is necessary" answered Iblis. "Do not be troubled. She is under our protection" Lord Treachery replied from under a black hooded cloak. Gall's right eyebrow raised into his forehead as the Lycan buccaneer kept the mystery of his appearance and parted the seams of his cloak to reveal a badge underneath. "Our enemies are at our doorstep and more will come if we do not find a way to avoid unnecessary attention. We already have a city detective here investigating our murders and inquiring about our brother Gall" said Lord Treachery. "Sorry to disappoint you brother, but our time is pressed after a killing. The Berserkers and ghost riders don't seem to understand we need time to bury them after a slaughter" Enemy amusingly replied as the Lycan buccaneers tumbled over with laughter. "Silence!" Iblis angrily shouted as he increased in size and eclipsed the lighted torches surrounding the lair. His bright red eyes became the only sight visible as he explained, "Total darkness! This is what awaits a careless soldier and within that, awaits me! Take heed to Lord Treachery's words before we have an army of mortals roaming about. A new underworld is within my grasp and any failure to seize it will bring you an eternity of pain. Tonight the ghost riders will spread through the area of the old forts. Odin will seek ground to properly bury Thor, but he will still continue the hunt. Within this time the ghost riders will be divided. King Arthur and I will lead a small army of Berserkers to hunt the grounds surrounding Fort Ticonderoga. I want Enemy's pack to fulfill their bloodlust upon our arrival and leave no one to tell the tale. Need I say more?" Iblis instructed as he returned to a normal size. "Our window of opportunity will be small so we must move in unison after the killings. You can make use of the Skidbladnir. Blackmarket Ginyel has already learned the mechanisms for flight. I will leave Enemy with a route that will assure a victory and safe return for his pack!" said Lord Treachery as he handed Enemy a map. A smoke screen slowly engulfed Iblis as he approached Gall. "You must obtain the flaming sword!" Iblis advised before scattering into the flames of the surrounding torches. "If you were not involved I would've been sitting in front of the fireplace enjoying a nice cup of tea" said Akantha. Gall thanked her with a mild embrace. "Then tell me why am I worthy of such concern?" asked Gall. "The sword of your next opponent is of great importance. There is much you need to learn before facing it. Excalibur is possessed by Chimeras and I have little time to prepare you for them" answered Akantha. "We must drink for our Bloody Bartholomew Smyte now resides in Davey Jones locker and celebrate for tonight we may join him!" interrupted Enemy. "Your last moment is just a few seconds away if you dare to interrupt me again!" snapped Akantha. "Is that a threat?" Enemy amusingly asked. "I am a Greek. We don't make threats. We prophesize!" Akantha boldly answered as Gall held out his arm. She politely accepted the gesture to leave and grunted as they passed Enemy.

Late that night a thick fog assembled at Lake Tear of the Clouds. It slowly parted as Berserkers carried Thor's corpse upon their shoulders and behind them were Odin's ghost riders. Odin signaled King Arthur and Iblis to continue the hunt as he slowly stepped out the fog. The remaining ghost riders surrounded a stone ship formation of tree limbs and stones while the Berserkers laid Thor in the center. As Odin looked over the body, Iblis lead King Arthur and a small army of Berserkers to the surrounding borders of Fort Ticonderoga. There Enemy and the Lycan buccaneers patiently waited in hiding until Iblis ended a wild goose chase that tired the Berserkers. "We most appease Odin with some sort of slaughter!" Iblis shouted with sarcasm as a coyote raced for the woods. "I will slay Lycans and only Lycans on this hunt. There is no cause for any other creature to endure blood loss or death. To seek vengence or harm against any other than a Lycan or slayer is against my code!" explained King Arthur. "We picked up the scent of a Lycan within the walls of the fort!" a scout interrupted. "Now I will show you how to atone for Thor's death" King Arthur responded as he gripped the reigns of his horse and charged through the fort's boundaries. As they cautiously circled the interior of the fort they came upon a lone Lycan. "Does your code of chivalry still stand for one measley Lycan?" Iblis heckled as the Berserkers circled. "You dare mock my

code!" King Arthur replied as he gripped the handle of his
sword and stepped down from his horse. "This beast will
fall to Excalibur!" King Arthur shouted as he unsheathed
his sword.

As King Arthur approached, Gall's plot unraveled.
When they left the hall and returned to his room Akantha
calmly sat Gall down for a tale. "I tell you the story of
another slayer. A greek male by the name of Bellerophon
faced the wrath of the creature that now inhabits Excalibur.
Its flame can blind its enemies and when in battle with
creatures of a mythical latitude it'll reduce them to ashes.
Like Thor, Arthur's power derives from his weapon, and
for him to fall you must defeat the spirit of the blade. On
the hilt of the sword is the design of a Chimera. *The spirit
of one inhabits the blade!*" explained Akantha. "So how did
Bellerophon defeat the creature?" asked Gall. "He speared a
block of lead in its mouth" answered Akantha.

A fiery light raced from the hilt of Excalibur to the
point as King Arthur rushed to attack. Gall immediately
responded with a howl of reckoning and boldly brandished
claws coated with lead. The howl also signaled Enemy's pack
and within seconds the Lycan buccaneers had surrounded
the small army of Berserkers. "It's a trap!" Iblis amusingly
shouted as King Arthur looked on dumbfounded. "This
devious plot will not save you Lycan!" King Arthur replied
as he struck the first blow. Gall quickly shielded his eyes with
his claws and deflected the blade as a fierce battle between
the Berserkers and Lycan buccaneers followed. To Gall the
battle was nothing more than a sparring match. He patiently
timed and deflected the blows from Excalibur until the lead

coating on his claws began to melt. It was at that moment a Marid Djinn emerged to deliver an obscuring fate.

A whirlwind of severed limbs circled around Gall as the Lycan buccaneers dissected the Berserkers from their pelts, and when Gall's moment had arrived the possessed Lycan charged at King Arthur with a series of quick strikes. While deflecting the attacks Gall smeared the lead coating on the blade of Excalibur. By the time Arthur had finally took notice the swords flame had been extinguished. While stunned from the sudden turn of events Gall sampled the one inch punch technique on his armor. The blow forced King Arthur to release Excalibur and as he fell to his knees, Gall spear handed his breast plate. The remaining droplets of lead slid from his claws and eclipsed the coronary artery. *"The Gall!"* Iblis boasted as Gall removed the organ and raised it to the sky. "Now comes the hard part" Enemy bellowed as Grit and Muzzle Blast carted out bundles of coroner bags.

While Enemy's pack cleaned their mess, Det. Rodriguez and Dep. Ellwood made their way to Lake Tear of the Clouds. "I don't need to be a city detective with an impeccable record to follow a trail of coroner bags. We should patrol Crown Point or Mirror Lake. Taking the time to randomly search this area is ridiculous!" Dep. Ellwood protested as he stepped out the patrol vehicle with a flashlight and shotgun. "To follow up on a lead would seem ridiculous *to you*" Det. Rodriguez replied as he sorted through a folder containing information about the case. "A lead? You mean a hunch!" snapped Dep. Ellwood. He switched on his flashlight and headed down a path leading to the outskirts of Lake Tear of the Clouds. "A hunch is an assumption of the way you think a situation might pan out. A lead is based on a prior fact or evidence. Your county coroner is missing a corpse that arrived in viking garments. One would face the possibility that it was taken for the same burial ritual that was earlier reported on the ram" explained Det. Rodriguez. "Shhh!" Dep. Ellwood interrupted as he picked up the sound of chanting. A surprised expression appeared on their faces as they crept along the brush and evaluated the situation. Berserkers raised their swords as Odin stepped out a small boat and signaled to set it on fire. "Call for back up" whispered Det. Rodriguez. Dep. Ellwood unexpectedly rushed from behind him. "It's payback time!" Dep. Ellwood shouted as he leapt from the brush. "This is the Sheriff's Department. Back away from the body with your hands over your head!" Dep. Ellwood commanded as he pointed a shotgun at the surrounding suspects. "Feel free to join me at any time partner!" Dep. Ellwood hinted as a crowd of Berserkers amassed around Odin. Detective Rodriguez quickly withdrew his sidearm and disappointedly backed the impetuous act. "You dare intrude upon this burial. Gwyn Ap Nudd make them yield before me!" commanded Odin. Gwyn Ap Nudd unsheathed his sword and slowly approached the officers. "My sword is one of the four treasures of Tuatha De Dannan and possesses the ability to make my enemies succumb to my demands. No one has ever escaped it in battle" boasted Gwyn Ap Nudd. "Put down your weapon!" warned Det. Rodriguez. "You will disarm yourselves and bow before Odin!" commanded Gwyn Ap Nudd. There was a brief pause and suddenly the lure of the sword quickly overwhelmed the thoughts of the arresting officers. Their eyes widened with a false sense of fulfillment as they obediently approached Odin and knelt before him. "You have forfeited your lives with this intrusion and will now sacrifice yourselves for this burial!" Odin shouted as he withdrew his spear. "Wait King Odin! This one only casts the illusion of a mortal. He is more!" Gwydion the magician interrupted as he stepped from behind Odin and confronted Dep. Ellwood. "What form of deceit does this creature hide?" Odin suspiciously asked as he positioned his spear under the chin of the deputy. "He is a Lycan and belongs to the pack we seek!" answered Gwydion. He held his hand over the deputy's face and waved it like he was erasing a chalk board. The motion faded the deputy's human appearance and displayed the Lycan features underneath. "Now my enemies are within my grasp. We shall have the location of their lair after she interrogates them!" said Odin. Herne the Hunter quickly bound and dragged the officers into the midst of the fog. There Odin placed his hands on their shoulders and commanded, "Go to Hel!"

The following day the dwarves decorated and prepared the halls beneath the Adirondack Iron works. A worried look appeared on the faces of the servants as Rottenvein dragged a corpse through the halls and into the throne room. "Rottenvein? What news do you bring with that stench?" asked the High Chief. His eyes showed concern as Rottenvien approached the throne and displayed the mummified corpse. "Is it Victorhelm?" the High Chief asked as he stepped down from his throne. "No. There is a matter that I must bring to your attention" answered Rottenvein. "Do not haste to speak. Tonight the princess and Freyr will arrive. If Victorhelm is not in attendance the head of his slayer should be!" said the High Chief. "I captured an ally to the blood drinkers. He claims Victorhelm was imprisoned because he failed to fulfill an agreement for the corpse" replied Rottenvein. "Victorhelm was grave robbing?" asked the High Chief. "The corpse in the possession of the thieves assured it. After I retrieved it, I searched for the blood drinker that Victorhelm was to barter with. Her soldiers had been searching the peaks above my lair for dwarf lipids. I followed them back to their camp and discovered they were in league with Freyr" explained Rottenvein. "Freyr? What was his purpose?" asked the High Chief. "That I could not uncover. He met his fate at the hands of the neighboring wolf packs" answered Rottenvein. "Freyr has fallen? What of Victorhelm and the blood drinker?" the High Chief continued to question. "There was no sight of either after Freyr's death and the slaughtering of their soldiers. The wolf pack also escaped with his vessel" answered Rottenvein. "This celebration has become a tragedy. The death of Freyr and the absence of Victorhelm will surely cause the princess to shun our community. In order to save face I must take action! Press a heel against the prisoner for more information. When he reveals all he knows, bring me his head!" commanded the High Chief. Rottenvein acknowledged with a nod and before leaving the throne room he caught sight of Victorhelm and Sitoel. "Father!" Victorhelm happily blurted as he rushed inside the throne room to greet him. "Victorhelm, your

actions and whereabouts have caused a great deal of grief"
said the High Chief. "I am fully aware of the matter father
and I will address it as a prince should when I gain the
hand of the princess" boasted Victorhelm. "I hope your
words bring promise. Only the guarantee of royal courtship
will make me overlook these past occurrences and the
unexpected intrusion of your guest" the High Chief replied
as he suspiciously looked over Sitoel. "The ally to the blood
drinker is most fortunate. He has escaped death twice"
Rottenvein amusingly mumbled. "What did you say?" Sitoel
curiously asked as she approached. "The ally to the blood
drinker has escaped death twice" answered Rottenvein. A
broad smile appeared on her face as she politely requested,
"Can you take me to the blood drinkers ally?" "Yes, I'm
sure my pet has grown weary of his company by now"
Rottenvein replied as he escorted Sitoel from the hall with
the corpse.

Late that afternoon, Rottenvein returned to his lair
with Sitoel and the corpse. The sound of her approaching
footsteps assured Banter of the company of another prisoner
before he discovered those high heel boots belonged to
Sitoel. "Well, what do we have here?" Sitoel asked while
she playfully shook Banter's rope. "Sitoel? I was just on my
way to resuce you!" Banter nervously replied. "Rescue me?
From that dungeon they put me in after you sent me to get
that corpse" Sitoel replied as a hungry growl roared from
the pit below. "Let me explain" pleaded Banter. Rottenvein
unsheathed his knife and handed it to Sitoel. "Explain to
us all!" interrupted Enemy as he charged into the cavern
with Gall and his pack. Before Rottenvein could react,

Enemy quickly extended a claw and positioned it above his Adam's apple. "You seem surprised? You can imagine mine after I returned from Fort Ticonderoga and caught sight of two Lycans I left to guard a corpse affected by that brain germ you laced your trail with. Fortunately for us, you couldn't cover the one you made in the air" said Enemy. A smirk appeared on Gall's face as he curiously made his way to the pit. "Fortunately for all of us it was a trail that even an old woman with my limited abilities could follow" Akantha interrupted as she entered the cavern with a lit torch. "What purpose would it serve you?" asked Enemy. "Before we proceed further I needed to clear the air between us" answered Akantha. She placed the torch on the corpse to set it on fire. It burst into flames while she continued to explain, "The two that stand before you Enemy are Fates. I don't understand why one is bound by his ankles but I can assure you they are crucial to Iblis's new underworld". "If they are Fates, where is the third?" Enemy questioned as he suspiciously looked over Rottenvein. "Gall do you care to answer that question?" replied Akantha. A stunned expression appeared on Enemy's face as Gall turned to face him with the truth. He boldly displayed the fetter wrapped around his waist and transformed into a monstrous wolf state. "My father told me another monstrous wolf would seek us out. He said I need only worry if I lash out against the Fate. So why didn't you tell me earlier?" Enemy asked as he released Rottenvein. Rottenvein rushed to extinguish the fire while Gall returned to his human form to explain. "I didn't sense a connection until I discovered the plot to assassinate you and your brother. I felt it was in everyone's best interest to keep it a secret until I learned a way to save your loved ones and mine" Gall answered as he turned to help Banter. "If they are friends of yours, they are friends of mine!" Enemy happily replied as he rushed to help Gall free Banter. "I'm not kin nor friend to any of you. Your friend's presence is no longer necessary, so please leave now!" demanded Rottenvein.

After they freed Banter, the group sought refuge in another discrete underground cavern to avoid Berserker patrols. The crackle of a warm flame accompanied a quaint conversation as the Fates caught up on current events. "So who appeared when Loki applied the solution?" Gall coyly asked Sitoel. "Richard Dawson!" Sitoel snapped with a blush. "The game show host?" Enemy suspiciously asked. "Yes, and fortunately for him I wasn't fooled by his charm or he would've met a fate similar to Sound's!" Sitoel defensively replied. "You also mentioned you were threatened by another?" interrupted Akantha. "The Govenor is her father" answered Sitoel. "Before his untimely demise Freyr told us that the Governor was Loki" added Gall. "Then that would make that woman Hel" said Banter as he tossed a few branches into the fire. "Hearing of Sound's demise is a relief to me, but having to face Hel is another. Is she as gruesome as tales depicted?" asked Enemy. "There was nothing gruesome about the woman I saw. She was beautiful and well toned. Her black and flesh colored hair was fashionably pinned like a princess" answered Sitoel. "It makes sense to me for Hel to be a red head, but why the lie about her beauty?" Banter asked Akantha. "Hel is the daughter of Loki and reigns in a realm named after herself. There an entire army is at her disposal, and it consists of the souls no one else would want. The fear of Ragnarok forced Odin to confine her to it. Loki just added a lie about her appearance to ward off suitors and further problems of abominations to Odin" explained Akantha. "If she's confined there and only allowed to keep souls no one wants, how am I to face her?" Sitoel continued to question. "A Norse god or ghost rider has the power to send you to Hel by the command, *Go to Hel!*" answered Akantha.

In Helheim, a prisoner shuttered at the sound of footsteps breaking a pavement of skulls lined outside his cell. When Hel entered, half her body bared the recent tattoo of her father's dragon appearance. It covered half her face and stretched to her ankle. "I see your interrogation tactics are still favored by Odin" said Loki as he looked over a severely beaten Lycan. "Their healing ability almost takes the fun out of it, but I still managed to get what I wanted" Hel boasted as she raised Dep. Ellwood's head. His body had been tortured to the point of a hybird state. "Odin and the ghost riders are invading the hidden cavern of the Lycan buccaneers as we speak. I only hope their slayer is worthy enough to end it there. Then I can face Iblis and that wretched vessel Sitoel" replied Hel. She walked over to a table and unraveled a pouch containing silver surgical knives laced with wolf's bane. "Do not underestimate them. King Arthur has fallen and the flaming sword is now his" warned Loki. "Then the timing of Odin's raid is fortunate for us. Whether he brings a victory or loses his life, neither him or the slayer will be in any condition to face us when it's over. We can easily claim the spoils!" Hel amusingly replied as she charged at the deputy and thrusted her blade in the center of his rib cage. Their laughter smothered the cry and as the blade burned his flesh, Det. Rodriguez recited verses from a pocket sized bible in a neighboring cell.

The following day Enemy's pack and the Fates returned to their lair. Before entering the hidden cavern Enemy's nostrils flared like a canine to the misplaced scent of death. "It doesn't belong to Lycans?" said Gall as he perked his nostrils in the air. "Let's find out why" replied Enemy. They quickly turned into their monstrous wolf states and rushed through the broken entry doors. Inside, severely burned and mutilated carcasses carpeted the floor. "The door held them at bay long enough for Prison Levelfield to lay his land mines, but was it long enough for him to get away?" Enemy worriedly mumbled as they made their way through the cavern. "A sorry bunch of buccaneers this pack is, and I won't bother to speak on the caliber of Lycan. For a pack to allow an army of Berserkers to waltz in their den and snatch Lord Treachery is simply untolerable!" scolded Agilroy Finalgates. "When your abilities surpass that of a demi god or Odin I'll allow you to judge our failure" replied Prison Levelfield. "It is not I who will judge your failure. It will be *our Enemy*" Agilroy Finalgates replied before a growl from Enemy gained everyone's attention. When Banter and Sitoel entered with the other Lycan buccaneers their Marid Djinns unexpectedly emerged. "There's still a threat present?" Banter suspiciously asked with the echo of a hiss. "No, your Marid Djinn's are aware of the presence of another nature" answered Akantha as she slowly approached a drawn rune casting on the wall. "Odin has left a portal. One that will allow his army to return to this cavern and regain the ground they earned" explained Akantha. "They also took all the mead! For this outrage they will receive a welcoming far worse than the one they made!" Enemy angrily shouted as he kicked over an empty oak barrel beside him. "Then let's not make haste!" interrupted Iblis. A stream of smoke emerged from the surrounding torches, and the roar of a revving chopper motorcycle engine followed. "Odin's vengeance and rage has made him ignorant to certain laws. He has taken a mortal prisoner before his time and his prayers will unbalance the realms" said Iblis as he emerged into the shadow of a Lycan. "Prisoners?" Enemy worriedly asked. "Your brother is still alive. The pack fought around him until sunrise was among them. They left Odin no choice but to send them all to Hel!" answered Iblis. "Then I will get him!" replied Enemy. "Am I the only one that cares to ask how will we return?" asked Banter. "Care is the key word Banter. As long as someone does Hel will have no hold on you" answered Akantha. "I will stay here and beacon a safe return for your crew" she added. "Crew?" Sitoel asked as Enemy signaled the pack to board the Skidbladnir. "You will be traveling aboard the Skidbladnir. The ship was made by dwarves to travel over land and sea. Its superb ingenuity will also keep it intact as you travel through the realms" said Iblis as he waved his hand to part the cavern walls. The motion revealed a lava slope leading into a pit within the earth's core. The Lycan buccaneers quickly boarded the vessel and after the crew took on their natural roles, Enemy raised the colors of the Lycan buccaneers. It boldly stated that little or no mercy would be given. When the sails were set, Gall looked down at the bow and seen Iblis removing Excalibur from within his robe. He handed the sword to Akantha and gestured to remove the lead patches before he placed his hand on the bow of the ship. Then he stared back at Gall and commanded, "Go to Hel!"

The vessel slid down the lava slope with sails set for Helheim and while traveling at high speeds, Gall was suddenly struck with the idea to kill two birds with one stone. After relaying the idea to Enemy the crew quickly retrieved the coroner bags from below deck and tossed them over the ship's rails to lighten the load. "We'll go under the cover of death. When we arrive at Helheim drop the anchors and toss us overboard" Gall instructed Enemy as he dropped four empty coroner bags on deck. "Brillant idea! A soul no one wants and still trapped inside the body will get us pass the gates guarded by Hel's hound Garmr, but then what?" asked Enemy. "Back the play of a Marid Djinn" Gall replied as he made a few minor adjustments to his bag. After foreseeing a fate, the familiar sound of heels tapping up the stairs from below deck brought an unnerving surprise to the crew. Sitoel slowly approached Enemy from behind and asked, "What do you call the solution you made in that pot. It smells great and I felt goosebumps after I rubbed some on my skin?"

The question immediately created mass hysteria aboard the ship as Freyr's solution suddenly came to mind. "Run for your lives! Do not look the beast directly in the face!" Enemy shouted across deck. Banter and Gall quickly tore a piece of cloth from their clothing and blindfolded themselves as Sitoel approached. "Run? Beast? What are you talking about?" Sitoel amusingly asked while the Lycan buccaneers blindly scurried around deck for safe sanctuary. "Did you honestly believe that a crew of blood thirsty buccaneers would be interested in beauty products?" Banter scolded as he stumbled over a Lycan buccaneer. "No, that's why I applied it to my mask" answered Sitoel. The air suddenly thinned and a thick mist crept over the deck as the ship's look out shouted, "Helheim!" "You just volunteered to be the first diver" Gall replied as he knelt down to lift a coroner bag from the floor. Filled with anticipation Sitoel snatched it from his hand and sealed herself in it. "You still think it's a good idea to take her!" Banter protested as he removed his blindfold. "We can use it to our advantage" Gall answered as he removed his bag and instructed the crew to free the ship of its cargo.

Shortly after relieving the Skidbladnir of its dead weight, the Lycan buccaneers tossed over Enemy and the Marid Djinns. A few grunts from the bags followed as they landed on the pile of corpses beneath. There they laid in wait for Hel's servants to carry them in. Delay, Slowness, Surprised, Violence and Rage made their way out of Hel's gates to retrieve the coroner bags. They dragged them through a cold stormy road that paved a way to the gates of Helheim and upon arrival, felt the nostrils of Garmr pressed against their chest. Everyone cautiously held their breath until the pulling of their bags continued into the Hall of Eljuonir. After a long stillness, Enemy and the Marid Djinns cut through their bags. After putting on her mask Sitoel cut an additional piece to mask herself while the others shied away and looked over their surroundings. There were several passageways in the hall, and as they looked overhead they seen the throne room nine levels above. "I can only guess that on the top floor Hel decides what is to become of the souls she keeps" said Banter. "My brothers are there!" said Enemy as his nostrils flared in a direction paved with broken skulls. "I'll go free them with Sitoel. You can occupy Hel with Banter" instructed Gall. Enemy acknowledged with a nod as he transformed into his monstrous wolf state. "I suggest you hold on tight" Gall advised as Enemy lowered his head and gestured for Banter to mount him. After doing so, they raced up a long spiral marbled staircase to the throne room. "You can unlock the cells when we pass" Gall told Sitoel as he transformed into his monstrous wolf state. "I believe you have a few more obstacles to overcome!" a voice interrupted from behind the pillars of the doorway. The sound of a sword being unsheathed gained their attention as Gwyn Ap Nudd stepped into the light. "Were you so ignorant to believe that Odin would leave a monstrous wolf without an adequate guard?" said Gwyn Ap Nudd.

Before he could give a command, Sitoel quickly unmasked herself. "Lower your weapon and come to me!" Sitoel demanded as she displayed the appearance of Creiddylad. A forbidden love that Gwyn Ap Nudd abducted and had been cursed to fight for every year until doomsday. "Creiddylad? Why are you not with your father?" Gwyn Ap Nudd asked as he sheathed his sword. "I had to inform you of matters of great concern" whispered Sitoel. She gently pushed Gall forward to proceed with freeing the prisoners while her Marid Djinn emerged to weave a fate of sapiential interpretation. "Tell me you'll never leave me!" Gwyn Ap

Nudd demanded as he embraced her. "You will never leave here. *Live by the sword, die by the sword!*" the Marid Djinn replied in a tone that carried a hiss. She unsheathed Gwyn Ap Nudd's sword and pushed him back before she followed with a thrust that confirmed the statement.

When they had reached the top level, Enemy returned to his human form to remove a small glass vile from his waistline. "What do you intend to do with that?" Banter suspiciously asked as he withdrew his silver hunting knife. "I intend to use it against Hel!" replied Enemy. They cautiously approached the doors of Hel's throne room while Enemy raised the vile over his head to prepare himself for a sudden entry. "Wait! We don't know what's in there. We should wait until we see what's on the other side!" advised Banter. "Fast and lethal has always been my motto" Enemy eagerly replied. "If it is, you'll be creating another problem like Sitoel did aboard ship!" warned Banter. Enemy took a brief moment to give thought to the warning and extended his claws to back Banter's play. After counting to three they charged through the doors. To their surprise they found Hel patiently waiting on her throne while Eavesdropping and Curiosity whispered in her ear. "She dared to show her face here!" Hel angrily shouted as she stood and removed the pins from her hair.

Her braids unraveled to reveal the blades she kept hidden within as she quickly removed two to spear the vile Enemy held. The first blade struck his hand and forced him to release it, and as Banter desperately reached out to grab it, the second blade shattered the vile in mid air.

It was at that moment Hel leapt from her throne to

greet the Marid Djinn she had desired since her childhood. She soared through the air with a slow stirring growl and tackled Banter *without the effects of the lotion*! "I shall return my love" Hel seductively whispered in his ear as she pounced on Banter's chest and gave him a stare that pierced its way to the Marid Djinn. She briefly paused from her natural instincts for a bigger prey as she removed a Chinese folding fan strapped to her leg.

Banter and Enemy nervously watched as she raced from the throne room and dived over the spiral railings of the stairs to a flock of prisoners escaping beneath. When she was within range of the last three levels, she unfolded her fan and gracefully landed on Gwyn Ap Nudd's head. "What kind of host would I be if I just allowed you to kill and leave?" Hel boasted as her step crushed the skull beneath her feet and landed on the pavement. She coyly waved her fan as two monstrous wolves exited the corridor and circled. "Leave us!" Sitoel demanded as she removed her mask. Gall and Lord Treachery obeyed the request and raced through the hall as Hel asked Sitoel, "Have you seen my fate?" Sitoel's eyes darkened in color as she gave her answer, "Yes". "I guess it's only fair since I always plotted yours. I can't tell you how many times I sent Careless and Forgetful to those awful magic shows. I guess if you want something done right, you have to do it yourself!" Hel angrily replied as she approached Sitoel. The shadow of a dragon passing overhead halted the attack as Loki interrupted, "Do not jeopardize our arrangement. You must wait until the agreed time!"

The entire foundation shook as Jormungandr the serpent circled overhead and merged into a jotunn. A disturbance

that also alerted Banter and Enemy in the throne room.
"This is the perfect time to leave!" Banter shouted as they
dodged a crumbling pillar. "After your advice nearly cost
us our life, you can only aid me by not showing your face!"
scolded Enemy. They ran to the stairwell and caught sight of
Jormungandr prying through the roof with a pair of walrus
shaped teeth. An enormous fireball cleared the opening and
followed the falling stones as Loki gracefully descended in
his human form. "She came to me!" Hel defensively replied.
"She came to free those that will end Odin. You will allow
them to leave. All of them!" commanded Loki. He smiled
at the crushed skull by his feet while Banter descended the
staircase on Enemy's back. "Let's go!" Banter shouted to
Sitoel. A broad smile appeared on Sitoel's face while a small
mist of steam blew from Hel's nostrils. Her eyes lustered
the color of rubies while the fire within evaporated the gulp
of spit she had to swallow. "Abracadabra and Presto!" Sitoel
amusingly replied as she strolled past and mounted Enemy.
She boldly left Hel the sight of her embracing Banter by the
waistline as they raced from the hall. They were the last to
board the ship and while doing so, the Marid Djinns looked
back at their future opponents. Jormungandr shielded the
storm at a height that towered one hundred and twenty
stories tall and ten leagues wide. Burgundy and green scales
covered his body and surrounded his face like a chained
head skirt. He feverishly licked fangs that were filled with
venom as the dragon Loki flew above his head with Hel
as a rider. Her eyes still beaconed rage as Loki landed on
Jormungandr's extended arm like a trained falcon.

   As the crew set sail an image of Excalibur appeared

in the skies above them. "There's Akantha's beacon!" Sitoel shouted as she pointed at the image of the sword. "Obnoxious Koss give us a tally" demanded Enemy. "We lost one Lycan named Clovis. It grieves me to say that he was the same Lycan that gave the location of our lair" replied Obnoxious Koss. "A Lycan under the tutelage of Lord Treachery gave information of our whereabouts?" Enemy doubtfully asked. "Aye. Hel accepted the challenge with surgical tools laced with wolf's bane. The corpse told the tale of a lobotomy and upon discovering the body, Clumsy removed a crow from an incision on his stomach as if it were a second anus. It grieves me to say the wentch will bring out the best in all of us for an obnoxious cost!" explained Obnoxious Koss. "I missed an attempt on her life!" Enemy snapped in Banter's direction. "Do not be displeased with the outcome Enemy" said Iblis. A roar that mimicked the sound of a revving chopper motorcycle engine followed as he appeared on the bow of the ship with Gwyn App Nudd's sword in hand. "Hel's fate was not meant for your hands. These realms are still govern by laws of a higher authority. If you would have interfered you would have met the same demise as your father" explained Iblis. "What do you know of my father's death?" Enemy suspiciously asked. "There are three types of beings that threaten the existence of a Norse god. Two of them are the Fates and offspring of Loki. In order to keep his children alive Loki agreed to place them in confinement. When your father evolved passed his boundaries Odin swayed Loki to ride against him. It was the only way the monstrous wolf would lower his guard. On that same day, Loki returned with his corpse and secretly

vowed two things. The death of Odin and the reign of all
outer worldly realms. Those are the stakes that keep them at
bay. The third type of being that can interfere is an avenging
angel. One was on its way to rectify Hel's holdings. If he
had arrived and learned of my plans everything would be in
jeopardy. The rescue was sentimental to you, but necessary
for me" explained Iblis. "Which one of us would've been
responsible for that?" Enemy continued to question as the
Lycan buccaneers gathered on deck. "The man I speak of
is the descendant of a saint" answered Iblis. "I've known
these buccaneers for centuries, and a few Lycans my entire
life. Believe me when I tell you, none of them are worthy
of a saint's status. Especially while at sea!" Enemy jokingly
replied. "This man is no Lycan or buccaneer. Isn't that
so Det. Rodriguez?" Iblis asked as the large crowd of
Lycan buccaneers looked amongst each other. "We have a
stowaway!" Enemy replied as the crowd parted and circled
Det. Rodriguez. "I don't recall any relation to a saint?" Det.
Rodriguez nervously answered as he cautiously looked over
his surroundings. "How ironic. You always seem to receive
the assistance of one" answered Iblis. "I can't take all the
credit for the work you've sent my way. You also have a
helper. One that likes to call me praetorian!" Det. Rodriguez
angrily replied as he gripped his pocket sized Bible. *You ran
into junior?"* interrupted Ninety-six Nine. "He made scars
too big for neosporin to fix. I intend to settle the matter
with him one day!" answered Det. Rodriguez. "For more
reasons than you know" replied Iblis. "All this law official
needs to know is that he is a stowaway on a buccaneer's
ship and we follow buccaneer laws. Get the rope and set the

plank!" commanded Enemy. Unchained Gauge obediently complied to the command and gathered rope before Iblis interrupted, "I warned you to leave this man alone!" He grabbed Unchained Gauge by the throat and tossed him back into the crowd. "A thousand pardons. I thought that warning only applied while we were in Hel's realm. We are now sailing over Aesir" Enemy replied with sarcasm. "You can follow your laws when you return to your plain. There you can proceed without interruption" instructed Iblis. "I'm afraid he will not be satisfied there either" said Lord Treachery as he parted the seams of his robe to reveal the badge underneath. "We lost a Lycan buccaneer and seven prospects. We'll need every man for Odin's retaliation" added Lord Treachery. "Your brother is right. Odin would want to finish it tonight" said Gall as he made his way to the detective. "I will hire the services of the dark elf and seek you out when it is over" Iblis instructed as he emerged into a thick mist of smoke and floated away from the vessel. "Ahoy! The portal to Midgard is ahead" Agilroy Finalgates shouted as the image of Excalibur increased in size. It divided to reveal an entrance back into the hidden cavern, and after the ship released its anchors, Gall happily jumped from the deck to greet Akantha. A proud smile appeared on her face as she displayed the luster of Excalibur. "I see your trip was successful" said Akantha as the crew and Marid Djinns exited the vessel. "Gwyn App Nudd has fallen and Det. Rodriguez has returned with us" replied Gall. "I'm almost tempted to pull that hood from your head to see who you really are" said Det. Rodriguez as Enemy escorted his brother down the ramp. "I never doubted your courage

detective. Don't make me question your intelligence. The
investigation is over. The killers we have sought to capture
will be here by the end of the night. If you care to see another
day take the advice given to you earlier. When in Rome, do
as the Romans do!" advised Lord Treachery. They looked to
Akantha as she handed Gall Excalibur. "This is a great sword,
but I have no use for it" said Gall. "The use of Excalibur in
battle pertains more to politics" replied Akantha. "Another
political campaign? What office is Gall supposed to run
for?" Det. Rodriguez amusingly asked. "Odin's army will
follow legends foretold by the Norse god's. It was said that
a dark jotuun would engulf the world in a flame while
wielding his flame sword. Many of them will lay down their
weapons and follow you if you weild such a weapon during
Odin's fall" explained Akantha. Gall acknowledged with a
nod and slid Excalibur between his back and vest. "What
do we have here?" Enemy asked as Morbid Medley dragged
a line of gun turrets from a neighboring cavern. "I made
use of the Ak-47's the Damphirs left behind" answered
Morbid Medley. He held up one of the automatic rifles with
a severed hand attached to the handle. A string of sheep gut
was sewn to the trigger finger as Morbid Medley placed
it on one of the twenty gun turrets. "Clever idea, but why
worry about forensics when your captain runs the town?"
Det. Rodriguez suspiciously asked. "I didn't place a severed
hand on the handle to elude officials. I did it because I like
the sound!" Morbid Medley boasted as he loaded a drum
cartridge into one of the automatic rifles. Det. Rodriguez
quickly took cover as he pulled the trigger finger string and
unleashed a drum roll of fire while singing Yankee Doodle.

A sinister smile appeared on Lord Treachery's face as he helped Det. Rodriguez back on his feet and sang, *"He stuck a feather in his hat and called it macaroni!"*

Later that night a strict curfew gave the Lycan buccaneers the privacy they needed to ready Fort Crown Point for Odin's attack. They conviently left a trail from their cavern in Highfalls Gorge to the Fort of Crown Point while Banter placed a phone call to Tobias. He joined them shortly before midnight. "Special delivery!" Tobias yelled as he entered the ruins of the fort with a large aluminum case and back pack. Banter eagerly grabbed the case and opened it to assemble his M-110 sniper rifle. There was a sigh of relief as he fastened a cartridge belt filled with the ammo he had previously designed in his lab. "Did you bring what I asked you for?" Sitoel asked as she opened the back pack that was placed on the table. "I brought everything on Banter's list" answered Tobias. A smirk appeared on Sitoel's face as she excitedly removed a black Venetian mask with an ace of spades design. "Here's something we don't see every day" said Tobias as he looked across the room and observed Det. Rodriguez reading from a small pocket sized bible. "Did he find his faith after finding out about you?" Tobias asked as Gall entered the barracks. "You can't blame me for that one. He had religion way before I came into his life. Maybe you should stick around and compare verses or have a bible study" Gall amusingly replied. "Maybe I will!" Tobias responded as he withdrew a pocket sized bible from his back pocket and joined the detective. "I wish I could be here to see the expression on his face" Banter whispered as he grabbed his mask and left the barracks. Outside the perimeter of the fort, Enemy waited in his monstrous wolf form with a newly recruited Rottenvein. Banter quickly mounted him and headed to a secluded brush where Iblis's plot would unravel.

At midnight Odin's army had arrived and scouts immediately picked up the trail from the hidden cavern beneath Highfalls Gorge. A thick fog accompanied Herne the Hunter as he scouted with a small army of Berserker wolves and bears. They gave chase like a pack of rabid basset hounds to the Crown Point area while Odin followed with Gwydion the magician, King Nuada and Iblis by his side. "It appears they decided to make a stand on the grounds where we first held camp" said Gwydion the magician. "Then we should allow the hunter and King Nuada to storm the abandoned fort first" Iblis advised in an attempt to divide the attack. "I will not hand this slayer another opportunity to escape. If you want to cower, fall back and allow a Valkry to take your place by my side!" Odin angrily replied.

As Herne the Hunter rode across a small plateau within a mile from the fort a Marid Djinn emerged to crown him with a fate. Three boomerangs soared passed the hunter's head. He dodged two before the last one unexpectedly knocked off his magical crown of antlers. While Herne looked for the fallen item, a Marid Djinn fired his rifle to replace it with another. Two fragmentation and an incideniary round penetrated the frontal lobes of Herne the Hunter's cranium. The impact pushed him off his horse and while in the air, it created a rigid design of a crown that erupted a veil spectrum of light as the incideniary round reflected off scattered pieces of fragmentation. The

Berserkers that followed Herne the Hunter returned to their human form and kneeled to the sight of a mind blown as the effects of Rottenvein's nurtured Naegleria Fowleri took its toll. "I've endured enough of these vermin. Storm the fort!" commanded Odin. A howl of reckoning answered from within the walls as Gall scaled the front wall of the fort and brandished the flame of Excalibur on a roof pillar. Grit and Muzzle Blast carted out Morbid Medley's rack of gun turrets to the main road to back the bold display, and after he pulled several strings they opened fire on the first wave of the assault. The Blast Brothers steadily reloaded the drum cartridges until the barrels had a meltdown. At that moment the flame ignited a second string of sheep gut that was extended from the wrist of the severed hands to a string of Prison Levelfield's gas land mines.

When the second wave of Berserker's had reached the plateau in front of the fort, Bopo Lava stepped into the pathway and ignited another wave of fire to back Gall's statement. "What was that?" Tobias nervously asked as he ran to a broken window to see the explosion. He witnessed a wave of fire circle the fort and blow ashes from bones through the air like dust smacked off a carpet. "Stand clear of the door and windows!" Det. Rodriguez advised as he cautiously withdrew his firearm. Tobias obediently complied with the warning as ash flooded the ruins of the fort. "I should've known!" Tobias angrily shouted as he climbed out of a pile and waved a clenched fist at Gall. As Odin watched from the perimeter he caught sight of Gall leaving the fort to Banter's location. "The slayer!" shouted Odin. He started a pursuit into the woods and it lead to the neighboring lake. Gall quickly transformed into his monstrous wolf state to keep a safe distance and picked up Herne the Hunter's antlers along the way. His grey spiked mane glimmered in the moonlight as he raced a mile from the fort and up the tree of a neighboring brush.

At that moment Gall's Marid Djinn emerged into his Lycan state and scaled a tree to camouflage himself from an approaching Odin. "Mangy hound! Do you think you can avoid my wrath up there!" Odin shouted as he withdrew his spear. He slowly galloped to the base of the tree and seen the possessed Lycan standing under a few branches. "After your death I'll ride to Hel to torment your soul with several others!" Odin yelled as he threw his spear. The possessed Lycan howled in agony as the impact caused him to tumble from the tree. "The slayer has fallen!" Odin boasted as he dismounted his horse and watched several branches collapsing over the Lycan. Gwydion the magician immediately seized the attack and pursued the call of their king. Before King Nuada could follow, Iblis unsheathed his knife and pulled him from his horse. The blade on the knife increased to the full size of a scythe blade as Iblis placed it under his arm pit and cleanly severed King Nuada's arm. "No need to trouble yourself over relinquishing your weapon. I take the lot!" said Iblis. Another strike from the blade separated the head from the body as Iblis continued his pursuit.

Under a tree a broad smile appeared on Odin's face as he slowly removed his spear from the expected corpse. Suddenly without warning the possessed Lycan stirred from under the batch of branches and stood upright before Odin.

"What type of wizardry is this? My spear is Gungnir! It never misses a target and kills whatever manner of creature it strikes!" Odin scaredly mumbled. As his wound closed, the possessed Lycan pulled Herne the Hunter's crown of antlers from under the broken branches and crowned himself so Odin could remember their purpose.

Herne the Hunter received the mystical crown of antlers while he was hunting with King Richard. He had endured life threatening wounds while trying to save the king. To reward him for his sacrifice, a local wizard bestowed a magical healing power upon the antlers with the expectation of one day saving his life or that of another king. It was at that moment Odin discovered he had foolishly relinquished his weapon to fate his inane rule. Before Odin could escape, two monstrous wolves leapt from the cover of darkness to complete a fate woven for the next of kin. "This is for our father!" Lord Treachery shouted as he punctured Odin's neck with his fangs. "And this is for my mead!" said Enemy as he followed the attack with a one inch punch technique. When Odin fell to his knee's Enemy spear handed the still heart and tossed it to Gall. After Gall impaled it on his claws he returned to a monstrous wolf state to feast in front of Odin's Berserkers. The sight successfully funneled a fire that birthed a legend and subdued the remaining Berserker's as a Valkyrie shouted, "Odin has passed the gates of Valhalla!"

They willingly laid down their weapons to a legend foretold as their Norns unlocked the secrets of *that which became, that which is happening, and that which will become.* After Gwydion the magician caught sight of the slaying he started his own retreat. He quickly raced back toward

Lake Champlain to return to the depths of an awaiting fog. As he crossed through the ridges of the plain a Marid Djinn emerged to erase the illusion of escape. Gwydion the magician waved his hands to cast four mirror images of himself as Sitoel stepped in front of his path and withdrew her weapon. She had broken the four jointed sections of her stick into four spear like weapons and when Gwydion was within range, the Marid Djinn weaved a fate of prestidigitation. After dodging the stampeding riders, Sitoel threw all four spears into the back of the magician on the far right of the road. The impact made the other illusions disappear and the magician fell victim to his wounds. "Clap, don't applaud" Sitoel requested in a tone that carried a hiss.

When the Marid Djinns returned to the fort they were greeted by a familiar voice. "I should've known!" Tobias shouted as he angrily waved his bible and peaked through the barracks broken window. They could also hear Rottenvein as he saddled two large potatoe sacks filled with gold escudo coins on Jolly's back. "This still does not compensate for the suffering of my bear!" complained Rottenvein. "Jolly was like that when we found her!" Lord Treachery amusingly replied as the bear lowered its head to his presence. The roar of a chopper motorcycle revving its engine interrupted as Iblis returned with the bounty of the battle. "You will dock your ship on the lake and prepare it for departure after you secure these weapons in my war chest" Iblis instructed as he tossed the weapons of the fallen generals at Enemy's feet. "Where will we be departing to?" asked Enemy.

The silhouette of a black horned scaled dragon eclipsed the moon and landed in front of Iblis to answer. "You have fulfilled your end of the agreement and delivered Odin's fate, but that is as far as your reign will go" said Loki. He returned to his human form and adjusted the tie to his suit while looking over Gall. "Do not toy with me Loki. State your terms so I can complete the prophecy and achieve my destiny!" demanded Iblis. "I am well aware of the prophecy, but your slayer is no Surtr! He will face my son Jormungdr and Hel will face Banter. I will face the female Fate" replied Loki. "You are more cunning than wise. You would have a female Fate battle for the throne when no woman has ever benefitted from the attempt?" asked Iblis. "You know nothing. To appease her *Hunger*, Hel was awarded nine realms. These are my terms and you will abide by them" Loki instructed as he returned to his dragon state. After Loki took flight Gall asked Iblis, "He said I was no Surtr?" "The dark jotunn Surtr was foretold to engulf the earth with his flaming sword during the events of Ragnarok. None would doubt you, but Loki has twisted the outcome. You will not face the successor and Govenor of their dark realm" Iblis angrily replied. "Meaning what?" asked Sitoel. "War!" blurted Iblis. "The other Norse gods and goddesses would have willingly accepted my rule if the dark jotunn that possessed the flaming sword did away with their king and his successors during the events of Ragnarok. To achieve this goal by any other means would guarantee a rebellion and a constant challenge to my authority. Loki created a twist of fate between you and Banter" explained Iblis. "Now you will need an army to take over their realms" said Banter. "You act as if I do not have one!" replied Iblis. A devilish grin appeared on his face as he approached Lord

Treachery. "It is time for your *Avalanche of Protection*" Iblis eagerly requested. "It's too soon! We've been training them in small packs but their blood thirst has yet to evolve, and without any battle experience they pale in comparison with the Lycan buccaneers I've sailed with. They're just town's people learning to adapt to their Lycan abilities" explained Lord Treachery. "That may be true, but after I lay hands on them they will be *possessed Lycans*. Send your pack to convert the remaining Berserkers and summon everyone to your lair for tonight we set sail!" demanded Iblis.

The population of the Adirondack's was estimated at one hundred and thirty thousand people. During Lord Treachery's stay he converted a large portion of that number into Lycans. Iblis spent an entire day converting over sixty thousand people into blood thirsty killing machines. He sped through the large group that gathered by the cavern and demonized their souls. When he was done, the Lycans had increased in size and strength. Their need for combat experience had been replaced with malicious and murderous thoughts that hungered for an unquenchable blood rage. The Lycan buccaneers also made use of the magical ingenuity of the Skidbladnir by expanding it to a size that accommodated all passengers. After they secured their cargo, Lord Treachery proudly handed Enemy Heimdalls horns.

The crew raised their colors while Enemy blew the horn to summon all those who challenged Iblis's rule to Vigrid. Akantha, Tobias and Det. Rodriguez watched from a balcony in the cavern as the walls slowly parted and swallowed the departing vessel. "I can sense it. Their departure troubles

you as much as it does me" said Akantha. "You're very
perceptive, but I cannot stop an army of supernatural
beings. The request will be as senseless as Lord Treachery's
campaign. I wasn't assigned this case. I overheard Banter's
company name and felt I could do something to take the
burden of Gall saving my life off my chest. While in pursuit
to save his, I narrowly escaped with my own" answered
Det. Rodriguez. "You came out here to save Gall's life?
You would've had better luck apprehending his enemies"
interrupted Tobias. "The idea crossed my mind. Now let's
take a moment to reflect on past events. There was the one
guy I ran past in hell with a sword sticking out of his chest,
and the others I knew about have several limbs hanging
from that ship that just set sail. That just about covers the
list of enemies. I can't predict the outcome of the war, but
after seeing his army I'd say his chances are good. The only
benefit for me to hang around now is to pay back a Jinn that
likes to take hold of people and call me praetorian" explained
Det. Rodriguez. "You came out here to save a life but I
came out here to save many. Including those that I've raised
since their birth. If Iblis wins this war the outcome will be
disastrous for other gods and realms. As for your thirst for
revenge, the being you speak of is drawn to legendary battles
and wars. He utters the word praetorian when losing a fight
because it reminds him of the guard that failed to protect
him. You would have surely found him on the battlefield
if you had set sail" replied Akantha. "Now you tell me!"
the detective snapped as the Skidbladnir sailed to the field
of Vigrid with torn carcasses hanging from the side rails
and Odin's heartless corpse dangling from the front mast.

When the Skidbladnir anchored on the bordering waters
of Vigrid, Odin's son Vidar caught sight of Enemy tossing
pebbles through his father's chest wound. "Why do you
insist on provoking unwanted anger? It may fuel them and
turn the tide of war!" scolded Lord Treachery. "Have you
looked down there brother? There are but a few thousand
Aesirs below. I doubt if we will have to lift a finger before
the day is over" replied Enemy. "Things are not always as
they seem!" warned Iblis as he pointed out another vessel
approaching from the opposite end. It was recognized as the
Naglfar. A ship constructed with the fingers and toenails
of the dead. Every Norse god and goddess feared the day
it would set it sails because it was another sign of their
demise. On deck, Loki boldly stood with all Hel's servants
and Odin's horse Sleipnir. Beneath the ship, a large snake
like wave repeatedly rippled as Jormungandr raced past
and approached the shore to merge into his jotunn form.
When the ship docked Loki transformed into his dragon
state and quickly scooped Sleipnir in his claws. "Prepare
for boarding" Iblis shouted as Loki flew to the ship's deck.
He gently placed Sleipnir on his feet before returning to his
human form. "Sleipnir will take the Fate to Hel's realm.
They will battle there!" Loki instructed as the Marid Djinns
and Lycan buccaneers surrounded him on deck. "What type
of sorted scheme is this? All of her servants are present and
she wishes to do battle alone in her realm?" Iblis suspiciously
questioned. "You've miscounted. Take another look!" Loki
amusingly answered as he jumped into the air and returned
to his dragon state. Iblis quickly ran to the ship's rails to take
another look as Banter mounted Sleipnir. "*I was mistaken!*

Hunger, Forgetful and Rumors are missing?" mumbled Iblis. Before he could warn Banter, Sleipnir kicked up its feet and charged through the crowded deck. In the blink of an eye the horse had dove from the deck and into a black hole in the sea in route to Helheim. "I faced Hel's servants before with Banter. I fail to see how they can be a threat" Enemy commented as he looked down from the deck rails. "You might have faced them in Hel, but these beings are at their worst in spirit form! The harm they can cause when they inhabit vessels can easily diminish our numbers and turn the tide of war!" warned Iblis. "Then what do you suggest we do?" asked Lord Treachery. "That answer now rests on how fast Banter can fate Hel" answered Iblis. He took the ship's wheel and anchored it near land. After releasing the anchors, Iblis, Loki and Vidar commanded their armies to attack. A large dust cloud amassed on the field as all three armies engaged in their destinies.

In Helheim, Sleipnir carried Banter directly to Hel's throne room door. After dismounting the horse he cautiously raised his rifle to a firing position and kicked open the door. Banter looked through the scope of his rifle for a head shot, but after seeing a broad smile on Hel's face decided to aim for the heart. The scope settled in the center of a black fur corset before the blood rage eyes of Fenrisulfer unexpectedly appeared. "Allow me to introduce you to *My Hunger*" said Hel. His soul leapt from Hel's body and funneled through the barrel of Banter's rifle as he discharged his weapon. It ate the bullet in the chamber, and then consumed the rounds in the clip while Banter repeatedly squeezed the trigger. After Fenrisulfer appeased his hunger, Forgetful discretely toured

Banter's vessel in spirit form. "Do you know why you're here" asked Hel. "No. I can barely remember anything?" replied Banter. Hel grabbed Banter by the hand and escorted him to the personal chamber behind her throne. There she undressed Banter and pulled him into her bed. She dragged him into the center while Rumors crawled from between her sheets and Hunger blanketed the bed like a quilt. After Hel removed her undergarments she placed her right hand over Banters chest.

She slowly stirred her index finger over the coronary artery while she explained, "As a child my brothers and I were gathered by the Norse gods because of the threat of Ragnarok. Odin exiled Jormungandr to the seas and oceans of Midgard. The jaws of Fenrisulfr were bound by a fetter, and I was given my own realm. Nine more were bestowed upon me and it felt like a great honor. I was also given the task of caring for the old and sick. As a child I did not recognize the torture and walls of the prison. Then one day I crept to the border's of my realm and seen Iblis building an army of Jinn's. One of three Marid Djinn's gained my attention. I secretly plotted schemes to bring him into my realm and slowly entered the reality of the prison. I was a woman and my body was barren. My realms were plagued by the sick and dying. A home filled with souls that no one wanted withered my dreams to be with you like rotted fruit. The Norse gods secretly laughed behind my back, and in the midst of this darkness they overlooked one minor detail. After the death of Fenrisulfr he joined the ranks of my unwanted souls. His hunger became mine! When my brother curled his frame around my barren body he discovered the famine that plagued my realms and I had nothing to feed his hunger. At that moment everything in my realms changed, *and so did the hunger!* I made an army and gave the unwanted souls a name and a purpose. I built great walls for the sick and dying, then fed them to my brother. For wandering eyes I left Deception and Deceit in their place".

Hel briefly paused to mount Banter. At the edge of the bed the head of Fenrisulfr emerged from the quilt to burp the fragmentation and incendiary projectiles he had devoured from the gun clip. His hunger had forged the shape of a flamed crown before it shattered on the marble floor. It was at that moment a Marid Djinn emerged to fate Hel with a spark of life. "Now go spread the word and when she comes to investigate, take hold!" Hel commanded Rumors. Rumors raced from her chamber and made way to Valhalla where it merged with an unsuspecting Valkry. Then it rushed to the fields of Vigrid to begin Hel's bidding. "The Marid Djinn known as Banter has fallen!" the Valkry shouted. The entire crew of the Skidbladnir paused and nervously watched as the news scaled the tide of war. "Now merge!" commanded Loki. Hel's servants immediately responded by touring Lycan vessels on the battlefield. The Aesir's and Vidar quickly gained ground as the mighty army before them slowly turned into a mass of buffoons. Vidar could barely contain his laughter as he gripped his double edged axes and plowed through Lycans toured by Age, Delay, Lazy, Clumsy and Stupidity. Clutter was the biggest threat of all. He merged with Jealousy, Hate, Deceit,

Betrayal and Deception before ramming through a herd of Lycans that quickly turned on each other.

Loki boldly flew overhead and rested himself like a trained falcon on Jormungandr extended arm to continue the next wave of the attack. "Proceed!" Loki commanded Jormungandr. The jotunn advanced through the battlefield and stomped on every Lycan between him and the Skidbladnir. The Lycan buccaneer's angerily watched as rivers of blood and corpses amassed on the battlefield. A sight that provoked a Marid Djinn to pierce the scorns and howls of agony with a flaming sword. "Enough!" Gall angrily shouted as his Marid Djinn emerged and unsheathed Excalibur. The crew immediately took their battle stations as he boldly made his way to the plank and raised the sword to provoke a confrontation. "Finish him!" demanded Loki. Gall jumped into the battlefield as Jormungandr took steps in his direction. Below deck another Marid Djinn readied herself. "Now!" Sitoel shouted with a hiss. Tiki Sangre and Blush responded by opening the cannon's hidden portholes. "I didn't just decorate the ship with corpses!" Enemy boasted as Lord Treachery took the wheel. A devilish grin appeared on Rottenvein's face as he loaded spherical projectiles filled with his nurtured Naegleria Fowleri. "Fire at will!" Lord Treachery commanded as he advanced to an aerial position. With increased speed Sitoel ignited an entire row of cannons. The barrage of fire kept Jormungandr at bay and after witnessing the effect of the brain germ, he headed for the neighboring seas. Gall stabbed Excalibur into the dirt of the battlefield and transformed into his monstrous wolf state. When he was done, he locked his jaws around the handle of the sword and gained pursuit. The possessed monstrous wolf dissected every opponent between him and Jormungandr with the flames of Excalibur extended diagonally from his jaws. When Jormungandr had reached the seashore he emerged into his serpent form. His large coiled body slowly slithered into the sea, but before submerging he unexpectedly turned to face his pursuer.

Two enormous fangs extended as Jormungandr opened his mouth and devoured the attacking monstrous wolf leaping from the shore. Before he could close his jaws a fang fell into the water and the outpouring of venom served as a combustible. The possessed monstrous wolf cut clean into the root of the fang, and made an incision from the jaw to the throat to weave an equatorial fate. Jormungandr raced franticly through the realms as the possessed monstrous wolf continued to burrow through his intestinal organs, and the excruciating pain forced the serpent to bite his tail. After completing what seemed to be an endless plight Gall cut his way out the mouth and fell into the prime meridian. When he swam to the surface of the Pacific Ocean he discovered that while circling Jormungandr's intestines, he also circled the earth and engulfed it in a flame.

"*I can't ASurtr?*" boasted Gall.

On the battlefield of Vigrior, Loki repeatedly dodged cannonball fire while setting the field below in flames. "Steer over his left flank!" Sitoel's Marid Djinn commanded as she withdrew two spear shaped iron sticks and walked onto the blank. The sight of her provoked a charge from Loki and as he prepared to fire, a Valkry delivered a disturbing message. "Jormungandr has fallen!" the Valkry shouted. Stunned by the news, Loki quickly dove beneath the vessel to avoid a head on collision. As he passed under, Sitoel dove from the plank to navigate him to an impeccable fate. The Marid Djinn conveniently landed beside a small horn implanted at the center of Loki's head. After piercing both sides with the dart ends of her sticks she proceeded to uproot it. Loki's eye lids stretched to the center of his forehead as the Marid Djinn pulled back and forced him to fly upward. After uprooting the horn Sitoel rolled onto the back of the dragon and Loki unleashed the fireball he was consuming. The burst of flames impacted a string of cannonball fire and scattered flesh with bone as he charged through it. "Loki has fallen!" shouted the Valkry. Sitoel surfed the dragon's headless body back to the ship as it fell from the sky. When she was within distance of the Skidblanir she raced across the dragons back and leapt onto the plank. She looked down at the fallen carcass and discovered she had not only decapitated the dragon, but the head of Hel's army. Hel's servants raced from their vessels and franticly ran toward the sea as Enemy, Lord Treachery and Iblis entered the battlefield. The brute force of Iblis's army quickly gained ground and razed the remaining Aesir's as the trio pursued Odin's heir. Vidar's armor pulsated as he panted within the chewed and battered metal. After the Lycans cornored him, he willingly removed his helmet and displayed his father's features. "I do not fear you! The taste of my flesh will come with steel and I will dine in Valhalla after taking you with me!" Vidar bravely shouted. He gripped the handles of his axes as the Lycan horde slowly parted for Iblis. "Take him!" commanded Iblis. Before Vidar could complete a swing the monstrous wolves attacked him from both sides and anchored their jaws into his forearms. Vidar's eyes broadened with fear as they held him down for Iblis. "There will be no Valhalla or any Norse realms after you leave this world. You will find that only purgatory awaits you and all your kinsmen until I recreate them. You were only right about one thing. I can't have you causing up a stir while my plans are in motion. So your flesh will come with the taste of steel!" replied Iblis. He kneeled to remove Vidar's tongue. A clean slice through the mouth left Vidar with the expression of a lost soul as Iblis removed the organ and placed it in the center of his right palm. "Praetorian!" it uttered as Iblis positioned it to talk back to him.

The Skidbladnir hovered overhead and Sitoel leapt from the plank into the battlefield with a request, "I want to see Banter!" "You're not the only one. He is not dead and a Valkry has yet to call Hel's name!" Iblis angrily responded as he tossed the severed tongue to Morbid Medley. "Take my army and march on Asgard. I will begin my campaign there!" Iblis commanded Lord Treachery. As his army moved on, he returned to the ship with Sitoel and the Lycan buccaneers. They set their sails as he placed his hand on the deck rail and shouted, *"Go to Hel!"*

When the group had arrived in Helheim they cautiously sailed around the torn walls of her domain until a light beaconing from behind her throne caught their attention. They quickly anchored the ship and descended rope ladders through the opening Jormungadr had previously made to investigate. When they entered the personal chamber behind her throne they found Banter's bare frame resting on a feathered mattress. "Banter!" Sitoel and Iblis shouted as they rushed to his bedside. Banter slowly opened his eyes as Iblis grabbed him by the neck and raised him from the bed. "Do you know what your little rendezvous has cost me!" Iblis shouted as he slammed Banter back into the center of the mattress. "I had her in my sight? I came to do battle!" Banter defensively replied as he slowly recalled his moment of entry. "Battle? Is that what you call it? I warned you about this one!" Enemy replied as Banter's Marid Djinn emerged. Sitoel's Marid Djinn also emerged in response to her mixed emotions and without warning, Rumors had discretely left his hiding place. "He's lying! They were in love and always will be. He did this to save her life. The Marid Djinn is the man and the man will always follow the Marid Djinn. *Abracadabra and Presto!*" Rumors whispered in Sitoel's ears. "I don't know what happened after that" Banter angrily replied with a hiss as he struggled to get dress.

"Do we seek her out?" Enemy asked as he glanced around the room. "No need to bother. This foolish act has solidified her realms. There were only two ways to gain rule over her domain. Death or marriage. Banter has failed to complete the one of my choice!" Iblis disappointedly answered. "I don't recall committing to the other!" replied Banter. "He maybe telling the truth. After the loss of her father and brother she would sooner stab you with the scepter than wed you to it" said Enemy. "Then why would she bother with the act. Her body is barren?" replied Iblis. "I want to leave now!" Sitoel demanded with a hiss. "Where do you wish to go?" Iblis suspiciously asked. "Home. Back to my kumpania" answered Sitoel. Iblis complied with Sitoel's demands and returned everyone but the Lycan buccaneers to their homes.

On the border of Helheim, Hel reunited her family with a phrase that governed her realms. *If anyone speaks against him or refuses to cry in the world, he shall remain with Hel forever!*" Hel recited while she watched the soul of Jormungandr the serpent circle her nine realms and bite his tail to keep them linked. When he was done, the soul of Loki flew threw the center of the ring in his dragon state and merged with the dragon tattoo on Hel's body. Hel's power and strength increased to a tremendous level to solidify the stature of a queen while Fenrisulfr wrapped himself around her frame like a quilt. When the process was complete, Hel removed the Chinese folding fan fastened to her leg and made way to Mount Olympus.

The following morning, no matter how bright the sun shined in Akantha's residence it could not out do the radiance of an Olympian. "I figured Hel would look past the

underworld and go straight to the top of Mount Olympus"
Akantha disappointedly responded as she turned to address
Zeus. "What troubles me is that you didn't come to me
first!" Zeus replied as he removed the hood to a long white
glowing cloak. "I did not want to alert you to a matter that
did not concern you" Akantha worriedly answered. She
coyly strolled to her coffee table and poured a cup of tea.
"Does not concern me? Asgard is crumbling as we speak and
regretfully it will not be enough to satisfy that megalomaniac!
Furthermore, the arrogance of his henchmen. One has
already crossed a boundary by polluting Poseidon's waters
with Jormungandr's ashes! The Norse goddess has made a
very clear point. Order must be regained and these lowly
beasts must learn to respect authority!" Zeus harshly replied.
"Their road to power was foretold through prophecy. Even
the mighty Zeus can recall when Cronos was warned of
his coming. The very things he did to avoid the fulfillment
of the prophecy are the very things that brought you into
power" explained Akantha. "No oracle gave a foretelling
of these creatures, so I need not worry. I have sent Pandora
to avenge the offensive acts committed within Poseidon's
waters. To discourage any further acts Ares will follow!"
Zeus explained as he pulled his hood back over his head.

"The beings you seek are possessed by Fates!" warned
Akantha. "Then they already know the outcome" Zeus
boldly replied as he emerged into a small glowing sphere
and disappeared into the sunlight.

...And so began a second Titanomachy for the Greek
gods, but that is another story.

To whom it may concern:

Three Marid Djinn's are a work of fiction. Names, characters, businesses, places and events and incidents are either products of the author's imagination or used in a fictitious manner. Any connection to any person living or dead, or actual events is purely coincidental.

Design of fates are displayed through illustrations of German Expressionism and depict their own tale about the characters when paired together.

Author
Juan Berry

ABOUT THE AUTHOR

Juan Berry has been a fan of supernatural stories since his childhood—an interest that eventually moved on to films. One of the reasons he decided to create characters of his own and write books is that he someday intends to adapt his stories into movies.

Printed in the United States
By Bookmasters